THE DEVIL'S THERAPIST

J.E. SERRANO

ISBN 978-1-961358-04-1 (paperback)

Printed in the United States of America

CONTENTS

CHAPTER 1

MORNING RITUAL

The sun softly pierced the tinted bedroom windows of the apartment of Doctor Peter Dayyagi. the silver-grey-haired man with a medium build rolled over in his bed, shutting off the alarm that insisted he awakens. The one-bedroom loft that he called home was immaculate. Hardwood floors with a vaulted ceiling. It is a jewel on Grand Street, just two and a half miles from Peter's job. Rolling out of bed, he hit the floor and began Counting off his pushups. Completing his ritual of one hundred, he snatched up the phone, putting in a breakfast order of egg whites on wheat toast from the deli across the street. "Yeah, hey Patty, could I ask you to have that ready in a half hour, please, a ten spot if that's a yes." Peter cajoled. "Of course, doc." Was her reply. Hanging up the phone, Peter jumped in the shower. Peter felt indebted to the boss that recruited him. Peter had a successful practice before he was approached by Doctor William Payne. a very successful psychiatrist from New York. Knowing Peter's success in treating depression and Hyperactive disorders, William flew to England to recruit Peter for a flagship project he had just put together. Graduating Magna cum Laude from the distinguished Imperial College in London with Ph.D. in psychology, Peter enjoyed a few years of ever-increasing recognition for his work. Since joining Doctor Payne, Peter has enjoyed a great salary and excellent living conditions. The Grand apartments were luxurious and worth the money. After his shower, the Doctor put on his bicycling gear over his athletic build. He exited his apartment and bound down the stairs. Stepping out of his building into a brilliant day, Peter shielded his eyes from the sun as cars zipped up and down Grand street. Running across the street, a car zoomed past Peter, blowing his angry horn. "Watch where the fuck you're going, asshole." The driver in the speeding vehicle shouted. "Yeah, good morning to you as well." Peter shouted at the driver. Smiling, he continued to the deli where his breakfast waited. Entering the store, a bell rang, announcing his arrival. Patty greeted him with what was becoming a ritual salutation. "Hey, Doc. I got a pain in my ass this morning. What do you prescribe for it?" Patty Gomez, The pretty, red-haired co-owner with her husband Pedro, a short, wiry, mocha-complexioned gentleman, Of Gomez Deli, shouted. Peter laughed. "A divorce." He joked in return. Peter loved this about New York. People loved getting on one another nerves, but it was all in jest. "Hey. What kind of Doctor are you advising such nonsense?" shouted Pedro, the other half of the dynamic duo. "who said I was a doctor? I'm a window washer." Peter jibed while picking up his food, handing Patty money and a wink. "Hey, what about that prostrate exam I let you perform?" Pedro quipped, stepping out from the back office. Peter, walking out of the door, called over his shoulder. "Hey, you asked for it. I tried to tell you I wasn't that kind of Doctor." Peter joked, hearing what he knew to be Spanish expletives being hurled at him. Smiling and eating his sandwich, he strolled back across the street, finishing the sandwich before going to the bike rack, which rested alongside the building. Peter loosened up, stretching his long legs. standing six feet two inches, he learned early in life that a good stretch minimized the likelihood of cramps. Unlocking his bicycle, he rode down Grand street for the two-and-a-half-mile ride to Stuyvesant ave. There the beautifully refurbished "Less stress therapy clinic" stood. Peter loved the ride. It was a neighborhood setting that differed from the sister Borough of Manhattan. Brooklyn still had a lot of charm and had not yet industrialized. Dismounting the bike, Peter was greeted by one of his colleagues who was getting out of his expensive Mercedes. "Good morning Peter." Doctor Bruce Sable greeted. A man who had garnered moderate wealth in the stock market(due to his father's connections), Bruce graduated from Harvard University. there, he met the founder of the Less stress clinic. "I see you still insist on a pedestrian mode of transportation." Bruce said condescendingly. Peter could hear the snideness in Bruce's disingenuous greeting. Not one to rise to such denigrations, Peter responded. "Yes, I prefer my dopamine through mutually beneficial exercise as opposed to pills or other artificial means." Doctor Sable tilted his head. "What are you insinuating?" Sable demanded. Peter played coy. "Whatever do you mean, Doctor Sable? I was only.." At that moment, they were joined by their employer, Doctor William Payne, a six-foot-six imposing figure of a man with graying hair and deep blue eyes. The founder of the "Less stress" clinic. During the Covid pandemic, he watched several friends, and colleagues suffer from depression and exhaustion. Payne a graduate of Harvard with Summa cum Laude honors, brilliantly set up multiple therapeutic disciplines in the establishment. From standard talk therapy to massages, mud baths, hot pools, ice pools, audio-visual stimulation, and a nutrition store. Peter thought the ideal revolutionary. "Well, gentlemen." In a finely tailored gray suit, William, looking more like a wall street C.E.O., greeted them. "Good morning, sir." Doctor Sable greeted stoically. "Good morning, boss." Peter responded casually. Williams looked at his two employees and queried the perceptive psychiatrist that he was. "I'm I missing something here?" Doctor Sable remained quiet. Peter smiled. "No sir, just Doctor Sable was commenting on my mode of transportation." Really?" Doctor Payne replied. "If I were not already settled in my routine, I would do just as you are, Peter. It must be very refreshing." Doctor Payne observed. Peter smiled. "Only because you made it possible, sir. What other job can a person ride their bike, arrive sweaty, and jump into a high-pressure shower?" Peter exclaimed. "You flatter me, sir." Doctor Payne jested. Peter's smile deepened. "Yes, sir, but we all need such treatment occasionally, wouldn't you agree, Doctor Sable?" "Yes, of course." Sable, who was spoiled, somewhat lazy as his bulging stomach suggested, grunted. Doctor Payne punched in the security code, unlocking the door. Peter carried his bike into the spacious basement. Placing it in the bike rack, Peter stripped off his soaked tank top and flung open a closet door where the employees had a personal, sectioned-off locker space. (more like walk-in closet space.) Peter picked out a gray suit and a black shirt, snatched a pair of Stacy Adams shoes, and retreated to the shower. Minutes later, he brushed his hair while his assistant reviewed the morning docket. "Well, doctor, you have a nine-twenty with Mister Collins and then an eleven o clock with Miss Montoya." She reported. Peter looked up, expecting more. "Well?" Peter hinted. "Is there anything else, Miss Rogers?" Nancy grinned nefariously. "That is all you have in the office, sir. You are scheduled for a one o'clock with your dentist." She related with a wicked grin. Peter frowned. "Nancy, I find it disturbing that you would find sublime joy in my discomfort." Peter playfully complained. A ritual formed from the past three and a half years of working together, Peter was fortunate to have hired Nancy. she never complained about working late. She volunteered for assignments when the therapists did pro-bone work for underprivileged clients. Her organizational skills were second to none, and her research capabilities were top-notch. Peter glared at her. "You're lucky your so good at what you do." Peter grumbled. Nancy smiled in return. "Be mindful, sir. You know you sprained an ankle the last time you complimented me in such a heartfelt manner." Peter looked at her with a serious expression. "You know there is a diagnosis for people that think all compliments are suspicious," Peter suggested. "Oh really?" Nancy responded. "Yeah, really." Peter echoed. "We may have to get you on the couch one day." Peter warned. At that moment Helen Zhang. Peter's colleague walked in and stopped. She slowly turned her head to Peter. "Doctor Dayyagi?" She posed in a lilting tone. "Don't start, Helen." Peter shot back. Nancy giggled, and Helen looked at her, smiling in appreciation for the chance to make Peter uncomfortable. "You see what you've started, Rogers."

Peter complained lightheartedly. Helen winked at Nancy and continued to her office. "Nancy, wait a moment, please," Peter called to his receptionist. Pausing, Nancy waited as Peter appeared to think. "Nancy, please ask Doctor Zhang if she would be willing to take over Lisa Montoya's case from me?" He finally requested. Nancy nodded. "Very well, Doctor." She responded. Doctor Payne entered the common area; the frivolities ceased upon entering. Peter grabbed his files and proceeded to his office. Helen was reading files in her office when Doctor Payne stuck his head in the room. "Are you just getting in? You're getting slow, Helen." Doctor Payne joked. "It's these damned heels." she complained. William laughed. "Do you have an open schedule today?" He inquired. She nodded in return. "This afternoon, is that okay?" Helen inquired. William nodded. "Absolutely. Buzz me when you have time." Helen assured him she would do just that. Her intercom rang a moment later. "Doctor Zhang, Doctor Dayaggi asked if you could take over a case for him?" Nancy related. Helen confirmed that she could. "What is the client's name?" She asked. "Lisa Montoya, I'll send the files over immediately; Doctor Dayaggi had an appointment with her this afternoon." Helen informed Doctor Zhang. Helen frowned at the impracticality of the request. "Very well. Send me the files and ask Doctor Dayaggi to call me before the client arrives." Helen requested. Nancy replied in acknowledgment.

9:30 am-Mister Collins

Peter sat at his desk preparing for a patient that was already late. His intercom buzzed, his receptionist announcing the arrival of his appointment. "Mister Collins has arrived, Doctor." She reported. "Send him in, please, Miss Rogers." Nancy smiled, relaying the message. "Doctor Dayyagi will see you now, sir." Collins looked over nervously at Nancy, uttering "thank you, thank you." while slipping past her. Peter greeted his patient with concern, as the delay was not part of his behavior patterns. "How are you, Merle?" Peter inquired. "Well, you know," He replied evasively. Peter smiled. "How would that be possible, as I've only just seen you now?" Peter responded. Merle shifted his feet. "Forgive me, Merle. Would you like to sit down, or shall we retire to the patio?" Peter asked. "The patio would be just fine, just fine." Merle responded. Peter led the way to a beautiful rooftop patio complete with comfortable furnishings. (a clever observation by Doctor Payne that people often felt relaxed in natural environments. He had trees and grass sectioned off on the rooftop alongside a recirculating brook, adding the calming effect of running water.) Entering the patio, Peter gestured to a chair that Merle stood in front of; then, ritualistically, he swiped at both arms and legs and removed chess pieces from his pockets. Specifically five pieces. The King, Queen, Bishop, Knight, and pawn. At their first meeting upon first producing the chess pieces. Peter once asked about their significance, and Merle had shut down for the remainder of the session. At the end of the session, Peter gently reminded him that the sessions were not mandatory and were requested by him. We could arrange that if he preferred a new Doctor because Peter inadvertently made him uncomfortable. Merle thanked him profusely but denied any need for changing therapists. All the while, he began shifting the chess pieces he had arranged on the table. Careful not to notice that idiosyncrasy, Peter responded to Merle's comment. "Thank you, Merle." Peter responded to Merle's unspoken vote of confidence. "So, How are you feeling?" Merle moved the pawn. "I think I might be comfortable with you, Doc, if you want to give it a chance?" Merle confided. (piece moved, knight.) Peter grinned. "I would like that." Peter acknowledged. "Me too, me too." Collins responded. "The first thing I must ask concerns medication." Peter explained. "What about them?" Merle asked. "Do you remember the last session you were going to decide if you wanted to try them?" Peter inquired. "Nope." Merle responded. (pawn moved back). Peter nodded. "No, you don't want them or don't remember?" Peter asked for clarification. "Don't want them." Merle insisted. "I see." Peter responded. "Allow me to explain My methodology." Merle nodded. "First, I avoid assumptions; I ask questions. I ask because we get to the root of an issue through honest questions and answers. Are you okay with that?" Peter inquired. Merle nodded again. (pawn moved.) "Good." Peter responded. "So tell us, Merle, How are you feeling? (Merle moved the Queen back. "Not sure how to explain Doc, (Bishop moved to check Queen.) We used to go to church a lot. "(King forward) "My Dad was an old testament type minister. He used to preach that the Devil would usurp the world with clever words. Still, if you believed in the word (knight to bishop), Then even the sinner could be saved (pawn forward), but beware for evil looks to imprison the weak. (Bishop flanks pawn) and the weak shall be taken from his redemption." Collins quoted. Merle seemed to withdraw into himself. Peter waited a moment before calling his name softly. "Merle?" Collins came out of his reverie. "Things aint the same, aint the same." Peter nodded. "Are you okay?" Merle smiled. "I'm Tired; I'm hungry." He responded. Peter smiled. "Would you like to call it a day and get something to eat?" Peter inquired. Merle looked confused. "Don't I have to stay for an hour or something?" Peter shrugged. "Do you want to continue talking?" He asked. Merle shook his head. "Well, that settles that. We're here to serve you, Merle, and if you can talk for a few hours, that's what we'll do, but if you only want twenty minutes, then that's what we'll take. Is that okay with you?" Peter asked. Merle nodded vigorously. "I like that, like that." He repeated. (moving the pawn forward.) Peter smiled. "Get something to eat and call Miss Rogers if or when you want another appointment. Merle gingerly put out his hand, and Peter gently shook it. "A pleasure to see you again, Merle." Merle smiled. "we'll see you soon." Merle swiped up the chess pieces sticking them in his pocket. King, Queen, Bishop, pawn, knight. Dayyagi noticed the order for possible future reference. Upon Merle's exiting, Peter sat and began his notes.

Patient: Merle Collins.

Possible diag: Patient exhibits uncontrollable compulsions relatable to O.C.D. (Obsessive compulsive disorder)

Symptoms include Speech repetition: Object, and spatial manipulation. (user's chess pieces when relating incidents. Repetitive wiping of hands to sleeve to the pant leg. Precise in repetition (left arm, right arm, both legs simultaneously).

Affect: Gentle, amiable

Medication: Self reports N/A

Session #2-Ten minute session with the client engaged in light reminiscing

Placing his pen down, Peter reflected on the new client's behavior patterns momentarily before getting up and buzzing Miss Rogers. "Yes, sir?" The receptionist responded. "Who is my next appointment?" Peter asked. "Your next appointment is not for another hour and a half, sir." Peter looked at the clock and spoke to the intercom. "I'm going to grab some files and go to the patio. who is the next client?" Rogers responded promptly in a clipped tone. "It would have been Lisa Montoya, Doctor. But you referred her to Doctor Zhang, who would like you to call her at your first opportunity," Nancy informed him. Peter smiled. "Thank you, Miss Rogers." He responded, mimicking her tone. Peter dialed Helens' extension. She answered a moment later. "Doctor Zhang." She responded."

Helen, this is Peter. Thank you for taking Miss Montoya's case on such short notice. Peter expressed his gratitude. "No problem, Peter, but why the sudden switch?" Helen inquired. "This woman has suffered terrible physical and emotional abuse, some of which I'm concerned she might be too embarrassed to discuss with a man."

Peter related. "Very well, your receptionist just sent me the files. I believe she has a one-thirty appointment." Helen clarified. "Yes, she does, and I apologize for the short notice." Peter evinced. "Would you like me there for the introductions?" Peter asked. "That won't be necessary, Peter. Go get those teeth cleaned." Helen teased. Helen took the files she had just received and decided to review them on the roof. Entering the rooftop, Helen found a comfortable seat near the recirculating water (which acted like a stream). Once on the top, Helen sat in a shaded area, continuing to read her files, fascinated by the events reported by her new client. Her perseverance was astounding. The abuse she survived was nothing short of miraculous. As a child, she lost both her parents in a robbery. Both were accidentally shot when police attempted to capture the perpetrators, which began this woman's woes.

CHAPTER 2

PUPPETS

Doctor Payne sat with Helen Zhang. A brilliant therapist, a graduate of Yale University, with the honor of making the Deans list. She was of Chinese ancestry and was born in Connecticut. She was athletic, an excellent communicator, standing five feet seven inches, one hundred twenty pounds, and had a slender build. She had shoulder-length black hair with rum brown eyes. She is a single mom and very active in her community. William was lucky enough to engage her services when the world shut down because of the Covid pandemic. Her previous employment as a communication specialist was an "empty experience." As she liked to put it. When asked why she felt empty, she responded, "It was more sales than communication. I have degrees in therapy, not sales." She clarified. William reached for a pot that was boiling. "Would you like some tea?" Doctor Payne offered. Helen shook her head at the offer of tea. She shifted nervously, curious why Doctor Payne had requested to speak to her. "You may be wondering why I asked you here." William began as if reading her mind. Helen nodded in the affirmative. William began pouring tea into two cups. The Doctor's face took on a serious aspect as he handed her the proffered tea. "Well, let me begin by saying that having you here has benefited us. Undoubtedly, your skill and professional insight rank among the finest in our profession." William paused to sip from his cup. Helen kept her composure. She was familiar with Doctor Payne's methodologies. She was also aware he would often regale people with positive attributes they believed about themselves, confirming in their minds the validity of his observations. before reversing course and revealing concerning behaviors, he noticed. Accepting the tea he poured and handed her, she set it aside. William was capable of dismantling most people's defenses. His methodology was powerful as it made the person doubt their decision-making skills. "It is a beautiful day, wouldn't you agree?" William posed offhandedly, looking around the enclosed garden patio. Helen kept in step, barely phased by William's methods of disorientation or the fact he imposed upon her despite her denial of tea. "Doctor Payne, if there is something you wish to discuss, I should inform you I have a client in half an hour." Helen was informative and professional about her obligations, using it to move Doctor Paynes' discussion along. Payne drew a deep breath as if he were sorry the moment didn't last long. "There is that understanding again. Didn't you want the tea?" He asked innocently. Helen remained staring at him silently. "No on the tea then, very well. I asked to see you because I realized that I don't need four therapists while reviewing our financial records." William observed, pausing again to sip from his cup. Helen sat immobile, disbelief etched on her face. "Has my job performance been unsatisfactory, Doctor Payne?" She inquired. William looked at her, mildly shocked. "Not at all. Why would you say or think that?" He decried. Helen whispered. "William Payne, I don't understand why you are so cruel. If you want to fire me, say it." Helen demanded. William took another sip of tea. "What are you going on about, Helen?" He inquired, appearing baffled. Doctor Zhang composed herself. "William, I've seen first-hand how you manipulate through dissembling. I would prefer you did not treat me like a patient." Doctor Zhang demanded. Doctor Payne's features softened. "I apologize, Doctor Zhang, Helen. Perhaps it is becoming second nature for me. allow me to get to the heart of our conversation." William expressed without clarifying. Helen shrugged in frustrated miscomprehension. William waved his hands in dismissal. "Let me start again." He urged. "In plain English." Helen complained. William smiled. "Of course. Doctor Zhang, because of your exemplary work performance. With your ability to effectively communicate with the entire staff and your excellent therapeutic and managerial skills, I'd like to offer you a promotion to Supervising therapist. With the promotion comes a sizable raise, and if you'd like a company car." William concluded with a smile. Doctor Zhang stood suddenly. She was quiet for a moment. "William, you jackass!" She exploded. "A man of your education putting me through a verbal ringer like that; you have a dark heart, young man." She scolded. "So you don't want the job?" William teased. Helen cocked her head to the side. "Is that any way to speak to your Supervising therapist?" Doctor Payne smiled. "No, ma'am." Helen smiled in return. "Thank you, Doctor." She said gratefully. William nodded in response. Standing, he extended his hand for a congratulatory handshake. In response, Helen stood, smiling, and she grasped his hand with misty eyes. "Thank you, Doctor Payne. This raise means so much to me, to Mei and me." William smiled. "Well, Mei was one of the factors in my decision to give it to you. I mean all that complimentary stuff I said, phew." He exclaimed teasingly, holding his nose. Helen locked eyes with him. "Are you a child William?" She asked condescendingly. "Yes, ma'am." William agreed to grin childishly. Helen tilted her head to the side while making a face of impatience. "Is that all? because some of us have work to do." Helen inquired. "Yes, Doctor Zhang, and thank you." A smiling William said dismissively. Helen walked to the rooftop door; opening it, she paused. "Thank you, William." She said in earnest. William smiled. "Our good fortune, Doctor." He replied with equal sincerity. Doctor Payne smiled, pleased it went so smoothly. Deciding whether to make his next task equally smooth or to save that for last, he chose the latter, knowing that this next conversation may prove more dramatic. Picking up the intercom, he dialed Doctor Sable's extension. Bruce picked up on the third ring. "I hope I did not disturb you, Doctor Sable?" William said, expressing concern. "No, not at all, Doctor Payne. I was momentarily indisposed." Bruce offered as an explanation. "Yes, business all must attend." Payne admitted. "I was wondering if you could take the time to speak with me?" William asked in his manner. "Of course, Doctor Payne. When did you have in mind?" Bruce inquired. "I see you have time in the next half hour." Payne mentioned knowing Doctor Sable's schedule. "Of course, William, I'll be in your office at.." Payne interjected. "No, no. It's a lovely day; let us meet on the patio." Bruce nodded to no one (as he was alone). "Of course, a half-hour is then." Bruce's mind raced, trying to ascertain the reason for the impromptu meeting. He exited his office and saw Helen in the staff lounge eating yogurt, sifting through some files, and humming. Bruce walked in, greeting Helen. "Good morning Doctor Zhang." Helen looked up from her work. "Good morning Doctor Sable. "How's the workload today?" He posed in an attempt to strike up a conversation. "I'm sorry. Did you mean my workload or the office workload?" She asked. "Which-ever, does it matter?" Sable asked snidely. "It does Helen responded. She laid her spoon down on a napkin. "If it were me you were asking about, that would show at least a facsimile of concern for me, as opposed to the latter, which reveals you don't acknowledge that I'm a therapist. but a receptionist whose job it is to know office workload." Helen clarified. Sable stood mute for a moment. "What do you want, Bruce?" Helen asked directly. Bruce shuffled for a moment before asking. "Do you know why William wants to see me this afternoon?" He inquired with piercing eyes. Helens' brow furrowed. "How and why would I know that?" She retorted. "Well, we've gathered that you are William's favorite." Sable complained. Helen tilted her head in wonder. "Bruce, please remember we treat people here with paranoid delusions. We don't employ them." Sable stared at her. He took a breath and muttered. "I apologize, Helen. This sudden call from William when I know he's seriously considering office staffing is problematic." He admitted. Now it was Helens' turn to get upset. "How long have you known he was.." Bruce looked at his watch. "Oh my, look at the time;

better not keep the boss man waiting." He expressed beating a hasty retreat from the lounge area.

Sable's disappointment

William sat reviewing his charts on his employees. Convinced he made the right choice with Helen, he now prepared to meet with his talented yet narcissistic employee. "Good day Doctor Payne." Doctor Bruce Sable announced himself as he walked up to where Doctor Payne sat. "ahh, Doctor Sable, how good of you to come. Please join me." Doctor Payne invited, gesturing to a chair for Bruce to be seated. "I must say your call was unexpected." Bruce said as a conversation starter. "Was it?" Doctor Payne asked. Doctor Sable took a deep breath. "May I be straightforward with you, William?" Doctor Payne hid a smirk. "One would certainly hope so." He responded. Bruce leaned forward. "I've wanted to share a concern with you but was unsure how to approach it." Sable confided. William sipped his refreshed tea. "Try being concise." William suggested. "Oh, may I offer you some tea?" He asked offhandedly. Bruce declined. Doctor Sable seemed to consider William's suggestion about being concise. "William, you have undoubtedly created a fine organization with lofty ambitions." Sable observed. "You think so? It is kind of you to say." William responded cautiously. "Please forgive me if I speak out of place, William, but this is as concise as possible. It appears you'll run yourself ragged, trying to do everything yourself." Sable observed. William took another sip from his cup. "I see." William responded. "Well, allow me to thank you for being perceptive enough to take notice of my dilemma." William said, expressing gratitude. Bruce lifted his hands in protestation. "No disrespect, sir; they're only my opinions." William lifted his hand, warding off such notions. "Be assured, Doctor, no offense taken." William reassured him. "I am pleased by your perception and will not deny your observations. It has been difficult wearing so many hats." Payne admitted. "Do you have any suggestions?" William asked. Sable looked pleasantly surprised. "Seriously?" He asked in disbelief, which was disingenuous. William nodded. "Of course, I'd like to see how closely our minds work in resolving an issue." Payne clarified. Sable looked very pleased over William's statement. Pausing for dramatic effect doctor, Sable stood and paced on the rooftop. William sat back, sipping more of his tea and enjoying the theatrics. After a moment of what William assumed was deep consideration, Doctor Sable stopped pacing. He paused, then turned to William. "I apologize. I'm overthinking this. I think the solution is obvious." Sable espoused. William sat up from the lounging position he had assumed. "Really? Do tell." He encouraged. Stroking a hairless chin, Doctor Sable began his assessment. "It appears we need a restructuring on an organizational level." Sable offered. William paused as if giving the notion some thought. "What exactly would that look like?" Doctor Payne asked. "Well," Sable began while anxiously rubbing his hands together. "First, I think we should consider if it's practical to have such a large therapeutic staff," Bruce paused for any interjections Payne wished to inject. With none forthcoming, he continued. "Second, I would create a new position that oversaw the work of the therapy staff. cut down on their record review time and better-triaging prospective clients to ensure maximum efficiency." Sable suggested. William smiled. "Excellent ideas Doctor. Do you have any suggestions as to who should fill such a spot?" William asked. Bruce paused, surprised that the position was not automatically offered to him. Concealing his disappointment, he paused as if considering. "Well, there is Doctor Dayyagi. He's an excellent therapist." Bruce suggested insincerely. "Yes, you're right." Payne agreed. Doctor Sable tried to cover his look of disgust. "But as you observed, Doctor, he is an excellent therapist, and I don't want to distract him from that." Payne observed, much to Sable's relief. "Well," Sable said reluctantly. "There is Doctor Zhang." Sable half-heartedly suggested. William looked at Sables' expression of apprehension. "Yes, Helen Zhang, why did I overlook the obvious?"

Payne asked himself. William could see the internal struggle doctor Sable was going through. "Bruce, is something wrong? Do you think the recommendation unacceptable?" Payne inquired. Bruce absentmindedly scratched at his neck. "I would never second guess you, sir," He began. "What do you mean, Bruce? It was your suggestion." Payne pointed out. "I was just going down the list, sir." Sable responded. "Yes, and I noticed you didn't consider your name. William paused as he refilled his tea cup. "I must say I am very impressed with both your modesty and candor." William acclaimed. A confused Doctor Sable looked at William. "Sir?" He asked, refusing to comprehend. "Well, knowing that Doctor Zhang has excellent skills in the requirements for this new office, I agree with you, Doctor Sable. Managing other therapists' scheduling and the struggle of follow-ups and planning meetings is not what you signed up for. Is it?" William posed. Bruce silently shook his head. "Thank you for your time and valuable input Doctor Sable." Payne said dismissively, going back to his paperwork. Bruce stood stunned for a moment. "Was there anything else, Doctor Sable?" Payne inquired, looking up and seeing Sable standing there mutely. Sable shook his head. "No, sir." Bruce muttered. Slowly, Bruce turned and walked toward the rooftop door. Payne stared at the retreating back and shook his head, satisfied with the meeting. He picked up the intercom and dialed. Two rings later, he heard Doctor Dayyagi's office." The roar of a siren drowned out whatever reply may have been given. After a moment, Peter heard, "Doctor Dayyagi." William was repeating loudly. "Doctor Payne, I hear you, sir." Peter responded. "Would you be kind enough to meet me on the patio?" Payne requested. "Sure, boss." Peter replied. "When were you thinking?" He asked. "Now, I don't imagine this will take longer if you have a moment." William said reassuringly. "Be up in a second, boss." Peter assured him. William hung up, feeling the meeting would go well, as Peter was the most relaxed, confident staff member. He didn't have the worries of raising a child as Helen did, nor the vain materialistic concerns of Bruce. Three flawed individuals, each uniquely gifted. The door to the rooftop opened as Peter bound out with his usual high energy. "Hey, boss." Peter greeted seeing Doctor Payne. "Peter." Richard greeted in return. "How is your day going?" William asked. "Had a client in a short session as he was reluctant to open up." Peter shared. "And that was?" William inquired. "Merle, Merle Collins. O.C.D.-initial diagnosis." William nodded in recollection. "How was the session terminated?" Payne delved. "Rescheduled at his convenience, he left somewhat agitated, but I think he will return." Peter reported. "Excellent, Peter." William commended. "Peter, the reason I asked you up here today is simple," Payne paused and saw no anxiety reactions, nervousness, or fear exhibited by Peter. "Doctor, I must inform you I've developed a new promotional position here. A Therapy supervisor for our clinic." William informed him. Again, no tics or nervous sweat. Payne pushed forward. "It's a nice pay raise," He paused. Still no reaction. *In for a penny.*" William thought. "I gave the position to Helen Zhang." Payne advised awaiting a reaction. Peter smiled. "Good for her." Peter sincerely cheered. "She's great at her job, and I'm sure she'll do what we need around here." Peter boasted. William looked at Peter sideways. "I thought you might be upset." He confided. "I would have been if you tried to give it to me, or worse yet, that prima-donna Bruce." Peter exclaimed honestly. "You don't like Doctor Sable?" William asked. Peter shook his head. "It's less him and more his type as if he could measure life on a spreadsheet." William nodded. "I understand. Can this be kept on a professional level?" Payne asked seriously. Peter nodded vigorously. "Of course, boss. I'm here to do a job, not make nice with Doctor Sable." William nodded. That will suffice. He agreed.

CHAPTER 3

THE DEPRESSED

Mason stood outside of the clinic. He was watching birds fly from tree to tree. He imagined that he felt the sadness of the birds. "Don't be so sad little sparrow; one day, you will die, and it will be over." He whispered gently, almost as if a prayer. Mason suffered what some mistakenly called a Napoleonic complex—wishing to be appropriately evaluated brought him here—standing only five foot six inches. His two-hundred-and-forty-five-pound frame gave him a stout look. His green eyes stared at the sign on the building, *Less Stress therapeutic center.* he read to himself. Unsure, Mason entered a softly lit entry that opened into a reception area. A receptionist sat behind her desk. Approaching her, Mason cleared his throat. "Excuse me." The Receptionist looked up from her work and revealed a dazzling smile. "Good morning, sir. How can I be of assistance?" She asked warmly. "Yes, umm. My name is Mason Brice, and a friend suggested this might be a good place to," Mason paused as if embarrassed. "To perhaps talk about some things concerning you?" The Receptionist offered. Mason smiled, nodding shyly. The Receptionist returned the smile and handed Mason a form. "If you would fill this out, we'll check you in." Mason smiled. "Thank you, ma'am." He responded courteously. "You can call me Miss Drake." The Receptionist replied professionally. Mason sat to fill out the form. Upon completion, Mason handed the Receptionist the forms. She took the paperwork and glanced at it. She then picked up the phone and mumbled briefly into it; hanging up, she looked at Mason. "Mister Brice, Doctor Sable will be with you momentarily. Perhaps I can give you a brief tour?" She suggested. "Don't you have to stay at your desk?" Mason asked shyly. "Perhaps I misspoke. It would be more like an explanation of where everything is, and if you decide this is a good place for you, I guess you'll get the complete tour." the Receptionist informed him. Mason smiled, nodding his understanding. "This spiral staircase." She gestured to the stairs. "Leads up to the roof where we have a fully furnished deck with lawn chairs, tables, a dining area, and a meditation garden. To the right of the entry is a staircase that leads to the locker rooms, showers, and mud and ice baths. Alongside the baths are the massage rooms, she informed him. Doctor Sable entered the reception area from an office off to the side of the Reception desk. "Well, here is The doctor now." She said to Mason, who was gazing around. "Doctor Sable, this is Mason Brice." The Doctor extended his hand in greeting; Mason gingerly shook it. "It is good to meet you, sir." Sable began. "Would you like to come into my office?" He invited Mason, who cast his gaze to the floor, responding. "Okay." Sable smiled. "If you would follow me, please." Doctor Sable led Mason to his office. Mason stopped at the doorway and looked into the Doctor's office. Bruce stood inside, looking at Mason; he inquired, "Is this okay?" Mason nodded and slowly entered the office. Sable motioned to a chair, "Please sit down." He offered. Mason looked at a chair and then at a couch. "Ain't I suppose to lay down?" He asked innocently. "Would you be more comfortable laying down, Mister Brice?" Sable inquired. Mason shook his head. "No, it's just what I heard is done." He responded naively. The Doctor smiled. "This is unlike any place you've been before, Mister Brice." Mason cocked his head in confusion. "How do you mean Doc?" Sable's smile deepened. "First, you don't have to call me doc unless you want to." Sable clarified. Mason tilted his head in response. "oh, what should I call you then?" He posed. "My name is Bruce Sable." The Doctor replied amicably. "Mason Brice, pleased to meet you." Mason replied. Bruce responded. "Likewise," Mason shuffled his feet momentarily, looking around the room. "Well, how does this work?" Mason asked. Sable nodded. "If you don't mind, I'd like to ask a few questions to get us started, and you can tell me whatever is on your mind. Is that alright?" Sable asked. "Yeah, sure." Mason answered. Picking up a pad and pen, Bruce inquired. "Have you ever seen a therapist before?" Mason shook his head. "Please respond with a yes or no, and if you don't understand what I'm asking, just tell me so I can explain better, okay?" Mason nodded again, then caught himself. "Yes, I understand." He responded as requested. "Thank you for that." Bruce acknowledged. "Now, let's make the first question an easy one. Do I call you Mason or Mister Brice?" Bruce asked. "My daddy was Mister Brice. Call me Mason." He responded. "Very well, Mason, it is." Bruce acknowledged. "That'd be fine." Mason nodded in confirmation. "Well, let me ask you what brought you here, Mason?" Bruce probed. "Well, some of my friends say they have noticed I've changed. Bruce nodded. "I see. Did they specify how you've changed?" Bruce probed further. Mason seemed to think a moment before responding. "Mostly, they say I've gotten reticent and take things too seriously." Mason shared. Bruce nodded. "Can you give me any examples?" He asked. Mason drew back on memories. "Well, movies I used to laugh at, I now take seriously." Bruce nodded. "Is there any you can think of?" Mason thought a moment. "Well, there is a movie called the hitch-hikers guide to the galaxy. You ever hear of it?" Bruce smiled. "42." He responded. Mason grinned, "Exactly." Mason tilted his head. "what's different?" Bruce inquired. "Well, when I first saw the movie about ten years ago, I laughed when they sang thanks for all the fish." Mason explained haltingly. "And now?" Bruce asked. "I cry." Mason admitted. Bruce nodded. "If you believe that a change is taking place within you, when do you think it started?" Bruce inquired. Mason thought a moment. His expression grew somber. "I think it is true, I am changing, and it began in the second year of the pandemic lock-down. All those people are dying, and we seem to care more about our economy than people. What kind of ass-end back-ward thinking is that?" Mason complained. "How is anyone supposed to feel safe, loved, or wanted?" He complained bitterly. "They talk about mental health like they give a damn about you. Then you're told not to get close to people because of how contagious the illness is, and yet they have events that people close to one another. I just don't get it." Mason complained with a raised voice." Sable scribbled on his pad. "Is there anything you do that helps you when you feel this way?"

At first, Mason began laughing, almost giggling, but it grew in force and volume. Mason stood and walked to the door; he looked back at Doctor Sable gravely. "How does one stop the incarnation of Evil Doc? He's here, walks among us, and has brought the vile stench with him." Before Sable could open his mouth, Mason opened the door and left. Walking past the Receptionist, who looked up as Mason hurried past her. "Mister Brice?" She called out, but Mason stormed out of the front door.

Sable sat at his desk and began his session report:

Client Mason Brice- Male Caucasian- Age:52

The client exhibits symptoms of depression, Mild anxiety as well as a form of religious persecution. (the stated belief that the Devil walks among humanity.

The client exited abruptly in an excited state. I will contact the health provider requesting court-appointed sessions.

Damaged:

Lisa entered the Less stress clinic as Mason charged out, mumbling about time running out. Not a good sign as far as she was concerned. Approaching the Receptionist's desk, Molly looked up and greeted her. "Good morning. How may I help you?" Lisa looked around the beautiful office. "I have a referral to see Doctor Dayaggi."

Lisa exclaimed. "And what is your name?" Molly asked. "My name is Lisa Montoya, and I have an eleven-thirty appointment." Molly looked through the appointment book and found Lisa's name; she looked up, smiling. "Here you are. Doctor Dayaggi reviewed your file and thought you might be more comfortable with Doctor Zhang if that suits you?" Molly informed. Feeling relieved, Lisa nodded. "That would be fine." She acknowledged. 'Excellent. Doctor Zhang will be a moment. Would you like a tour of our facility?" Lisa shook her head as she sat to wait. "No, thank you, I'll just wait here." She declined. Molly contacted Doctor Zhang to inform her that her appointment had arrived. Molly hung up the intercom. "As I said, the Doctor will be there in a few moments." She conveyed. Lisa nodded her gratitude. After a moment, Doctor Zhang emerged from her office. "Miss Montoya, I'm so glad you came." Helen greeted her. Lisa looked around the office, "This place is beautiful; I'm not sure I'm in the right place." She exclaimed uncomfortably. Helen smiled and gestured to her office. "Please, come into my office, and I assure you you're in the right place." Lisa looked suspiciously at the Doctor as she walked toward the Doctor's office. "How could you possibly know that? I mean that I'm in the right place?" Lisa insisted. "You don't know me or what I'm about." She demanded. Helen entered her office and gestured for Lisa to join her. "Please, a moment of your time. If you don't like what I say, you can do as you see fit." Helen entreated. Lisa cut her eyes at Helen. "Fine, I'm here. What you got to say?" Lisa posed. Helen took a moment to compose herself and took a breath. "I read your file, and while it doesn't tell me everything about you, it does tell you you've suffered physical and emotional abuse." Helen began. Lisa interjected. "Wait, are you talking about my childhood?" Helen held up her hand. "If I may finish." Helen requested. Lisa nodded. "As I was saying, I see a young lady who refuses to sit. She looks very uncomfortable and keeps looking out the window, but not as if she is waiting for someone. No, my instinct tells me that she is hiding. I see in this attractive woman's beautiful brown eyes fear. Lisa interrupted. "Tell me, what else did you see, bruja?" Lisa complained sarcastically. Helen smiled, recognizing the reaction. "Well, I see desperation, fatigue, a sense of loneliness, and anger." Helen concluded. "Is that right?" Lisa demanded with anger in her voice. "Am I wrong?" Helen asked. Lisa looked exhausted and finally plopped into a chair. "No." Lisa admitted. "I was, am, all those things." Helen smiled. "You're safe here. Would you like to tell me what's happening in your life that might be driving your feelings?" Helen inquired. Lisa eyed the Doctor suspiciously. "Why do you want to help me?" She pushed. "That's a fair question; it is for a simple reason. My boss is dedicated to helping people with emotional or mental issues. When I look into your eyes, I feel you are the kind of person my boss is talking about." Helen explained. "What, is he some sort of saint or something?" Lisa exclaimed. Helen shook her head. "No, I think he is a good man with a good heart and doesn't like to see people suffer." Lisa shook her head in disbelief. "There is no such thing as a good man." Lisa expressed vehemently. "Why would you say that? Have you had bad incidents with men?" Helen asked gently. "If you count being molested by your Father, then yes, I've had a bad experience or two." Helen frowned. "I'm sorry to hear of your suffering." Helen sympathized. Helen sat quietly for a moment, giving Lisa time. "Why are you looking at me like that?" Lisa demanded. Helen took a breath. "I was wondering how strong you must be." Helen stated. "Strong?" Lisa gasped. "I'm nervous all the time! Everywhere I go, I expect to be attacked." She sputtered. Helen nodded in understanding. "Are you doing anything to protect yourself?" Lisa tilted her head curiously. "Like what?" She asked. "Well," Helen began. "You can take martial arts, buy mace, buy a rape whistle," Lisa laughed. "Did I say something funny?" Helen inquired. "What tune do you want me to blow on the whistle?" Lisa asked sarcastically. "Well, I," Helen began, only to be interrupted. "And how long do I need to take martial arts before I learn to kick someone in the balls?" Lisa huffed. "Lisa, I meant no.." Helen tried to de-escalate Lisa's irritation. "No, Doc." Lisa continued irately. "If I need protection," Lisa reached into her handbag and pulled out a 380 caliber pistol. "I will blast the next fool who tries to hurt me!" Lisa concluded with murder in her eyes. Helen took a deep breath. "Lisa, be very careful with that. You know New-york has some stringent gun laws, and if you get caught with that," Helen let the warning hang. "Why? Are you going to rat me out?" Lisa demanded. Helen shook her head. "Of course not. There is a thing called Doctor client privilege which precludes me from sharing information." Helen informed. Lisa cut her eyes at Helen. "Yeah, but I'm not your patient." Lisa pointed out. Helen smiled. "The moment we closed that door, and you began relating issues with me, you became my patient. If you have no desire to continue, I am still under the condition of the HIPAA law. It prevents me from revealing to anyone the things we've discussed unless you pose an immediate threat to yourself or the public. Do you pose an immediate threat?" Helen asked. "Only to a rapist." Lisa admitted. "You know I like you, Doctor Zhang. I'm just not sure I can afford treatment in a place like this." Lisa admitted. Helen smiled. Remember about that boss I was telling you about that likes helping people?" Lisa nodded, vaguely remembering Helen mentioning something. "Well," Helen continued. "He has set up funding for needy people and convinced the State to fund that program." Lisa smiled. "medicare will pay for it so I can come back?" She asked innocently. "We have an arrangement with them, and I pray you come back." Helen answered sincerely. Lisa stood. "Thanks, Doctor. Can I make an appointment now?" Lisa asked anxiously. Helen smiled. "The Receptionist, Molly Drake, can help you with that. Lisa looked relatively comfortable and smiled as she exited. "Thanks, Doc. I'll be seeing you soon." Helen returned the smile. "Looking forward to it." Lisa replied. Lisa left looking a bit more relaxed.

Helen sat at her desk to write her report

Client: Lisa Montoya- Female

poss. diagnosis: Rape victim suffers from paranoia, poss-p.t.s.d. has confirmed continued treatment.

Entry: Distrustful- anxious

Exit: The patient appeared relaxed and not as nervous. To be continued.

CHAPTER 4

PINS & NEEDLES

Errol stepped off of the bus at Grand and Fulton. It was another hot, humid New York day. he glanced around nervously, turning south and continuing his stressful venture. The Xanax he took earlier was barely working. Since he was diagnosed with an anxiety disorder, the six foot five slenderly built man at one hundred fifty pounds has been looking for a suitable clinic for his illness. After trying a couple of possibilities, he saw a commercial for the Less Stress Clinic and called to arrange an appointment. Errol began walking, occasionally glancing up and looking at addresses.

The downtown Brooklyn traffic (both vehicular and pedestrian) was thick, agitating him. Scratching his bearded face (a coping mechanism), he saw a sign that bore a name on the sought-after address. "Less stress clinic." Errol opened the door and was met by a blast of cool air. With a sigh, Errol entered and presented himself to the receptionist. "Good afternoon. I have an appointment with a doctor Dayaggi." Errol said quietly. Molly looked through the appointment book. "There we are. Is this your first time here?" Molly inquired. Errol nodded affirmatively. Molly handed Errol a questionnaire. "If you would be kind enough to fill these out, I'll inform the doctor that you're here." Errol nodded, took the offered form, and sat filling it out. After a few minutes, Errol heard Peter's voice. "Errol." He called the waiting patient. Errol looked up and timidly waved at his therapist. Errol weakly shook his hand as he approached him. "Hello Doctor Dayaggi." Errol said in greeting. Peter shook his hand gently yet firmly. "Hello, Errol, please come inside." Dayaggi greeted in return. Errol hurried into the office and promptly sat. Noting his appearance, the Doctor queried about Errol's emotional state. "Well, Errol, how are you feeling?" Errol flashed a shy smile. "I am well, thank you for asking." Errol responded gratefully. Peter smiled. "Why don't you tell me what that is like for you? I mean, feeling well." Errol scratched his beard. "Well, that would be when my stomach isn't in knots." Errol replied timidly. Peter smiled in response. May I ask what it is that what are some of those things that, as you say, puts your stomach in knots?" Peter probed softly. "Truthfully, I get nervous about going outside, especially after dark." Errol admitted. Peter nodded in response. "*What* is it about the dark that makes you dislike it? do you go out at night at all?" Peter gently inquired. Errol looked around the office, Noticing Peters' pictures of hiking and white water rafting. Although Errol was Somewhat reluctant in the beginning, Peter's style of therapy was just what Errol needed. Errol leaned forward and told Peter about denying someone who asked him if he wanted female companionship. That the woman would show him a nice time. Peter looked kindly at Errol. "How did that make you feel?" Peter queried. Errol looked to the ground bashfully. "I knew what they meant. Errol nearly whispered as if embarrassed by the recognition. "I believe you did, but how did you feel about it?" Peter repeated. Errors smile faded. "I felt embarrassed." He admitted. Peter tilted his head." Why do you feel embarrassed?" Peter pressed. A part of Errol's smile returned. "Yeah, I know why, Doctor." Peter smiled. "I honestly don't, Errol. Do you want to tell me?" Looking away from Peter. Errol whispered. "Because I wanted to be with her." Knowing the effects of Errol's condition. Peter understood the difficulty this Client was battling to not only leave his apartment but engage in a conversation with a stranger who offered Errol the service he desired. Peter paused, "Errol, when did this happen to you?" Peter probed.

Earl smiled. "Last night, when I threw out my garbage. Leaving his apartment At night was a significant step. "Tell me, Errol, What did you do?" Peter inquired. Errol began fidgeting. "I said no thank you and went to the store for beer." Errol reported. Peter nodded in acknowledgment. Changing the subject, Peter asked. "How was your commute here today?" Errol cast his eyes down, sitting silent a moment; he mumbled. "Not so good." He admitted. Peter nodded. "That's okay, Errol, you're safe here. Why don't you tell me what was not so good about it?" Peter inquired. "Well, Doctor, the first two people were gabbing in a language I didn't understand. and they just kept going on and on. Then there was a huge and smelly guy who sat next to me. I felt like I would choke on his stink, and then there was this kid with a loud radio. People asked him to lower it, and he wouldn't, and then, Peter held up his hand. Errol stopped speaking as Peter thought he would. Peter discovered that Errol shared the penchant among the anxious to express themselves to the point of incoherence. "Errol looked up meekly. "Sorry, Doctor." Errol apologized. Peter smiled again. "Errol. there is nothing to be sorry about, You're doing very well, and I appreciate your honesty." Peter complimented. "Ya think so?" Errol asked doubtfully. Peter tilted his head. "Well, let's review. You say you don't like being around people. You claimed they make you very nervous and believed they were out to get you. Have you ever hired neighborhood kids to run to the store because you hated going outside? Errol nodded in confirmation. Well, today, you reported going outside at night. That in itself is a huge leap. You spoke with a stranger; you also told someone no. Has that been easy for you? Errol silently shook his head. "Would you please respond with words?" Peter requested. "Why? Why do I have to say it?" Errol softly demanded. "Because Errol, when you leave here, I still think about the things you tell me, and I don't want to get anything you say wrong, so I record it. I want to give you the best advice possible, Errol." Peter explained. "Is that Okay," Peter asked gently. Errol responded quietly, No, it isn't easy for me." Errol admitted. "What hasn't been easy for you?" Peter probed, catching

Errol's attempt to be evasive. "It isn't easy for me to say no to people." He admitted grudgingly. Errol, I find it amazing that you can open up to me as you do." The Doctor smiled, showing approval. Errol frowned. "Yeah, but today on the bus.." He related sadly, disappointed at his reaction to the behavior of the other passengers on the bus. "Mister Tandy, how long have you been feeling this way?" Peter probed, trying to gauge his clients' length of inner turmoil. Errol scratched his head in thought. "As far back as I can remember, I've always been this way, Doctor." He replied. Errol, Thinking your lifelong habit will be cast aside after only a few months is unfair. You spent a lifetime distrusting people and isolating yourself, mutating into an anxiety disorder. One thing to remember is that you can't control other people's behavior, only your own. Another way to look at it is perhaps they are fighting their issues the only way they know how." Peter expressed. Nothing is wrong with you; a combination of talk therapy, meds, and a good support group can't help. Are you currently taking anything?" Errol dug into his pocket, took out a small bottle, and handed it to Peter. Peter read the label and frowned. "May I ask where you got these, Errol? Peter gently asked. "A doctor I saw before coming to this clinic. "He disclosed. "Errol, would you mind if I send you up to see my colleague Doctor Payne?" Errol's eyes shifted nervously. "Why? Why do you want to send me away?" Errol asked, sounding dismayed. "Errol, it isn't anything you've done. The medicine that Doctor gave you is not the best for you. I think my colleague can give you some medicine that would be more helpful. Peter related. Errol had a huge grin on his face. "Thanks, Doctor, If you think it will work better because sometimes I eat these like their candy. Peter smiled. "Well, we want you to get better. Errol grinned broadly, revealing a pleasant smile. Errol nodded and stood. "Well, thanks for letting me rant, Doctor Dayaggi." Errol said, expressing his gratitude. "Thanks for letting me help Errol. "Would you like to talk again?" Peter inquired. Errol nodded vigorously. "Yes, please." He confirmed. "Just make an appointment with my receptionist." Peter reminded him. Errol waved and marched out to the receptionist's desk. Peter sat at his desk and opened Errol's chart. Patient preliminary report: Errol Tandy. Age 55. Presented with high Anxiety- possible agoraphobia- exhibited misanthropic behavior- may suffer from unresolved childhood trauma. This therapist recommends that Mister Tandy consults with Doctor Payne regarding medication to aid his Anxiety. Current medication: Xanax. Recommend SSRI as a replacement. Peter looked out of the office door Mister Tandy had left open when he departed and saw his receptionist busy with him. Peter buzzed the front desk. "Yes Doctor Dayaggi." Molly responded. "Molly, is Doctor Zhang available?" He inquired. "One moment, please." Molly requested and buzzed Doctor Zhang's office. Debra Lynx, Doctor Zhang's receptionist, answered. "Hey, Molly, what's up?" Debra inquired. "Deb, is Doctor Zhang in for Doctor Dayyagi?" Molly queried. "She won't be back until later this afternoon." Debra, a five-foot-five fiery, proud Native American with long, flowing black hair and soft brown eyes, took guff from no one and was the perfect receptionist for the gentle Doctor Zhang. Returning to Doctor Dayaggi, Molly reported that The Doctor was not at her desk. "Would you like her voice mail, Doctor?" The receptionist asked. "No, that's fine. I'll catch up with her later." Dayyagi exclaimed. "Very well, Doctor."

Something Wicked

Donning a Panama hat, the man wore a black suit and a red tie. soft, leather Italian loafers on his feet. He smiled at his reflection, revealing his pearly white teeth and smoldering brown eyes. He winked at himself. "You a bad motherfucker Lou." He exclaimed, pointing at himself. He spun gracefully, walking to the door. Lou's six-foot frame was slender, like a dancer. He was light on his feet. He weighed about One hundred and sixty pounds of what he liked to call lean muscle. Entering the elevator, the man pressed himself to the back of the cramped space. One floor down, an attractive woman stepped into the elevator and stopped short as she glimpsed at the man in the rear of the small elevator. A sense of discomfort compelled her to speak. "Good morning." She muttered. The man in black flashed her a brilliant smile and replied smoothly. "Good morning, and how are you on this beautiful day?" The woman felt her body flush at the sound of his voice. Confused by her bodily reaction, she responded timidly. "I'm fine, thank you for asking." She looked into the man's eyes and felt her defenses melt away. "Yes," She said as a distraction. "It looks like the Lord gave us a beautiful day." The man in black snickered. "So he gets all the credit?" The woman tilted her head, curious about his remark. At that moment, the elevator doors opened on the ground floor. The woman stepped out and hurried about her business, unaware of what had happened to her on the elevator. The man in black stood in the center of the lobby staring as if seeing something no one else could see. An employee of the hotel stopped as he saw the man staring into space. "Are you okay, Mister Cyphur?" He asked. The man in black looked at the bellhop. "Yes, I'm fine. I was here many years ago. The change is remarkable." The man appeared taken by nostalgia. The bellhop nodded. "You must have been here back in the bad old days." The bellhop observed. This time it was the man in black who turned to nod. "Yes, very bad indeed." He agreed. "Will there be anything special you need, Mister Cyphur?" The bellhop inquired. The man in black looked at the bellhop. "You may call me Lou." The man affirmed. "Will you need anything, Lou, a cab, reservations for dinner? Anything?" The bellhop inquired. "No," Lou paused a moment. The bellhop caught his meaning. "Tommy, sir. My name is Tommy. "Very well, Tommy, it is, and no, I won't need anything. I think I'll go out for a stroll. it's been so long since I've returned to one of my favorite cities." Lou conveyed. Tommy nodded. "Just be careful out there, Lou; the city is still dangerous." Tommy warned. Lou giggled. Tommy's eyebrows furrowed as the giggle seemed out of character for the tall, well-dressed, and good-looking gentleman. Lou saw the lobby as it was before its renovation. He could smell the decay and perversions that once plagued this hotel. "Well, they did a good job cleaning it up." Lou mused loudly. Strolling out of the front door, Lou took a deep breath. A passing cabbie noticed Lou and made the mistake of locking eyes with him. Much to the Cabbies' dismay, he couldn't look away, causing the inevitable crash. The cab smashed into a Volkswagen at a stoplight, pushing it into the middle of the intersection. A truck going in a westerly direction T-boned the cab, barely missing the Volkswagen. Lou smiled, hearing the scream of on-lookers as fellow pedestrians rushed to help the cab driver. Others ran to help the occupants of the accident. The Volkswagen did not get hit by the truck but appeared injured from the rear-ended smash by the cab. Holding back a laugh, Lou proceeded down forty-second street, deciding what to do next. Noticing a homeless man, Lou projected a thought at him. *That man in the dark blue suit in front of you just showed you a big wad of cash and called you a fucking bum."* The homeless man ran up to a man minding his business and smashed a bottle over his head, screaming. "Who's a bum, you fuckin piece of shit!" People scattered, thinking the homeless man was insane. Lou continued his stroll as police quickly descended on the assailant and wrestled him to the ground. Crossing the street, Lou was disappointed at New York's clean-up transformation. Seeing this handsome man look sad, a passerby stopped and asked. "Are you okay, Mister?" Lou looked at the concerned citizen and asked, "What happened to this place?" The stranger looked at Lou curiously. "What do you mean?" He inquired. Lou waved his arms around, encompassing the area. "I mean, what happened to the character, the gravitas?" Lou responded to the stranger. Trying not to be offensive to this potential maniac, the stranger thought he might be able to help. The stranger spoke softly. "Look, Mister; I didn't understand what you meant by your question." He explained. Then why the fuck did you ask?" Lou demanded. The stranger was convinced he should have minded his business when he saw this handsome gentleman standing in the middle of fifth avenue, looking confounded. Lou did not like the affect the stranger displayed. "Are you disappointed?"

Lou inquired. "The stranger was taken aback to be read so easily. "what do you mean?" He asked, feigning ignorance. Lou laughed. "I have staff in my employ that put on that same face when they've been caught doing something unauthorized." He exclaimed. The streets began to fill up with emergency vehicles. The stranger, who turned to look at the gathering of police, turned back to Lou only to find him gone. "Damn!" The stranger thought. "I finally met a good-looking guy who looked like he could use my help and disappeared in a New York minute. God must hate me to introduce someone so beautiful to me only to snatch him out of my life. what kind of luck do I have?" The stranger blindly asked, not knowing with whom he dallied. Lou continued along, enjoying the Summer air. Lou decided to go down a subway staircase at Times square. In the tunnel system of one of the biggest cities on the planet is a world unto itself. Philosophers, artists, musicians, hustlers, would be holy men, and the homeless all could be found in an ever-shifting migration. Some went to work, others at work in the subway, others made it their home, and others made it to hunting grounds. Lou slowly stepped down the muck-covered steps savoring the decadence infused in the steps. He was descending a stairway that led to the upper Manhattan train service. The tunnel staircase was rank with the odor of urine and desperation. Lou stepped unto the boarding platform. People pushed and shoved, waiting for a train to spew forth from the darkness of the tunnels. Lou marveled at the loosely controlled chaos that allowed such a crowd to gather in the musty tunnels. Lou smiled as he sensed the quiet dismay. An air of desperation mixed with desire. A vagrant, obviously drunk, staggered from person to person begging for money. "Excuse me, sir, can ya spare a dollar for coffee?" The man politely slurred. The man, the drunkard, had asked for money, wore a gray suit and a look of disdain. "Get a fucking job, man." The suited man replied. Lou smiled. "Hey!" The vagrant complained. "Who the fuck ya think ya talkin to?" He slurred loudly. The suited man tried to ignore him. "Hey, I'm talkin to ya." The vagrant shouted. Lou felt the rush of heated air that was the sign of an incoming train. A light could be seen in the depths of the tunnel. The train horn sounded, signaling its arrival. Lou whispered in the vagrant's ear. "He's not listening to you." The vagrant looked around, unsure where the voice originated. "He thinks you're a fucking bum not worth his time." Lou whispered. "What? Ya think ya better than me." the vagrant shouted over the sound of the train bearing down on the platform. The suited man stepped away from the vagrant and closer to the lip of the platform creating distance between him and the crazed vagrant. Unfortunately, he also left no room to evade the drunkard. "Look." Lou whispered. He thinks you're such a shit he won't even look at you." He goaded. "Ya think your special mother fucker!" The vagrant yelled and rushed forward, pushing the suited man who was too close to the lip of the platform. leaning over, he tried to regain his balance, only to be hit by the massive train sending his broken body flying across the platform. Blood sprayed passengers as he cartwheeled through the air. The scream of the train as it applied its' emergency breaks, as well as the horrified witness, filled the tunnel. Smiling, Lou walked up the stairs and headed for the platform across the tracks.

Momentarily exiting the station, Lou bought a hot dog and walked back down the stairs that led to Brooklyn. He ran into the E.M.T., who looked slightly confused, and Lou stopped and pointed to where they needed to go. Approaching the turnstile that led to the Brooklyn bound platform, Lou glanced left and right before hoping the turnstile and casually walked to await the train. On the other side of the platform, he watched as chaos ensued.

CHAPTER 5

THE VISITATION

Peter arrived home, stripped off his biking gear, threw the sweaty apparel into a hamper, and jumped into the shower washing the city grime and sweat the bike ride home gifted him. Finishing, he dressed in silk pajamas, opened his refrigerator, grabbed a prepared plate of meatloaf, he popped it in the oven. He sat and reviewed his daily notes, waiting for his dinner to cook. After finishing his plate, he placed the dish in the dishwasher, sank into his coach, and put the T.V. on. Watching the news, he was shocked to hear of the incidents that rocked Manhattan. The reporter spoke about an accident involving a cab running a stoplight and rear-ending a V.W. that was then T-boned by a truck. While the V.W. was not involved in the T-bone accident, both drivers were taken to the hospital by first responders. In another incident reported on a man struck by an uptown train. The man was reported dead on the scene. Meanwhile, police are searching for a man witnesses say was arguing with the victim. Identity will be withheld pending notification of relatives. "What the fuck is going on in the city?" Peter mused. Peter shut the T.V. off, did his evening exercises built himself a light sweat. Completing his routine, Peter rinsed himself off and prepared for the next day. After laying his clothes out, Peter prepared for bed. Sinking into his luxurious bed, Peter was asleep in minutes; however, it was not a restful sleep. Visions of horrendous events kept injecting themselves. Violent scenes, blood, screams. Peter saw the silhouette of a man sneering while all the violence was occurring around him. The silhouetted man seemed gleeful at the havoc around him. Peter awoke in a pool of sweat with the wicked laugh of the silhouetted man ringing in his ears. Looking at his clock, Peter saw it was Five in the morning. The false dawn was beginning to break. Disgusted by his lack of sleep, Peter dropped to the floor doing his daily routine. Finishing his push and sit-ups, he jumped in the shower, dressed in his bike shorts, putting the clothes he laid out the night before in a suit bag. He went downstairs and crossed the street to his favorite deli. Patty greeted him with her usual enthusiasm. "What the hell happened to you, man?" She inquired sardonically. "What do you mean?" Peter asked. "Man, you look like stir-fried shit." She exclaimed. Peter grinned. "With that kind of support, it's no wonder Pedro isn't the head of some major company." Peter replied sarcastically. "He would be if he wasn't so fucking lazy." Patty snapped. "Whoa," Peter complained. "You kiss your mother with that mouth?" Peter jibed. "You'd be surprised what she can do with that mouth." Pedro exclaimed, coming out of the back of the store. "Okay, that was more information than I needed this morning." Peter complained. "Biking to work today?" Patty asked. Peter nodded affirmatively. "Be mindful; it's supposed to storm later this afternoon." She warned. Peter smiled. "Yeah, gotta be careful; you know sugar melts." He teased. Peter ordered his favorite breakfast sandwich. "It's going to take a few minutes since you didn't call. Patty posed in what was supposed to be a complaining tone. Peter paid his bill and waited a few minutes before the sandwich was done. Peter thanked her. As he was leaving, Pedro called out to him. "Hey, Doc." Peter turned to speak to him. "What's up?" Pedro shuffled his feet as if embarrassed." Peter allowed Pedro a moment to say what he wanted to say. "Is it possible for me to stop by your place tonight to talk?" He inquired. Peter's curiosity rose as Pedro had never made such a request before. "Sure, man. Is eight o clock okay with you?" Peter asked. "That would be great, thanks, Peter, and uhh, can we keep this from Patty." He inquired. "Anything you say to me falls under a confidentiality clause." Peter informed. "Great!" Pedro exclaimed. "See you tonight." Peter nodded. "Tonight, then." Peter exited the store, carefully crossed the busy street, and headed for his bicycle. Unlocking his transportation, Peter slung his suit bag over his shoulder and began his two-and-a-half bike ride to work. Peter loved the ride as it helped to clear his head. He was becoming familiar with not only the route, but there were some faces he was coming to know. Peter waved to a local shop owner. The busy streets forced his mind to stay sharp. However, the disturbing news from the previous evening kept repeatedly playing in his head. A car horn snapped his attention back. Peter shook his head. It was not like him to be so distracted. He began to wonder if he had been doing the therapy game too long as he was finding it difficult to focus. While he considered himself a Humanist, Peter was not very sentimental. He believed discipline was more trustworthy than emotions, which was one of the reasons he was so upset. He could not forget the ringing laughter of the silhouetted man in his dreams. He might talk to William about it for some feedback. Pulling to his workplace, Peter dismounted his bike, walked up to the door, and punched the security code. Entering, Peter headed straight for the showers to make himself presentable for his workday. Carefully unfolding his suit bag, his receptionist Nancy walked into the clinic. "Good morning, boss." She called out. "Nancy, I'm about to jump in the shower. Would you be kind enough to check my suit for wrinkles?" Peter inquired. "I don't do laundry." She quipped. "No one asked you to do anything but check the clothing." Peter shot back." Nancy dug in with her complaint. "And if I find a wrinkle?" She could hear her boss sigh making her smile. "For the love of everything holy, just tell me I'll take care of it." Peter responded. Nancy's smile grew. "What, you don't want me to remove your wrinkles, Mister Dayaggi?" She twanged in an indistinguishable accent. "No! Don't touch my suit with anything but your eyes, and I'll press my suit." Peter rebuked, "Oh, and it's Doctor Dayaggi." Peter exclaimed.

Nancy laughed. "You're so sensitive." She teased. Peter mumbled something indistinguishable. Nancy laughed while checking the suit. "Seems fine." She called out. "Seems or is?" Peter queried. "It's fine, your highness." She retaliated. Turning the shower off, Peter donned a robe and stepped out of the bathroom to find Nancy. "Good morning, boss." She repeated with a smile. Peter returned the smile and greeting. "Good morning Miss Rogers. Would you be so kind as to see if William has a moment for me this morning?" He inquired. "Of course, sir. Anything else?" Nancy asked. Peter shook his head. "Not right now." Peter informed her. Nancy nodded; let me ring Doctor Payne and see if he's available." She said, heading for her desk. After a moment, she returned. Doctor Payne is unavailable until tomorrow afternoon but is willing to cancel an appointment if the matter is urgent. Peter shook his head. "No, that's fine." Peter responded.

Arrival of Darkness

The conductor's garbled voice could barely be understood above the noise. "This is Grand street, Grand street." He repeated. Lou felt a tug suggesting he get off at this stop. Lou exited the train and, shortly after that, the station. Lou sniffed at the air. *"Ahh, a familiar smell."* He mused silently. He followed the odor, surprised to find such a smell in this corrupt city. "How unlikely that in this city of sin I would find the smell of.." Lou paused and looked at a sign that said Less stress Clinic. "Sanctuary." He whispered. He slowly approached the building, getting a mixed sense of good and bad. Lou opened the door and felt cool air rush over him. "I don't like this place already." He complained. Entering, Lou approached the receptionist's desk, where Molly sat working on the computer. Feeling the shifting air current made by the opening of the door, Molly looked up and was struck by the handsome man approaching her as if in slow motion. He was graceful as if he was an apex predator on the prowl. Molly did a small shaking of her head as if to clear it of a mesmerizing effect. Her eyes cleared, and she looked into golden-brown eyes that seemed to envelop her. The two stared at one another for a moment that lasted an eternity. Peter sat in his office, becoming mildly frustrated after repeated attempts to reach the receptionist. He called his secretary on the intercom. "Nancy, is someone covering for Molly?" Peter inquired. "Not that I'm aware of, sir. She should be at her station. I can check if you'd like," Nancy offered. "That won't be necessary; I'll check myself." Peter declared. From his desk, Peter went out to the reception area to find Molly gazing into the eyes of a stranger as if entranced. "Is there a problem, Miss Drake?" Peter asked, slightly bewildered by Molly's behavior. Surprised by the sound of Peters's voice, She turned, gesturing to the stranger. "Oh, Doctor Dayaggi, this is.." It struck Molly that she never asked the stranger's name or the purpose of his visit, in other words, her job. "I'm sorry, sir, I never got your name." She declared embarrassed by her unprofessionalism. The gentleman with the smoldering eyes smiled a blinding smile and softly responded. "That's quite alright. My name is Lou, Lou Cyphur." He proclaimed as if expecting trumpets to accompany the vocalization of his name. Molly fought to keep a grip on a wave of desire for this moca-skinned, brown-eyed hunk of flesh. "How may we be of service?" Molly nearly whispered. Peter was watching the exchange, curious about the effect this man elicited from Molly. "The fact of the matter is I'm not sure why I'm here, Miss Drake." Lou responded softly. "Could you tell me what you do here?" Lou inquired. "Well," Molly began. "We, sir," Peter interjected. "Are a mental health clinic." He responded concisely. Lou turned his gaze upon Peter, whose heart skipped a beat when Lou looked at him. "Doctor Dayaggi? Is that right?" Lou asked flippantly. "How can we help you, Mister Cyphur?" Peter asked, not liking the feeling he was getting from this man. "Well, I'm not sure how you can help me, Doctor, as I'm only now discovering what the function of your clinic is." Lou proclaimed. "I see." Peter replied. "And now that you know?" Peter inquired. Lou looked around, pointing to the steps that led up he asked. "Where do those steps lead?" Peter walked beside Molly answering Lou's question. "That, Mister Cyphur, leads to the roof." Peter replied. "I see." Lou responded. "And this clinic is designed to assist people with mental disorders?" He asked. "Not all of our clients have what you call a disorder; some just come to talk." Peter clarified. "Just talk?" Lou asked, sounding confused. "Just talk about what?" Lou inquired. "Just about anything that could be effecting their emotional, mental or physical well-being." Peter informed. "You mean to tell me people can just come in and bitch about their problems?" Lou asked, sounding perplexed. Peter shook his head. "Not at all. Suppose they are not recommended by another professional and are walk-ins like yourself. In that case, we sit for a half hour to evaluate whether the person has an issue that needs to be addressed. Or if it is something they could resolve with a definitive action plan." Peter explained. Lou nodded slowly, stroking his chin while gazing around the office. "Are you unfamiliar with the therapy process Mister Cyphur?" Lou looked astonished. "Well, where I'm from, we don't have anything like this," Lou said honestly. Peter tilted his head. "And where might you be from, Mister Cyphur?" Peter inquired. Lou held up his hand. "Please call me Lou." Peter nodded. "As you wish. Where are you from?" Peter repeated. Lou slowly faced Peter. "Is it expensive? The therapy, I mean, does it cost much? I ask because we are in one of the most expensive city's in the world and this place is beautiful. I can't imagine the lease rate on such a spot." Lou declared. "Oh, we own the building." Molly, who had grown silent while trying hard not to stare at Lou, seemed o jump at the chance to contribute to the conversation. "Really?" Lou exclaimed, sounding surprised. "Well, actually Doctor Payne, our boss, owns it." Molly admitted. "The rates are on a sliding scale." Peter interjected. Lou gave a confused look in response. "You pay what you can afford." Molly piped in. "How can your Doctor Payne maintain such a place?" Lou asked in disbelief. Molly opened her mouth to speak. Peter stopped her by placing his hand on her arm. "We've managed so far and seem to do some good." Peter returned.

"Undeniably." Lou smiled. He looked at Peter with a look of curiosity. "How would one begin the process of becoming a patient?" Lou inquired. "Client, sir, not patient." Peter clarified. "I fail to see the difference." Lou admitted. "The former comes with another professional's direction for a diagnosed ailment while the latter voluntarily has not met criteria suggesting such a status." Peter explained. "Lou grinned, tilting his head in doubt. "If you say so." He charged. "So what do you think?" Peter asked. "Whom would I get to speak to? Is it you, or is there another Doctor I can choose from?" Lou inquired. Molly quickly handed Lou a pamphlet describing the facility and its staff. Lou quickly glanced at the pamphlet before his eyes returned to Molly. "Will you speak to me then? Can it be you that helps me explore my issues?" Lou asked with a flirtatious tone. Molly, uncharacteristically blushed. At five feet eight inches, Molly was considered tall. She wore her blonde hair at medium length and had striking blue eyes. She was pretty but, for whatever reason, single. She would argue that she was focused on her career. Peter was somewhat embarrassed as this was not the first time she had confronted such flirtatious behavior exhibited by clients. It is, however, the first time she cannot control her reactions. "Oh, no, sir.' She quickly said. "I'm a receptionist here; I am going to night school to earn my degree." She motioned to Peter. "Doctor Dayaggi is an excellent therapist, and if he doesn't suit your needs, there are others you may choose. "Well, Lou, what do you think?" Peter asked. Lou appeared to think for a moment before declaring. "You know, as long as it's reasonable, why not? I've got alot to confess." He exclaimed with an evil leer. "Just a reminder, we're not a church. We don't offer absolution." Peter confirmed. "Oh," Lou challenged. "What do you offer? Peter smiled. "Resolution." Peter responded, causing Lou to smile. "I'll take that bet." Lou snapped. "And will I see you again upon my return, uh?" Lou let the question hang. "Molly, Molly Drake." She sputtered. "Well, miss, is it?" Lou inquired. Molly shook her head eagerly. "Excellent. Miss Drake, I look forward to seeing you again. "So you've decided to utilize our facility. Peter exclaimed.

Lou shook his head. "No. I've decided to pay a visit and see if It is something I would find helpful in my endeavors." Lou clarified. Peter nodded. "I see; well, your seeming penchant for clarity would make it a brief visit." Peter claimed. "And why is that?" Lou asked. Peter smiled. "Half of the problem in therapy is lack of clarity. We frequently spend many hours getting our clients to admit their issues. Once admitting, we must sort through the many barriers people set before we strike the root of their issues." Lou smiled. "Fascinating. I look forward to our next meeting, Doctor." Lou expressed. "Did Molly take your basic information, sir?" Peter inquired. "Excuse me?" Lou responded. Peter grinned, shaking his head. "My apologies; Molly has a form to fill out if you wouldn't mind. "No, of course not." Lou responded, allowing Peter to escort him back to the front desk. "Molly, please allow Mister Cyphur to fill out an admission form." Peter asked flatly. Embarrassed by her lack of professionalism, Molly handed Lou a form he quickly filled out. "Well, I must be about my business, is that all?" He directed at Molly. "Yes sir, please excuse my.." Lou lifted his hand, signaling for her to stop. "Please, I had the pleasure of being in a beautiful woman's company. There is never a need to apologize for that." Lou complimented. Molly blushed. "Thank you, sir, until.." Lou signaled again. "That would be Lou, not sir." Molly smiled. "Of course, Lou." She said, hesitating tingly. Lou waved. "Until next we meet." he said in departure.

CHAPTER 6

DELI KING

Peter dismounted his bicycle and locked it up for the night. Looking across the street at Pedro & Patty's deli, he saw the store contending with its evening rush. *"I wonder what Tony wants to talk about?"* Peter mused. He proceeded to his apartment. Entering, he began shedding his clothes, preparing for a shower. Turning on the television, his attention was snatched by late-breaking news. "Good evening, This is Lance Brady with breaking news. Today on Fulton avenue, a man was violently beaten. An eyewitness clarified the reason for the attack. Let us go now to our reporter in the field, Ted Jackson, Ted." The scene changed to one Peter was familiar with. "Thanks, Lance. The incident occurred here on Kent avenue and south third, near Misi Italian restaurant. According to an eyewitness." Suddenly Peter was looking at the face of the man that introduced himself as Lou Cyphur earlier that day, speaking to the reporter. "I was walking from my Doctor's office when I heard a man shout something about the end of days and some nonsense about how he walks among us before throwing himself in front of a fast-moving bus." Lou stated, smiling at the camera. "When I asked the eyewitness how fast he thinks he way the bus was going, he shared it appeared to be going much faster than it should have." The reporter stated. "I sought out the bus driver, who told me that his brakes had failed and the bus had been accelerating for over a block before hitting the pedestrian. Back to you, Lance." Lance shook his head in disbelief. "What happens now, Ted?" The news anchor asked. "Well, there will be an investigation as to the exact cause of the failure, and the driver will be on paid administrative leave until the conclusion of the investigation, Lance." The news anchor shook his head. "Thanks, Ted. This has been an eyewitness news special report." Peter shut off the television. The telephone rang, startling Peter. "Hello." Peter greeted. "Hey Doc, it's Pedro. Just checking to see if we're still good for this evening." Peter checked his watch. "I was just going to jump in the shower." He replied. "Okay, you want me to bring some of Patty's spaghetti?" Pedro asked. Peter's mouth watered, and Patty made excellent pasta. "That would be fine." Peter answered with a grin. "Good enough, Doc; see you in an hour or so." Pedro replied. "Okay, I'll see you then." Peter confirmed. Peter jumped in the shower, glad he didn't have to worry about making dinner. After his shower, Peter decided to meditate to help clear his mind. The door intercom buzzed. Peter got up from his meditating position and glanced at the clock. Unaware of the passage of time, he answered the bell. "Who is it?" He inquired. "Delivery man." Came the response. "I've got some hot, kick-ass spaghetti here." Peter drooled slightly. "Okay, Spanish Pete, come on up." He joked. A few moments later, Pedro was at his door." Peter peeked through the eyehole and immaturely asked. "Who is it?" Pedro took a deep breath. "Delivery for the obstinate colonist." Pedro responded. Peter opened the door. "What's with the hostility?" He posed. "What's with the colonial penchant for renaming everything to suit your fancy?" Pedro responded. "What?, oh you mean the Spanish Pete remark?" Pedro's mouth twisted into a sneer, mocking Peter; he repeated. "Was it the Spanish Pete? Yeah, it was the Spanish Pete cabron." Pedro spat, feigning anger. Peter held up his hand defensively. "You do know Pedro is Spanish for Peter?" Peter complained defensively. Pedro looked at him sideways. "Yeah, I know, it's a weak argument. I apologize, Pedro." Peter said earnestly. Pedro smiled. Apology accepted, ass-hole." Pedro responded, slapping Peter on the back. Entering the apartment, Pedro looked around and whistled. "Nice place Doc. Must set you back a grip." Pedro observed. "Naah, I do okay." Peter countered modestly. "Yeah, that's what the rich always say." Pedro grumbled. "Did you come up here to complain about how much money you think I have?" Peter inquired. Pedro was quiet for a moment. "No, of course not." Pedro responded. "Would you like a beer?" Peter asked. Pedro smiled. "that would be great." Pedro accepted gratefully. Peter returned, handing Pedro his beer. "Lowenbrau? This is some good shit." Pedro complimented. "Glad you like it." Peter replied. Peter sat in his favorite chair, gesturing to a chair for Pedro to sit." Pedro glanced at it. "Looks comfy." He noticed. "It is." Peter responded. A moment of silence as Pedro avoided Peter's gaze. "The reason I asked for this meeting, it's Patty." Pedro fell silent. Peter waited patiently for him to start again. "She's been having these nightmares." Pedro shared. "What kind of nightmares?" Peter asked. Pedro stared at Peter intensely. "The kind that wakes a person up screaming." Pedro related. "What does she scream?" Peter probed. Pedro stood abruptly, walking to the picture window that faced downtown Brooklyn. "She screams about shit like "He's here, he's here, and death walks beside him." Peter waited a moment before asking. "Does she say who he is supposed to be?" Pedro turned suddenly. "The devil." He said. Peter was momentarily taken aback. "I'm sorry, what?" He asked. "You heard me." Pedro insisted. Peter considered a moment. "I didn't know Patty was religious." Peter admitted. "That's just it." Pedro countered. "She's not. When we first met, she used to complain about religious fools who kept praying instead of doing it for themselves. You can't imagine my surprise when she started this babbling." Pedro admitted. Peter nodded in understanding. "When did the nightmares begin? He asked, pulling out a pad and pen. Pedro looked at him suspiciously. "What are you doing?" Peter looked up. Writing some notes on what you're saying." He explained. "Why? Why are you taking notes? Pedro demanded. Peter sighed. Pedro, do you want my help?" Peter asked. Pedro nodded. "Then you must trust me, my friend. This is how we resolve things in my profession. We take notes, and the more we take, the more the story reveals itself if you know what to look for." Peter explained. "Is my Patty going crazy, Doc?" Pedro's concern for his wife reveals his love's depth. Peter shook his head. "I doubt that. She probably is very stressed. Is there something going on in the business or a family matter?" Peter inquired. Pedro shook his head. "Nothing she's shared with me." He stated flatly. Peter pursed his lips. "Have you spoken to her about it"? Peter questioned further. Pedro shook his head again. "No, I haven't." Pedro admitted. "That might be your first step." Peter advised. "How do I do that." Pedro asked. "Just ask if she has trouble sleeping and shares that you notice her tossing in her sleep." Pedro looked lost. "And then?" He responded. "If she admits it, ask her if she wants to talk about it. If she complies, I suggest she talk to Doctor Pete. Still, suppose she feels uncomfortable with that idea. In that case, I work with an excellent female therapist that might help her relax and resolve her inner turmoil." Peter suggested. "Inner turmoil?" Pedro repeated. "Something is bothering her if it has her screaming at night, my friend. Pedro nodded. "Thanks, Doc. I guess I'll go home and have a conversation with Patty. Pedro sadly remarked. "Keep your Head up, my friend. The first step on the road to recovery is recognition." Peter consoled. "Thanks, Doc; what do I owe you?" Pedro asked. Peter shook his head. "No, let us get our favorite cook back to her normal acerbic self." Peter jibed, sticking his hand out. Pedro shook the proffered hand stood, and Peter escorted him to the door.

Trouble trouble

Exiting the Holland hotel, Lou stopped and took a deep breath of the rank, New York air. It was a warm, clear evening, and Lou walked uptown. Striding through Manhattan, he Walked along Eleventh avenue. He wandered into an admixture of people enjoying the warm summer evening. On fifty-third street, he heard a violin playing. Lou followed the sound bringing him to Dewitt's/ Clinton park. A lovely performing artist caught Lou's attention. Her red hair and pale complexion complimented her bright green eyes. Her hands caught at invisible puffs of smoke as she danced to a well-played violin by a long-haired, somewhat bedraggled gentleman who played with a vigor that equaled her dancing. The beauty of the performance struck Lou. The park provided an excellent stage. A plateau of rocks served as an elevated platform to be admired (or jeered, this is New York). Unsure of how long he watched the couple's performance, Lou realized he was among the last of their audience. Watching them pack their gear, They noticed Lou standing there. "Hi." The petite dancer greeted him. Lou shyly gestured a greeting. "I apologize; I did not mean to stare; it's just that I thought your performance was lovely," Lou complimented. The pretty dancer smiled. "Thank you very much." She said gratefully. "And you, sir," Lou continued. "That was a well-played piece." Lou complimented the violinist, who acknowledged the compliment with a nod."It seems as if our performance touched you." The dancer observed. Lou nodded his head vigorously. "Yes, very much." He unabashedly agreed. "You see, I'm a historian. The music and dancing reminded me of an old musical piece. It's dancing accompaniment that has not been practiced or even taught anymore. I found it curious that you two perform as if raised in the culture which produced it." Lou explained. The dancers' faces lit up as Lou shared his impression. "Stephan, Stephan." The dancer called to her partner. Putting the rest of his gear away, Stephan joined them. "Yes, Ari, what are you so excited about?" The violinist asked. "Ari." Lou repeated. "What a beautiful name." He complimented. Ari curtsied. "Why, thank you." She responded, affecting a coy-shyness. Lou laughed a warm, welcoming tenor laugh. Unknown to his acquaintances, Lou's words were laced with a mesmerizing spell making them less inhibited. "Would you play for me again?" Lou asked. Stephan shook his head. "We would love to, but.." Lou dug in his pocket while staring at Stephan. After a moment, Lou asked. "Would a hundred dollars convince you it is worth the effort?" He cajoled. Stephan looked tempted, and Ari struck a pose. "Maestro, if you'd be so kind?" Ari gently requested. Caught in the moment, Stephan drew out his violin like a sword. Slowly he brought it to the play position. Lou applauded. "Very theatrical, bravo." He complimented. A compliment that had bound in it a spell of abandonment. All of Stephan's doubts about his playing abilities dissipated. Ari's inhibitions also were cut loose. Stephan plucked the strings in a manner that gave the impression of falling rain. Ari began moving, slowly, gracefully swaying her hips. She looked up at the sky and, in time with the plucking, began hopping as if avoiding the raindrops. Suddenly Stephan strummed a discordant note that Ari reacted to by throwing her hands above her head as if shielding herself from cascading notes. Ari threw her arms left and right as Stephan's staccato abruptly changed to long four-beat notes representing a mighty wind that tugged at Ari. People began to reform around the couple. Lou began to chant in time with the music. The gathering crowd bore witness to a spectacle. The performers, with the aid of an illusion of Pan-like festivities (made possible by the spell Lou was casting with his chant.) Lifting the audience's spirits. Enthralled, Ari struck a pose and looked at an audience member. "Baptize us, Father." She whispered. The bye-stander was surprised at the request and then realized that this was probably one of those performances that asked its audience to participate. A stranger walked beside Lou. "This is cool, huh?" He asked one of those questions that were looking for an agreement. "Very cool." Lou responded. "Do you think he'll do it?" The stranger asked. Lou shifted his gaze from Ari to the stranger. "What do you mean?" He asked. "The tourist. Do you think he'll participate?" The stranger clarified. "How do you know he's a tourist?" Lou inquired. The stranger smiled. "Oh, I didn't, but they did." He quipped, signifying the performers. "How do you know that?" Lou asked, genuinely curious. "Street performers know tourists because that is where their money is made." The stranger posed matter of factly. Lou nodded as it made perfect sense. He watched as the enchanted tourist ran out of the park to a row of parked cars. The boys hung around the vehicles until they saw a man come out of the park toward them. Thinking he might be the owner of one of the cars, the boys hastily left. As the man approached the spot where the boys stood, a bucket filled with fluid was beside one of the cars. Picking up the bucket, the man returned to the park and, laughing, began splashing the onlookers. "Gather one and all and give praise to the muse." Ari began to chant. The violin swelled to a crescendo sending Ari into a swirling dervish style of dance. The music swelled, Ari spun faster, and The audience joined the chant. "Give praise to the muse, give praise to the muse." The audience repeated the phrase several times as the violin somehow grew louder, even more powerful than a small instrument could play. Stephan was bathed in sweat; his breathing labored as he played far beyond his skill, too, was enraptured by the moment and the spell Lou cast. The moment every true performer sought, oneness with the audience. Lou smiled, seeing his incantation's effect, and began walking away. The audience was so enchanted by the music of the long-haired bedraggled, sweaty musician with piercing brown eyes and long matted hair. The dance of the pretty, pale, red hair, green-eyed Woman. The raw feeling of community was so overwhelming that no one noticed the odd smell of the liquid they used to "baptize" the audience. Everyone roared in approval when the lighting of a cigarette ignited the gasoline the audience had been doused in. The revelry quickly became pandemonium as The park filled with the screams of the burning. The level of their devotion was measured by the degree of conflagration they suffered. One such devotee, Lou, found it particularly amusing as she ran screeching with only her head ablaze. Ari, his beautiful little dancer, writhed on the floor, howling. Twitching and jerking, she gave one final, piercing scream of despair. The aspiring violinist Stephen Harris, caught in a hypnotic rapture, accompanied Ari's scream with one of his own as he played his final note and collapsed on the still, charred form that was once Ari Dubois, performing dancer. Lou smiled and continued his sojourn through the city. In his wandering, Lou ran across various villainy he reveled in. One dark ally held a pimp beating his whore with a great deal of pleasure. "Bitch! I told you not to fuck with my money." Lou heard the pimp shout. "Ya know now I gotta cut ya." The pimp threatened. Lou wanted to add a twist, not one to pass up a nice slashing. "Hey, tough guy." Lou called out. "What's your problem?" He asked. The pimp turned at the voice calling him out. "Yo, this aint yo business, so unless you want what she was about to get, I suggest you step the fuck off." The pimp warned. "Ohh, your such a tough guy." Lou responded sarcastically. "You either stupid, or ya got a death wish." The pimp observed. "The only wish I got is for that whore of yours to take that knife out of your hand and cut your dick off." Lou retaliated. "Dude, this bitch aint doin shit, and you about to meet yo maker." The pimp menaced. The pimp did not realize that when Lou uttered his wish, it was more a directed command to the prostitute who was badly beaten and suffered at the hands of this pimp. He had subjugated her body and mind. With no thoughts of consequence and Lou's prompting, the beaten Woman snatched the knife out of the pimp's hand and made a slashing motion severing the man's penis. In shock, the pimp grabbed his groin. Looking toward Lou, the pimp emitted a high-pitched scream that reflected the pain of his severed manhood and his reputation that would never recover from such a display of weakness. Laying on the ground in a pool of blood, Lou leaned over the bloodied pimp. "Just a suggestion, but you might want to find a new line of work." Watching the pool of blood get bigger, Lou qualified his observation. "That is if you live." Lou smiled and looked at the whore, who stood with the knife still in her hand. "You may want to get rid of that thing." Lou suggested gesturing to the knife. The Woman dropped the knife and ran. Lou smiled, continuing his journey. Content with the mayhem he was spreading.

CHAPTER 7

PONDERING

Peter sat alone, trying to make sense of the information Pedro shared with him. While Peter has known them for a brief period since he moved into his apartment. They had gotten fairly close in the last six months as he regularly bought breakfast sandwiches and occasional dinners from their deli. The relationship began developing with Patty's scorching sense of humor. A native New Yorker, she always seemed straightforward, except for her life growing up. When those conversations arose, they were quickly dismissed by her. "You know, same ole same ole." Peter wondered if it was a coping mechanism she employed to avoid serious discussion regarding that time in her life. Sadly Pedro knew little of his wife's childhood as she rarely referred to those times except, according to Pedro, as a warning. In the past, when Pedro brought up the idea of her seeing someone therapeutically, she would decline passively, claiming she had no such needs. If Peter took everything, Pedro reported at face value. It would be fair to assume that Patty suffered a sequence of events that left her vulnerable and possibly violated. Leaving her in a non-communicative state regarding her abuse. It was possible, Peter mused, that the dreams she was suffering now could be a convoluted and exaggerated attempt of her mind to exorcise those memories. Peter knew without Patty verbalizing her anxieties; there was little Peter could do for her. *It would be best if we could convince her to come and speak with me directly.* Peter thought to himself. Peter checked his watch. 10 pm. Peter turned on the T.V. to watch the late news. The reporter was ranting about a tragic act occurring in midtown. "Good evening. This is Lance Brady, eyewitness news with a late-breaking story. Tonight in Dewitt Park off of 12th ave and 54th Street was the scene of a horrific event. More now from reporter Ted Jackson who is on the scene, "Ted, can you tell us what's going on?" The camera showed The reporter trying to talk to an official. "Yeah, Lance. I keep trying to talk to officials and getting mixed stories. The gist of it seems to be the Emergency responders were called to Dewitt/Clinton park around 9:30 this evening when residents noticed an orange glow coming from the park. Upon arrival, officials found numerous badly burned and charred bodies. there is no official word yet as to what happened here. Was this a heinous act perpetrated against these people, a demonstration, or a protest? We are unclear at this time as there seemed to have been no eyewitnesses. Lance." The t.v. anchor shook his head in disbelief. "Have they counted how many victims there are?" Lance inquired. Ted shook his head. "Currently, they estimate over forty people; however, they will not release the final count until the investigation is complete. Lance." Lance drew in a breath. "It seems your pretty busy out there tonight Ted." Ted nodded. "No doubt, Lance, our city is having a restless night." Ted agreed. "Keep us updated as new facts are revealed, Ted." Lance mildly requested. "Of course." Ted confirmed. Peter shut off the t.v. wondering why he felt oddly close to all that was transpiring. Setting to his evening routines, Peter plotted his next day with the underlying feeling that something dynamic was occurring. Feeling slightly like a leaf caught in a storm, Peter jumped in the shower completing his routine. Unable to sleep, Peter lay in bed staring at his ceiling. Long shadows slowly shifted as the dawn approached. With a start, Peter awoke at the prodding of his alarm clock. Not knowing when he fell asleep, his body was spent as if he hadn't slept. Wearily he rolled out of bed and went about his morning work routine. fifteen minutes later, Peter called the deli to put in his usual breakfast order.

Exiting the front door of his apartment building, Peter Looked across the street at the Gomez Deli. Dashing across the busy street, Peter entered the store to get his usual sandwich finding the usual acerbic Patty more demur than usual. "Hey Patty-cake, what's shaking?" Peter asked nonchalantly. Patty looked at him without responding. Peter paused, "Are you okay?" He inquired. Patty's eyes narrowed. "Of course I'm alright. What kind of question is that?" She inquired. Peter shook his head. "Nothing, just a question. Patty lowered her head. "I apologize, Doc. I haven't been sleeping well and, well, you know." She complained softly. Peter gazed at her softly. "Patty, if there is anything I can do." He offered. Patty shook her head. "No thanks. Besides, what can be done?" She asked. Peter smiled gently. "You know what I do professionally, right?" He queried. Patty looked up suddenly. "Ya wanna shrink me, Doc?" She responded defensively. Peter shook his head. "no, not at all. We could start with a conversation." Peter minimized. Patty looked skeptical. "How does one relate a sense of impending doom?" She inquired. "Well," Peter responded. Just as you did now. Say what you feel without trying to know what it means." He replied. Patty looked at him sideways. "I thought the point was to figure out what it meant. Peter nodded. "Of course, eventually. But first, it's about voicing feelings. Once we can do that, then we start looking for meanings." Peter clarified. Patty laughed, a chilly laugh, one Peter had never heard her emit. "If you would like, we could do something private for your comfort, or you could come to the clinic. We have other therapists there you might feel more comfortable with." Peter offered. Patty shook her head. "Not likely, but I might take you up on the private consultation." She capitulated. Peter smiled. "Whatever you're comfortable with." Peter agreed. Patty nodded. "Let me talk to Pedro about it, and I'll get back to you." She added. Peter nodded. "Whenever you're ready." He agreed. Snatching up his breakfast sandwich, Peter bid farewell. "Gotta get to work. Let me know what you want to do when you know, of course." Patty nodded in agreement. "Thanks, Doc." She said gratefully. Peter waved goodbye and walked out of the store. He quickly ate his breakfast sandwich, unlocked it, and mounted his bicycle for the short ride to work. Clouds threatened the morning sky. Peter mounted his bike and cut through the traffic to work.

The clinic

Helen and Bruce sat in the lounge area of the clinic, watching the morning news. Helen was shocked at the incident report at Dewitt/Clinton park. Bruce sat watching stoically as the reporter encapsulated the details of the event. "Police have no leads nor motives at this time. No one can definitively say this was an act of violence perpetrated or a symbolic gesture, Mary." The anchor of the news team shook her head. "Dear god." He quipped. "Wallace, Do the police have any suspects?" The reporter shook his head. "As I stated. The police did not share such information; they asked the public if anyone saw anything suspicious in this area before or after the incident, no matter how remote, to call 555-tip. Your name will remain confidential. Back to you, Mary". "Thanks, Wallace. Well, it was a very active day in our city. Yesterday in the morning rush hour, a cab w rear-ended a Volkswagen and then pushed it into the middle of an intersection. The report was cut short as Helen shut off the T.V. "My Lord." she whispered. "God had nothing to do with it." Bruce exclaimed. "I bet you it's some drug-crazed kids who were doing some kind of gang initiation." He observed. "You think this was a gang initiation?" Helen asked, shocked. Bruce nodded affirmatively. "You don't think this is kind of beyond that." Helen inquired, disturbed at Bruce's seeming callousness. Bruce shook his head. "Live in this city long enough, and you'll see all kinds of insanity." He claimed. "Which is why we opened shop here, to help." William stated as he walked into the lounge. "Good morning, Doctor." Bruce greeted. "Good morning Doctor Payne." Helen echoed. "Good morning." William responded. "Has anyone seen Doctor Dayaggi?" He inquired. "No, sir." The doctors responded. At that moment,

Peter entered the clinic. "Sorry I'm late, boss, but it seems a neighbor is suffering a dilemma, and they requested my assistance." Peter informed him. "No problem, Peter; anything we can do to help?" William asked. Peter shook his head. "I don't think so. I informed them of our therapists and that we could accommodate them if they felt more comfortable. They requested that they speak to me only. I assured them it wouldn't be an issue." William nodded his head. "Well done; let us know if we can help." Peter nodded. "Of course, thank you, William." Peter answered. Doctor Payne smiled. "I'm sure everyone has seen the news and the events that took place last night?" He waited while his staff confirmed his assumption. "Let's prepare ourselves for our clients' possible reactions today." William requested. At that moment, Molly could be heard attempting to calm a client from the reception area. "I demand to see Doctor Dayaggi." Peter looked at his colleagues. "It sounds like Errol." He stated. Molly, the receptionist, spoke softly to Errol. "Mister Tandy, if you have a seat, Doctor Dayaggi will be with you momentarily." She assured him. Errol paced in the reception area. "Do you hear what's going on out there?" He asked loudly. "The city is going to hell." He exclaimed. Doctor Dayaggi walked into reception. "Errol, are we okay?" He inquired mildly. Errol stared at Peter. "Haven't you been watching the news?" He demanded. Peter nodded. "I have been watching the news, Errol, and yes, I've watched the reports. Can we step into my office and discuss this further?" Peter prodded. Errol reluctantly followed. "I'm telling you, Doc, this is different. I can feel it." Errol demanded. "I don't doubt that you feel something." Peter capitulated as he led Errol into his office and closed his door. "Man, oh man." Bruce whispered. Doctor Payne turned to look at him. "I'm afraid if this current uptick in crime continues, we'll see more of these reactions from our clients." William predicted. "That I don't doubt." Bruce agreed. "What is your schedule like today Bruce?" William inquired. Bruce flipped open his schedule book. "I have a possible one thirty and another at three o'clock." He responded. William nodded. "We might have to consider extending hours or being on call." William informed him. "Do you know for how long?" Bruce asked. William shook his head. "Until this crisis passes. He stated sadly. Bruce nodded. "Understood. William looked beside him where Helen stood quietly. "Doctor Zhang, will you please.." At that moment, the entrance doors were flung open, and Lisa Montoya hurriedly stepped in. "He's here. He's here!" She screamed. Helen rushed over to her. "Lisa, are you alright? What's wrong?" Lisa looked genuinely petrified. "He's here." She stated again emphatically. "Who is here, Lisa?" Helen asked. Lisa crossed herself. "El Diablo. He's here. She repeated. Helen took Lisa's hand in hers. Lisa's hands were cold and clammy. "Lisa," Helen prodded gently. "Did you remember to take your meds this morning? Lisa stopped panting and yanked her hands away. "You think I'm bugging out? You think this is because I forgot to take my meds?" She demanded. "You don't understand, do you?" She asked furiously. "The devil is here." She shouted, the terror returning to her voice. "Would you like to come into my office?" Helen asked. Lisa looked at her, disbelieving the apparent casual attitude. "fuck no. I want to get out of here. She complained. "But Lisa," Helen pointed out. "You just got here and came for a reason, right? Maybe because you feel safe here." Helen Helen espoused calmly. "You're not listening, lady. The reason I came was to warn you. He's coming!" Lisa demanded. "But how do you know he's coming here?" Helen begged. The front door entrance opened as if on cue, and a man dressed in black slacks. red shirt and black tie stepped into the building. Lisa seemed to shrink into herself. "Oh, my god." She whispered, which seemed to catch the man's attention. *"No, my dear, you know me."* Lisa heard in her mind. Lisa ran to the back of the building with Doctor Zhang called her name. "My oh my." Lou stated while walking up to the reception desk. "Mister Cyphur, welcome back." Molly expressed trying very hard to remain professional. "Well, greetings, lovely Molly." Lou stated in a mildly flirtatious, if not seductive, voice. "Mister Cyphur," Doctor Payne, having dismissed the meeting, entered the reception area and interjected. "How may we be of service." Lou glanced at him. "Ahh,

You must be Doctor William Payne. Harvard graduate and founder of this clinic. I thought I would be able to speak with Doctor Dayaggi today. Lou informed," Lou stated calmly. William nodded his head. "Is it something you feel needs immediate attention? As you can see, we're trying to contend with a few serious issues today, and if it's a mere chat you're looking for.." Lou tilted his head. "On the contrary, Doctor, have you seen the news?" Lou asked cryptically. William misunderstood the ambiguous statement. "I have. Are you alright? Do you feel anxious?" He inquired. "Oh, we're well beyond anxious." Lou responded, his tone contrary to his statement. "Doctor Dayaggi is currently with a patient. If you wish to see him, I must ask you to either come back later or please be seated, and the Doctor will attend to you as soon as possible." Payne informed Lou calmly. "Very well, I'll wait." He responded and sat down. "As you wish." Doctor Payne responded politely. "Doctor, Lou addressed William. "You never asked how I know about you." Lou teased. Doctor Payne smiled. "The magic of google, I'd imagine. He responded glibly. "Molly, please tell Miss Rogers that Doctor Dayaggi has a client waiting for him in the reception area." Payne requested. Molly nodded, not trusting her voice around Lou. The intercom exchange was brief. "Nancy, please inform Doctor Dayaggi that Mister Cyphur is here to see him." She related. Nancy gathered the information for her boss and intruded via intercom, informing him that Lou Cyphur wished to speak to him. "Tell him I'll see him when I'm done." Peter insisted. Turning his attention back to Errol, he was surprised to see Errol staring at him. "You're going to see him?" Errol queried. "See who, Errol?" Peter inquired. "The same guy I've been trying to warn you about." He exclaimed. "Errol, if you would," Errol interjected. "Is there a back way out?" Peter took a deep breath. "Errol, why wouldn't you leave out the front door?" Peter asked. "Because he's here, I can feel him." Errol whispered. Peter squinted. "Who is here, Errol?" He repeated himself. Errol's eyes looked frantic. "Do you have a back way out or not?!" He demanded in a voice laced with fear. Not wishing to push his client further, Peter acquiesced to Errol's demands and showed him the rear exit. Turning before leaving, Errol whispered to Peter. "I'll be back when that evil bastard is gone." He promised. Peter nodded. "Until then, please take care of yourself, Errol. Errol cackled. "It's not me being visited by evil incarnate Doctor." Errol turned and ran out before Peter could say anything else. Entering the reception area, Peter saw Lou sitting patiently. "Greetings, Mister Cyphur. Why don't we step into my office." Peter invited him. "After you." Lou gestured to the Doctor. Molly kept her eyes glued to the paperwork before her, fearing she might betray herself. Walking past the reception desk, Lou's hand brushed Molly's lightly, sending shivers down her back. Once inside Peters closed doors, Lou sank onto The afforded couch. When Lou entered Peter's office, Doctor Zhang escorted Lisa from the rear of the building. "Lisa, are you sure you don't want to stay and talk?" Lisa inquired. "No, thank you, you have the Devil under your roof, and you don't even know it." She reprimanded, exiting hurriedly. Molly looked up at Helen. "Everything okay?" She inquired. Helen shook her head. "I'm afraid not." She admitted. In Peter's office, Lou was enjoying confounding Peter. "Well, what do you think?" Lou asked. Peter tilted his head. "I'm sorry, but I'm not sure what you're referring to." Peter admitted. Lou smiled. "My work, of course." Lou responded. Confused, Peter admitted. "Mister Cyphur, because your form says you would be paying in cash, I'm unaware of what you do for a living. That's something our financial office would know." Peter clarified. Lou laughed. "I'm sorry. Did I say something funny?" Peter asked. "Only that you confused my job with my work." Lou hinted. "Your works?" Peter pressed, revealing his confusion. So you have not been watching the news?" Lou inquired. "I fail to see.." Peter began. "Yes, you do." Lou admonished. Peter inhaled slowly. "I'm afraid I'm going to need some clarification Mister Cyphur. With obvious impatience, Lou snapped at Peter. "Doctor, this is tiresome. You said you watched the news but didn't know what I'm talking about?" Lou snarled. "Yes, that's right, I have no idea." Peter admitted. "If you want to know my work, pay attention to the news; for once, they are almost right." Lou admonished. "Well, if that helps me understand you better, I'll do that." Peter conceded. "Please see that you do." Lou chastised. waving his hand around in a gesture of dismissal and rising out of his chair. "Where are you going, sir." Peter inquired. Lou leaned against the door as if exhausted. "It's a tough job, so I'll indulge in more newsworthy work." Lou jibed. Peter looked at the hand resting on his door. "That is an expensive-looking ring." Peter noticed. "Ahh, you have a good eye. yes, from the furnaces of my kingdom, no other like it!" Lou bragged. "Don't forget the news." Lou called over his shoulder as he left.

CHAPTER 8

STROLL OF DESTRUCTION

Lou continued his walk down the eleventh avenue taking in the sounds. Watching The Prostitutes ply their craft, Lou stared at one who felt his presence without explaining to her pimp, who was conversing with her. Leaving his side, she walked over to Lou, dropped to her knees, and began fellating him right there on the street. A few passersby laughed, took out their phones, and began recording the event. Others, pretending to be shocked, left quickly while glancing over their shoulders. The furious pimp walked up to Lou and began chastising him. "Yo man, I hope you got the ends for the curbside service?" Lou laughed. "You think to charge me?" He asked, mildly amused. "You motherfuckin right I'm charging you, and I tell you what, I'm gonna charge you extra for interrupting me, now pay up." The indignant pimp demanded. Lou stared at the pimp. "You work for me bitch." Lou threatened. "All that you have is by my doing." Lou hissed. Drawn by Lou's eyes, the pimp caught a glimpse of the fire of hell reflected in the Lord of darkness's eyes. Fear infused the peddler of flesh as he recognized the true master of Evil. Being a superstitious man, the pimp had no difficulty believing he was talking to the devil. "I'm sorry, man, what do you want? I can have my whole stable here for you if you want." The terrified pimp offered. "Whose stable?" Lou menaced. "Your stable. I meant to say your stable." The pimp capitulated. The woman finished Lou off, cleaned him up, and gently put his momentarily sated member back into his pants. "Not necessary." Lou declined the pimps' offer. "Go on about your foulness and make me proud." He laughed. The pimp reached for the woman and stopped to look at Lou. "Take her," Lou ordered. The pimp snatched at the woman. Come on bitch." He yanked her arm to escape the only being he ever feared. With a smile, Lou continued his stroll. Passing a couple of fine eating establishments, Lou gazed inside a restaurant. Watching the patrons gorge themselves, he decided to have fun with them and emitted a low-frequency whistle. Moments later, the customers in several eateries began to scream and rush out as a nest of rats, cockroaches, and bugs ran across the floors, the tables, and the food. Small crowds gathered to watch the spectacle. Lou heard comments of anger and smiled before continuing. Walking to Tenth ave and 26th street, his stroll led him to a district where he heard bass-driven tribal music. Night clubs with long lines of people waiting to enter called invitingly to him. Detouring Lou made for a club with a clown's face on its marquee. Approaching the entry, Lou was greeted by a possessed bouncer. Clearing a path for him, the bouncer bowed as Lou passed. "Master." The bouncer whispered respectfully. Nodding, Lou entered. A patron was waiting in line to join and complained of apparent favoritism. "Hey, what the fuck, man? Do you know how long I've been standing here waiting to get in?" He argued. The huge bouncer turned to look at him. Seeing Lou stroll in without paying the twenty-dollar admission fee, the patron screamed at the top of his lungs. "Hey, what the hell? That motherfucker doesn't even have to pay? I wonder whose dick he's sucking!" The bouncer, now joined by another colleague, snatched the complaining patron. "Would you come with us, sir?" The question/demand was met with misunderstanding on the patrons' part. "Well, it's about fucking time, so all I had to do for service was treat you like shit?" He complained to the bouncers, which led him to a side door. "ahh, is this the V.I.P. entrance the complainant queried.

"Yeah, V.I.P., that's what you're going to find, most definitely. The bouncer snickered. Walking down a darkened hallway that led to a poorly lit ally, the patron nervously stated the obvious. "Hey, this aint the way in. The bouncer/demons grunted. "You're right about that." They exclaimed. Terrified, the unlucky patron began backing up. "Now wait a minute, dudes, if I was out of line yelling, I'm sorry. I was pissed and just talking shit." The patron tried excusing himself only to back into another bouncer. Surrounded, the patron put his hands up in a position of surrender. "You ready for your V.I.P. treatment?" a bouncer asked. The patron paused, hoping for the best. "Do you mean you're not going to kick my ass?"

The bouncers began to laugh, which caused the would-be patron to join in nervously. "Naah," rebutted the bouncer. "We left kicking your ass alone when you asked for V.I.P. treatment." A bouncer explained. "Huh, what? I don't get it?" The patron complained fearfully. "Let me explain," A bouncer offered cordially, the tone of his voice helping the threatened patron relax a bit. "You see before you asked for V.I.P. treatment, we were just going to kick your ass." The bouncer said, smiling and pausing a moment. At that moment, the patron gulped. "And now?" The patron whispered. "Oh, Now we're going to give you a Very Intense Pounding." The bouncer laughed. The patron looked up, terrified and prepared to scream, but the scream got caught in his throat when he noticed the reddish tinge in the bouncers' eyes. His last thought was, *"I should have kept my fucking mouth shut."* Before the bouncers began beating the hell out of him. They left a bloody, broken body behind. They walked through the switchbacks until they were again at the club entrance. After a few moments, one of the bouncers signaled to an off-duty cop making extra money as evening security for the club. "What's up?" The cop asked.

"Yeah, a guy here a few minutes ago was beefing about how important he was and how much cash he had. Seeing he wasn't the type we wanted here, we sent him on his way." The cop looked unconcerned. "And?" He asked blandly. "Well," The demon/bouncer clarified. "He was bragging about how much money he had, and when we told him to get lost, he started walking that way." The bouncer pointed down the street. "And?" The bored cop repeated. "Well, I saw a couple of guys follow him." The cop looked down the road and saw nothing except people waiting in line to enter the club. "I don't see him." The cop said. "Yeah," The bouncer confirmed. "I'm reporting what happened, so we're not liable for the smart ass." The bouncer admitted. "No problem." The cop insisted and returned to his post beside another off-duty cop leaning against a car.

Inside the club, Lou was delighted by the music and the sensuality. "Hey, you want a hit of this?" Someone asked. Lou took the cigar and pulled on it. Exhaling, Lou whispered. "Ahh, nice." The dancer smiled. "If you want, we can go to the lounge and take it to the next level?" He invited, hopefully. Lou considered it for a moment but declined. "No thanks." He responded. "Dude." The dancer said. "You don't know what your missing." He coaxed. Lou laughed. "Is that right?" Lou asked. "Yeah, man, it's a touch of Heaven." The dancer claimed. Lou grinned.

"I'm too much a sinner to enter Heaven," Lou admitted. "But I can give you a taste of hell if you'd like." Lou invited. The dancer believed he saw the gates of Hell in Lou's eyes, and they seemed to welcome him. Scaring the patron, he stammered. "No thanks, man, I just wanted to party. Besides, the crystal I smoked earlier got me fucked up. The dancer rationalized. "I should go cool out somewhere." Lou grinned. "Perhaps you should go do that." He warned. The dancer quickly removed himself. The music blared through the massive speakers, and Lou allowed himself to cut loose and dance.

Admission: Less stress clinic

Lou smiled at Peter. Peter looked at Lou with a look of bewilderment. "I must admit that I'm not sure what your point is,

Mister Cyphur." Lou tilted his head, giving the impression of disbelief. Peter returned the look. "Why are you looking at me that way?" Peter inquired. "Im trying to figure out whether you're being deliberately obtuse or clueless." Lou responded. Peter smiled. "I assure you, Mister Cyphur," Holding up his hand to interject, Lou posed. "Please, call me Lou." He said in a gesture of intimacy." Peter nodded. "Very well, Lou. As I was saying, I never look to be obtuse. To avoid that, I spent most of my life studying one thing or another." Peter informed him. Lou put his hand on his chin. "Then I fail to see why you don't understand what I'm saying?" Lou responded, voice dripping with disappointment. Although trained for such circumstances, Peter heard and understood the tone and found himself hurt by the accusation. "I'm not stupid, Mist, Lou." He quickly corrected himself. "Then stop acting stupidly." Lou growled. Peter took a deep breath to regain his composure. Observing the action, Lou smiled. "Did that help?" He asked, slightly amused. Peter returned the smile. "More than you know." He responded. Lou clapped his hands in glee. "Very good. Now I'll place a figurative map for you to garner my meaning." Lou stated. "Please do." Peter responded. "Fine, Think. Think of everything I've told you so far. Now ask yourself, where does it lead?" Lou prodded. Reflecting on all Lou shared, Peter scanned the information for clues. Peter believed he reached clarity when he noticed Lou staring intently at him. With great effort, Peter shook off the desire to shiver. "Well?" Lou asked, seeing a bit of understanding in Peter's eyes. "If I were to take you literally, it sounds like you witnessed the events in Manhattan." Peter stated. Lou sighed, disappointed again. "So very sad that your rationale so binds you." Lou exclaimed. Confused, Peter inquired. "So, I'm wrong. Didn't you witness the events? The car accidents, The man hit by a train, or the burning of the bodies?" Peter asked. Lou's smile grew sinister. "Witness? I was the cause." He claimed, slowly sitting back. Peter's shocked expression gave way to one of concern. "Lou, please think of what you're saying; you're admitting to murder." Peter voiced in a serious tone. Lou's smile deepened. To murder and mayhem." Lou responded. Peter shifted in his chair. "Feel like you're in a hot seat?" Lou teased. Peter's tone grew serious. "Lou, do you realize I cannot sit still under such an admission? I am obligated to report a threat to the public." Peter warned. "Ahh, poor foolish man. You want to help so badly, so sincerely, those you deem mentally incapable of acting responsibly that the truth evades you." Lou said in despair. Peter stood up. "You fail to understand, Lou, that such serious claims are met with equally serious reactions. I was under the impression that you were a well-to-do gentleman needing counseling. Lou cocked his head. "Addressing that point, I am well-to-do but no gentleman." Lou claimed. Peters' face grew serious. "If all you say is true, then you're right. You're a murderer." Peter exclaimed. Lou laughed. Millions of times over, or rather the instigator of the acts." Lou clarified. "I fail to see the difference; wait, are you implying you're some kind of cult leader?" Lou asked, surprised. "How provincial." Lou exclaimed. "Most of what you call cults are formed in a poor imitation of my domain and rule." Lou's statement stuck Peter as ambiguous. "Lou, please stop with the ambiguous references and speak plainly?" Peter pled. "Not my style, but ask, and I'll be forthcoming." He capitulated. "Finally." Peter said in relief. Lou held up his hand. "If I may?" He asked. Peter nodded. "Please remember that although you asked for the truth, I'm reputed to be unable to speak truthfully." Lou warned. "Reputed by whom?" Peter inquired. "You mostly." Peter hid his shock. "Me? but I never." Lou held up his hand again. "Pardon me; I generalized when I said you." Peter nodded. "Who then did you mean?" He inquired. "Humanity." Lou responded. Peter squinted his eyes and shook his head. "Excuse me, what?" He asked, thoroughly confused. "I, my good doctor, have been accused of being unable to speak truthfully. I have been saddled by the moniker "The father of lies." I deceived Eve into biting the forbidden fruit in one of my many forms." Lou exclaimed. Peter stared at Lou. "Are you saying.." Lou interjected. "Yes, my good man, you are the Devil's therapist." Lou stated matter-of-factly. Peter seemed unimpressed. "You realize you are not the first to claim to be the devil?" Peter stated. Lou smiled. "Yes, but I am the first to be him." Lou responded. Peter thought a moment silently. "You know what I think, Lou? I think you've been watching a lot of news and got caught up in the wave of emotion gripping the world. With the Pandemic, the world's response to this illness, the seeming increase in violent crimes, and the global catastrophes have left you exhausted in seeking an explanation. Hence, you revert to the notion that you may be to blame." Lou cocked his head. "That's ridiculous; why would I do that?" Peter sat back down and grinned. "Well, if you're truly the devil," Lou interjected. "I am." Peter continued. "You would know under stress; humanity has done some foolish things to find reasoning for the nonsense occurring." Lou was quiet for a moment. "That is the first reasonable argument you've presented." Lou admitted. "That being said," Peter continued. "You can see why your claiming to be the devil is not only highly likely but also, more likely than not, impossible. Lou grinned. "Impossible, you say?" Peter nodded. "Absolutely." Peter declared. Lou's sinister grin returned. "I'm sure you heard told that the devil is a gambling man? Lou posed. Peter acknowledged Lou's claim. "I have heard that." He admitted. Lou's grin deepened. "How much of your professional beliefs will you put on the line?" Lou inquired. Peter shook his head. "It would be unethical of me to place a wager with a client." He responded. Lou laughed loudly. "Your type has almost as many escape clauses as I." Lou observed. "Lou, I don't think you understand." Peter began explaining. Now Lou stood up abruptly. "Coward. I give you the opportunity for irrefutable truth, and you run behind the skirts of ethics?" Lou accused. "it's not that simple," Peter began. "It is that simple." Lou retorted. "You have the opportunity to ascertain the veracity of my statement, but you cower behind a veil of protocol and ethics all to protect your blissful ignorance, pathetic." Lou stated bluntly. Peter considered a moment. "What type of wager are we speaking about?" Peter relented. Lou smiled. "Well, doctor, I might have been mistaken about you. The wager is this, you come out with me for one evening, and if at the end of that evening, you're still not convinced I am who I say I am, then I will do as you recommend." Lou offered. Peter looked intrigued. "Include a truthful rendition of the events you spoke of as well as honest sessions so we can look for the source of your delusions?" Peter inquired. Lou smiled. "Yes." He responded. "And if I lose, what do you get?" Peter asked. "Your soul." Lou responded chillingly. "Of course, silly question." Peter admitted. "Do we have a deal?" Lou asked. Peter thought a moment. "When?" He inquired. "Tonight." Lou responded. Peter shook his head. "I can't see tonight; I must help a friend." Peter stated. "Oh, don't worry about Patty. I'll lift my cloud of vapor from her; she won't remember feeling that way at all. Peter, for the first time, revealed a genuine surprise. "How did you know," Lou waved his hands in dismissal."Okay, fine, yes, her husband as well. He will have no recollection of ever discussing his concerns." Lou promised. For the first time, Peter had a doubt. *"How could he possibly know?"* Peter wondered. Lou rose to extend his hand. "Well, my good man, I will leave you to your work. Prepare yourself; it will be a hell of a night for you." Lou claimed with a smile. Peter nodded. "Shall we meet here?" Peter inquired. Lou nodded. "That will be fine. Shaking Lou's hand, Peter escorted him to the door. Upon Lou's exit, Peter realized his shirt was soaked. Pressing the intercom, he spoke to his private secretary. "Nancy, please bring me a fresh shirt from my locker." Peter requested.

CHAPTER 9

DAMAGE CONTROL

Lisa sat in Doctor Zhang's office, trying to keep her composure. "Listen, Doc; you're not getting it." Lisa complained. Helen Zhang was attempting to rationalize Lisa's very irrational fear. "Lisa, I understand that you believe in the devil. but you have to ask yourself, does it make any sense for such a being to come here now when everything is going how he would want?" Helen attempted to rationalize. Lisa shook her head strongly. "Bullshit. You don't believe in such things, but you must believe me. Not only is he real, but he walks among us." Lisa exclaimed. "He's been in this clinic!" Lisa insisted. Helen had treated zealots during her career, but Miss Montoya has been acting out in the extreme. She self-reported that she was drawing wards of protection on her bedroom door and decorating her apartment with mystical detection symbols. Seeing her condition deteriorating over the last month, Helen sought and received special dispensation for a home visit to observe first-hand the lengths to which Lisa would feel safe. However, as of late, these precautions appear no longer enough. On one visit, Helen noticed suspicious stains and discovered (through a nosey neighbor) that Lisa had brought a live goat into her apartment. Still, no one ever saw or heard it again. The assumption is she sacrificed it. Acknowledging she had to ascertain the rumor, Helen asked straightforwardly. "Lisa, what happened to the goat?" Without hesitation, Lisa said she sacrificed the goat to Orisa for protection. Helen was very concerned for her client as Lisa became increasingly agitated as the days passed. "Doctor Zhang, you don't understand." Lisa exclaimed. "What don't I understand, Lisa?" Helen asked. Lisa glared around the Doctor's office. "He and his minions are everywhere, and saying his name summons him." Lisa claimed. Helen shifted in her chair. "Who?" Helen inquired softly. Lisa shook her head violently and made the sign of the cross. "No, I will never utter his name, but he is here." She claimed, the pitch of her voice revealing fear. "I don't know what to do." She whispered as if merely speaking about him would summon him. "Lisa, you have nothing to fear." Helen attempted to reassure her. Lisa stared hard at Helen. "You work for him?" She asked and accused in the same breath. Helen tipped her head to the side. "Lisa, I work for you. I help you realize there is no place for such superstitious thoughts in the modern world." Helen said soothingly. Lisa stood abruptly. "You do work for him." She accused. Helen drew a deep breath. "Lisa," She began calmly. "It seems to me that with your past diagnosis of abuse, it's possible that you're overly sensitized and that any disruption to your routine sets off alarms. I assure you those alarms are false. Helen tried reassuring her. However, Lisa could feel it in her bones. She knew something was wrong and felt like she was in the middle. Helen sighed. "Is there something I can do to help you relax? Helen queried. "Yeah," Lisa admitted. "What, Lisa? What can I do to help you feel better?" Helen inquired. Without hesitation, Lisa said, "Send his ass back to hell." She stated flatly. Keeping her composure and seeking answers, Helen pushed the issue. "Send who?" Lisa did a double take. "Seriously?" She asked sarcastically. Lisa nodded affirmatively. "I can't send anyone anywhere if I don't know who." Helen answered in a measured voice. "Aint you listening?" Lisa asked, raising her voice. The devil. If you could send the devil back to hell, I'd feel better, but you can't. You can't because you don't believe in him." Lisa exclaimed. Helen took a moment. "You're right, Lisa. I don't believe in a supernatural devil, but I know that evil people indulge in it. Do you know this person, the devil, I mean?" Lisa looked at Helen with a frightened look. "No, but I know he's been here." She spat out. Helen jotted on her pad. "Do you mean in the world? the Country? Maybe even the City?" Helen inquired. Lisa leaned toward Helen. "No bitch I mean the clinic. Haven't you been listening? I meant here. Don't you remember the day I hid in the back? Who did you think I was hiding from" Lisa stated emphatically. Helen was at a loss for words for a moment. "Lisa, do you believe that?" Helen asked. "No." She declared. "I know it." Helen nodded. "But Lisa, if you don't know who it is, how do you know he's been to our clinic? As you said, you hid from him. Did you see his face or not?" Helen posed. Lisa shook her head. "No." She admitted. "Then how." Helen began before being interrupted. "Nature." Was Lisa's simple reply. "Nature?" Helen echoed. "Yeah, Nature." Lisa repeated. Helen jotted on her pad again, then returned her attention to her client. "And how does Nature inform you that the devil is here?" She asked. Lisa got a faraway look in her eyes. "One day, all the sparrows were gone, just gone." Lisa reported. "I fail to see why the absence of some birds," Lisa interjected. "There were worms everywhere that day." Lisa pointed out. Helen remembered that day which brought an uneasy feeling. "Lisa, I think you're taking a natural occurrence and making a link where there is none." Helen shared. "And I think you've allowed your education to blind you to something happening right under your nose." Lisa retorted. Helen nodded. "I see. How do you think we can resolve this?" Helen asked. "Simple." Lisa paced around the office. "By sending him back to hell." Helen jotted in her pad again. Infuriated, Lisa grabbed and threw the pad against the wall. "This isn't something your think or your meds can fix, Doc. I know you think I'm crazy, but I know what I feel, and he's coming for us." She claimed loudly. Helen nodded. "Lisa, please sit down." Helen requested. Lisa complied but sat on the edge of her chair. "I do not doubt your beliefs, and you're right; I don't share them, but that does not mean I don't understand. My job as your therapist is to help you rationally see this so we can focus on the cause of your anxiety. Lisa stood up. "Blah blah blah." All talk, but you'll see." Lisa warned.

The deli issue

Peter, somewhat distracted, was riding home on his bike when a horn blared. "Watch where the fuck you're going," The offended driver shouted. Peter swerved to avoid the car and did a double take as the driver looked like his client Lou Cyphur. Peter chastised himself, *shaking his head, saying, "Don't let him get in your head like that.* Arriving at his building, Peter jumped off his bike, locked it in the usual spot, and walked across the street to the deli. Entering the store, The bell rang, letting the proprietors know that a customer had arrived. Looking up from her reading Patty called out. "Hey Doc, how's life on the funny farm?" Peter squinted as he heard her speak as if nothing was bothering her. "Uh, hi Patty, how are you feeling?" Peter inquired, trying to hide his concern. "With my hands Doc, just like everyone else." Somewhat taken aback, Peter pressed the issue. "Is something bothering you?" He asked. Patty tilted her head at the odd question. "Besides my pain in the ass, husband, no." She responded. "No dark thoughts or feelings of anxiety?" Peter pressed. Patty's eyes narrowed. "What's with all the questions? You trying to drum up more business?" She asked suspiciously. "No, no.' Just want to make sure everything is okay with you." Peter replied. Patty leaned toward him. "Are you okay, Doc?" She asked. "Just busy at work." Peter answered. Patty snickered. "You must be. You've never come in here so sad before. Peter smiled. "I guess I'm just working too hard." He deflected. "Where is Pedro?" Patty pointed to the back of the store. "Stock room." She answered. Do you mind?" Peter asked, motioning toward the rear of the store. "Not at all." She replied. "Do you want to order anything?" Peter rubbed his chin. "Yeah, a roast beef sandwich to go." Peter confirmed. Walking into the stockroom, Peter saw Pedro inventorying the food. "Pedro." Peter called out. Turning, Pedro exclaimed, "You're not supposed to be," Pausing upon seeing Doctor Dayaggi, he replied in return. "Hey Doc, how you doin?" He asked in his Brooklyn accent. The Doctor looked at him closely. "I'm well, thank you, and yourself?" Peter asked tentatively.

"Same old bullshit." He responded. "What's up?" Pedro inquired, curious as to why The Doctor was in his storeroom. "Pedro, do you mind if I ask what you did last night?" Peter prodded. "Last night?" Pedro echoed. "Same as every night, worked until we closed, and then we went home." Peter looked disbelievingly at Pedro. "You mean to tell me you don't remember coming to speak to me?" Pedro shook his head. "I did no such thing. Are you okay, Doc?" He asked, concerned for his most steady customer. Peter nodded. "Humor me for a second if you would. Peter replied. "You mean to tell me you did not come and ask for my advice?" Peter asked, sounding unsettled. Pedro shook his head. "No, not at all. Besides, I couldn't afford a fancy Doctor like you." Pedro answered, laughing. Peter paused. The silence lasted a moment. "Hey, Doc, what's goin on?" He asked, becoming more concerned. Peter shook his head. "Nothing, Pedro, It must have been a dream." He responded dismissively. "What was the dream about?" Pedro asked curiously. "Nothing." Peter answered. "It isn't important." Pedro stared at him. "Doc, you don't look so good." Pedro responded, sounding worried. "Well, you're no prize either, buddy." Peter deflected. Pedro nodded. "True, but I still have a beautiful wife, and your alone spanking the monkey." Pedro joked. Peter laughed at the jibe. "She is beautiful, and you are a lucky man." Peter conceded. Turning to leave, he called back. "Sorry to bother you, have a great night." You to Doc, and maybe think about a vacation. I think you're working too hard." Pedro called out. "You may be right about that." Peter agreed. Walking to the front of the store, Peter picked up his sandwich. "Thank you, Patty." Peter said, handing over the five dollars for the item. "You talk to Pedro?" Patty asked. Peter nodded, exited the store, and crossed the busy street heading for his apartment. Pedro walked to where his wife stood at the cash register. "What did the Doc want, babe?" She asked her husband. Pedro shrugged his shoulders. "He asked me if I asked for his help last night. They both stared through the store's plate glass window at Peter's retreating back as he crossed the street. "I wonder what's goin on with him?" Patty mused. "I don't know, but I think when you fuck around in people's minds, bad shit can happen." Pedro considered. Patty nodded in agreement. Exiting the elevator, Peter took out his keys to open the door but froze when he heard sounds from his apartment. *I swore I turned everything off.* He thought to himself. He quietly opened the door and stepped inside. No one was there, but the t.v. was playing loudly. Reaching for the remote to put on the music channel, a reporter flashed on the screen. "A bizarre incident occurred last night when rodents and insects swarmed through some mid-town finer restaurants. All were up to code, and neither the owners nor City officials explained why such a thing would happen." Maybe if you cleaned your basements." Peter responded to the television. "In other news, a man was caught on camera receiving oral sex last night. The image of the two was blurry, as expected. While ordinarily, we would blur out such footage, and it would be interesting to note that we at eyewitness news didn't have to. The viewer who shared this claimed that he didn't blur it out, making this odd, to say the least." Shocked, Peter stared at the blurred figures recognizing a ring the man in the image was wearing. "In other news, the reporter continued. "A man was discovered beaten to death behind a local nightclub police have no leads now." Peter turned the t.v. off mumbling to himself. "That can't be him; it just can't." Peter thought he heard laughter. "And why couldn't it be me?" A voice asked. Peter spun, expecting to see an intruder, but no one was there. forgoing his routine, Peter got ready to shower. "I have to get a grip on myself. I must be losing my mind; I'm overworked, that's what it is." He consoled himself. "Or you're accepting reality." The voice whispered. Peter stepped into the shower and scrubbed himself raw. "Okay, Pete, you've been working hard, you have new clients in dire need, and you're bringing work home; just breathe and calm down; it's all in your head." Drying himself off, Peter stepped into his pajamas and sat to eat his sandwich. The usually delicious food Patty made seemed flavorless. He washed the tasteless meal down with water and crept into his bed. "It's all in my head, he repeated like a mantra. Closing his eyes, Peter was nearly asleep when the voice he heard earlier uttered. "The worst lie is the lie you tell yourself." Peter sat up abruptly, looking around the dark room. "It's just me in here?" He said to no one. Peter's dreams were filled with horrific imagery, people brutally beaten, set ablaze, and smashed in terrible accidents. Peter moaned as he tossed back and forth in his large, uncomfortable bed. Peter suddenly sat up in bed; the false dawn lightened the room gradually. "Huh, why didn't my.." Suddenly Peter's alarm rang. He decided he was going except for Lou's invitation for his proof of Hellish origin. *"Hopefully, we can shatter this illusion that seems to have a powerful grip on Lou."* Peter thought.

CHAPTER 10

THE SEDUCTRESS

Nadine was a whore who plied her crafts on the Las Vegas strip. She had done so for ten years until that fateful night when she was caught between two warring factions of crime families trying to take over the region. A stray bullet slew Nadine. She was beautiful, standing a petite four foot nine inches tall, with bronze skin, long black hair, high cheekbones on a chiseled face, and smoldering brown eyes. Nadine awakened in a bed of flames. Her screams were heard throughout the second circle of Asmodeus. In one torture session, Nadine was visited by Lillith herself. Of course, Nadine had heard of the cursed whore who was banished to Hell. "I have a special purpose for you, Nadine, an assignment, if you will. Suffer your brief punishment, and I shall reward you with a mission to escort the Master himself, but hold your tongue. The demons know the longer we punish someone, the more, shall we say, they are special. Hold fast and be rewarded." The demoness promised. Nadine was pleased that she was given such an assignment. To escort The Lord of Evil is the lowest dishonor any demon could wish for. The council of demon kings met soon after their Master's departure realizing He had gone alone. The demon kings were very concerned as their Master had an insatiable appetite that no mortal could ever sate. Upon Lilith's advice, the council assigned the task to a new convert to Lillith's clan of succubi. A recently deceased whore who, while suffering her punishment, had been drafted by Lillith, who had taken notice of her skills while she was alive. Impressed by her unabashed wanton behavior, Lillith decided to allow her to feel the flames of punishment before bringing her into the fold so she would know what awaited her if she ever disappointed Lillith. The biggest problem Lillith faced was fending off the demons that waited, mouths salivating to ravage the beautiful woman to their content. They protested loudly to Asmodeus, the Lord of lust, that having their way with her was their prerogative. Convinced by their argument, Asmodeus demanded Lillith explain why she denied the demons their privilege. "By what power do you withhold a damned soul from my demons to satisfy their lusts." Asmodeus demanded. Lillith, who was/is the first consort of the Lord of Evil, stared into the white eyes of the Lord of lust. "By the right assigned to me by the Master himself. "Upon the newly damned worthy of my desire shall you be mindful of." She iterated. This soul shall serve the Master; if you have a complaint, raise it with him." She stated flatly. Asmodeus knew the favor in which Lillith stood with the Unholy. Bowing, Asmodeus recanted. "As you say, Mistress, we serve his desire." Asmodeus returned to the complaining demons silencing their complaints. "The damned soul is assigned; find yourself another." He exclaimed with an inarguable finality. The demons hearing the tone of Asmodeus bowed and ceased harassing Lillith. Nayla was terrified and relieved when she was called forth from the fires of chastisement. She gazed in awe at the terrifying beauty of Lillith's chamber. Lillith sat on an ebony chair encrusted with rubies. Nadine instinctually kneeled. "I have chosen well." Lillith complimented herself. "Woman, what were you called in life?" She inquired. "I was called Nadine." The damned soul responded. "From this moment ever, you shall be Nayla of the clan of Lillith." The first consort declared. Nayla bowed her head. "As my lady desires." She cleverly responded. "I have an assignment for you, do it well, and you shall benefit well, fail, and your punishment shall be excruciating." Lillith warned. "What does my lady desire of me?" She queried. "Do not question." Lillith snapped. "Listen and obey." She demanded. Nayla bowed her head remaining silent. "You may do well here." Lillith observed. "I have decided to lift you from the flames to serve Hell's purpose." Nayla wisely stood silent. "I will not cast you among the lower demons to suffer their abuse, nor shall I give you to the Kings of Hell to suffer their jealousies, No. For you, I shall give you an assignment that will bring us a great reward if done well. Are you capable of such a task?" Lillith inquired. Nayla demurely raised her head. "My lady, you raised me from the flames, and for that, I shall serve you well." Lillith's eyes glinted in satisfaction. "Let it be as you say, Nayla. You shall ascend into the mortal world and escort our Lord and Master, quenching his desire as they raise, do this to his satisfaction, and you shall know comfort in Hell that few know." Lillith declared. Nayla bowed. Looking up, she found herself in s small but well-furnished chamber where a lesser demon stood to serve her. The demon bowed. My lady, I am Dazz, your servant while the Mistress wills it. He announced. After bathing in magma and cleansing herself of Hellfire, she ate a delicious meal and sought information from Dazz. "The food is delicious, Dazz; why is that:? She asked. "My lady, we have the finest chefs Mankind has ever produced, as many became gluttonous or practiced many forms of evil. Dazz shared. "Do you know of my assignment?" She asked the little demon. "I do, my lady." He answered quickly. "What do you know of it?" She inquired. "The grand Mistress ordered me to inform you as much as possible to increase your chance of success." The demon responded. "Increase my chances?" She posed. "As if I could fail?" She pursued. The demon nodded. "Most assuredly." The demon confirmed. "I don't understand if it's just satisfying his lusts.." She trailed off. Dazz waited a moment before responding. Nayla looked at him for direction. "The Master is very fickle, My lady; it is not just sex, but companionship, a sounding board, a cheerleader, a seductress to his cause." Dazz shared. Nayla nodded in understanding. "Is there anything I should avoid?" She asked. Dazz nodded. "The Master is jealous to the extreme, unless ordered never pay attention to another, always be at his beck and call. He has no patience for his desires, so don't make him wait." Dazz warned. "Do I have power?" She asked. "You do, my lady. You may reward those that aid us with material gains. Still, only those you can qualify as beneficial to the Master or Hell." Nayla nodded. I'm sure I'll become more proficient in time. Dazz tilted his head. "The confidence shall serve you well as long as you remember your place." Dazz warned. Nayla looked at Dazz. "My place was in the fire, The great mistress gave me a reprieve from the flames, and I will never forget that." Dazz nodded, hearing the sincerity in her voice. "If I may, mistress?" He requested. Nayla shook her head. "Please, Dazz, you have helped me; you may always call me Nayla as our Great Mistress does." Dazz shook his head. "No mistress, I am demon-born. My place is inscribed in my essence: you were human, born to rebel, born between good and evil, thus always open to corruption, and nothing corrupts like success. Nayla paused. "I shall serve my Mistress." She swore.

Open Eye

Peter awakened, did his morning exercise ritual, ordered breakfast, jumped in the shower, dried off, dressed in his riding gear, ran across the street to get his food, and gave a brief greeting to Patty and Pedro. Stepping outside, he wolfed down his breakfast sandwich. calling his answering service, it played a message left for him. "Hey, Doc." The message began. "I thought this evening would be a grand time for our stroll, so please don't make any plans. Cyphur out." The message ended. Peter paused, trying to recollect if he ever gave that number to Lou. Convinced that he didn't, Peter thought it best to seek advice, and the only person he trusted with such a delicate issue was his boss. Peter ran across the street to his bike and narrowingly missed being hit by a car. From the Deli, Patty, and Pedro watched Peter run, dodging traffic and almost getting hit. "I'm worried about the Doc. "Pedro muttered. "I know." Patty agreed. "He hasn't been acting right lately." she responded with concern. They watched as Peter came out of the garage on his bike, again barely missing a car and pumping the pedals on the bike as if it was an emergency. Arriving at the clinic, Peter skipping the usual shower, made his way to William's office. He walked passed Maria's desk, who called out to him. "Doctor Dayaggi, Doctor Payne is," Peter stormed into his boss's office. "William, we have to talk." Peter exclaimed with great urgency. William looked up. "I'm sorry, Harold, I must call you back." He said, hanging up the phone. "Peter?" William posed quietly, knowing Doctor Dayaggi was not prone to irrational outbursts. "Forgive me, William, but this is paramount." Peter claimed. William motioned to a chair. "Please sit down." William invited. Peter shook his head. "I'd rather stand if you don't mind." Denying the invitation to sit. "How can I help you, Peter?" William asked, hearing the distress in the Doctor's voice. "William," Peter began. "You're not going to believe a word I'm about to say, but I ask that you reserve your judgment until I'm done." Peter requested. William nodded in compliance. Peter took a moment to gather his thoughts. "William, I have a client that believes he is the Devil." Peter informed him. William nodded. "I see, and what do you think, Peter?" William asked. "Well, At first, I thought several things, from persecution and paranoid delusions to narcissism," Peter began. "But now?" William prodded. "Now I'm not so sure." Peter admitted hesitantly. "William peered hard at Peter. "Peter, you don't mean to say," Peter interjected. "I don't know what I mean, so I came to you. William waited a second before responding. Holding his hand silently, requesting Peter to be patient, William got on his intercom. "Maria, please hold my calls." Maria confirmed the request. "Yes, sir." She responded. Looking back at Peter, William inquired. "And what do you think?" William asked. Peter began pacing the office. "As a man of science, I know that my clients claim to be ridiculous and severely delusional at worst." Peter responded. "However." William added. Peter stopped pacing and stared at Doctor Payne. "However, he says and does things that no one would attribute to a mentally healthy individual." Peter complained. "And yet?" William prodded. Peter paused. "Well," Peter began slowly. "He speaks of being responsible for the mass immolation that occurred in Clinton-Dewitt park, of the multiple car accident that smashed a car into another car and then into a truck in mid-town." William interrupted. "Peter, he could have learned of that on the t.v. like the rest of us." Peter nodded. "True, if I may finish." He asked, sounding agitated. William gestured for him to continue. "He then claimed to cast a spell of delusion upon a homeless man that caused the man to attack an innocent man smashing a bottle over his head and sending him to the hospital. Peter glanced at William, who seemed more concerned about Peter and his mental well-being. Ignoring the look, Peter continued. "Then, on the news, there was a report of the infestation of the eateries of rodents and bugs. At first, I thought nothing of it, but then a subsequent report of a man being fellated a block away in the street," Peter," William interjected. "This is New York." He said calmly, seeing his colleague genuinely distressed. Peter nodded his agreement. "And usually that would explain it, but when it came over the news, the newscaster seemed confused because the image was blurred out, "Isn't that normal for such an obscene act?" William asked. "Yes." Peter agreed. "According to the newscaster, he claimed that no one altered the image." William frowned. "That seems unlikely." William protested. "No." Peter disagreed. "What was unlikely was that only one section of the scene was not blurred, and that was his hand." William tilted his head in curiosity. "And why would that be unusual?" He asked. "Because William, he wore a ring, a ring I noticed and mentioned in our first meeting. I have never seen such a ring!" He also knew that a friend of mine was distressed about his wife's nightmares. When I pointed out I couldn't because I had to meet with them, He told me not to worry about it; he would resolve the matter, and he did. Peter exclaimed. William took a deep breath. "Besides your obvious agitation, why are you sharing this with me?" William asked. Peter paused a moment. "He invited me to go with him on a casual stroll." Peter explained. "To what end?" William inquired. Peter's pause was longer. "To show me proof that he is the devil." He responded. William stared at Peter. "I have to be honest, Peter. Normally, I would say this is an opportunity to show your client that they are suffering delusional thoughts," Peter interjected. "But," William looked at his windows, noticing a crow that seemed to be staring inside at them. "But," He continued. "This sounds like a dangerous man Peter. He might regress to violence if you reject his so-called evidence." William pointed out. "I thought of that," Peter admitted. "Did he say when this venture might occur?" William asked. "Ah, another disturbing aspect." Peter admitted. "How so?" William prodded. "He left the day of it unscheduled." William frowned. "Why would that be disturbing? Maybe he realizes there-there is no way to prove his ridiculous claim." William pointed out. "If only that were so." Peter admitted. "Care to explain that." William asked. Peter nodded slowly, saying, "He called this morning, claiming tonight would be a wonderful night for our stroll." Peter explained. "Peter, you need to be.." Peter interrupted. "He called me on a number I never gave him." He concluded. William frowned. "The man is more resourceful than we are aware of." William admitted. "Perhaps you should cancel it, Peter. I do not like the direction this is going in." William conceded. "I thought of that, William, but that would be admitting that we, as therapists are incapable of treating truly mentally ill people." Peter protested. "I disagree," William stated. "It is more like recognizing that we are well aware of the crazies that populate our fair city." He argued. Peter smiled. "Is that your professional diagnosis?" Peter teased. William noticed the crow was gone when he glanced out the window. Seeing his boss's look, Peter chimed. "You noticed the crow is gone, didn't you? Yeah, I noticed him too. He's probably going to report to him now." He teased. William took another deep breath. "Peter, do not get entangled in this man's delusions." William warned. Peter nodded. "Will do, chief. Any other advice?" Peter asked. William reached into his desk drawer and withdrew a nine-millimeter pistol. "Take this, just in case." Peter laughed. "Boss, your straight-up gangster!" He scolded. "No, Peter, I'm a native New Yorker." He said straight-faced. Peter took the pistol and pocketed it. "Thanks, boss." He said gratefully. William nodded. "Be careful and call me when your stroll is over." He asserted. Peter left, leaving a very concerned boss who considered hiring a private detective to follow them.

CHAPTER 11

A WALK THROUGH THE VALLEY

Peter arrived home and listened to his messages. One was from William, reminding him he was under no obligation to do anything he felt endangered his life. Another was a stranger. It was not an actual message but rather sounds of moaning and distant screams before a snarl cut the message short. any other time he would have thought it a prank, but now? Now he realized just how rattled he had become. Peter sat at his dining table contemplating his situation. He tried shrugging off the feeling by meditating for twenty minutes before jumping in the shower to wash off the day's grime. Peter shampooed his hair, closed his eyes, and let the hot water help relax him. While soaking his head, Peter swore he heard a whisper, unintelligible yet audible. Peter opened his eyes. *"Boy, you let that man get in your head; now look at you!"* he admonished himself. Stepping out of the shower, he began to dry himself when the doorbell rang. getting into his robe, Peter went to answer the door. He looked through the peephole and saw a beautiful Asian woman standing there. "Who is it?" He asked. A silky voice responded. "My name is Nayla." She responded. "I'm sorry, but I didn't order any food." Peter replied. "Wow." The beautiful woman responded. "Racist much?" She asked. Embarrassed, Peter opened the door. "I apologize," He began before Lou, dressed in a blood-red tracksuit, pushed into Peter's apartment laughing. "Peter Peter, I would have never guessed it, you, a bigot." Lou laughingly stated. The beautiful woman was beside Peter running her fingers on his shoulders. "Nice robe, silk?" She asked. Peter fought to maintain his sense of balance. "Don't you have to be invited before entering someone's home?" He asked, bidding for time. He got a few moments as Lou stared at Nayla silently. The moment passed as Lou asked. "You want I should go out and do it again?" He asked seriously. There was another moment of silence as Peter didn't know how to respond. Lou and Nayla simultaneously burst out laughing. "Peter, we're not vampires; you have the etiquette mixed up." Lou pointed out. Trying to regain his composure. Peter asked. "How did you get here?" Lou shook his head. "If by here, you mean my current state of being, that, my friend, is a long story. However, you mean your apartment. I took the winding path of Hell to the junction of Mortality and Eternity. I took a right to my hotel room, where I changed into this snappy little outfit, Picked up Nayla, and walked here. Nayla posed by the window. The setting sun cast her in a flaming silhouette that looked incredibly enticing. Peter tried shaking the cobwebs out of his head. "No. I meant, how did you get into the apartment building? I never rang you in. "Sure you did." Lou countered. "No, I didn't," Peter claimed. "Well, no matter, I'm here." Lou stated. Peter narrowed his eyes. "Lou, I never gave you my address, let alone my apartment number. Nayla gazed at Peter. "Are you clueless as to whom you speak?" She asked intently. "Layla," Lou said quietly. "Do you remember what we spoke about before arriving here?" Lou asked in a warning tone. "Nayla nodded her head, remaining quiet. "You have to pardon Nayla Peter. She is one of my servants, and they are unaccustomed to not hearing me being addressed as befitting my rank." Lou explained. Peter gestured to his bedroom. "Do you mind if I get dressed?" He asked nervously. "By all means, my good man, as you say here, Let's get this party started." Lou announced. Peter quickly strode into his bedroom, dressed in black slacks and a pullover shirt. He looked at his bag that held the automatic pistol. "Where do you want to go?" He called out while retrieving the weapon. "Let's go to Chinatown." Lou laughed. Peter entered the living room. Lou gazed at him. "I like your color choice." He complimented. Peter slowly smiled. "Thank you; I thought it would be appropriate, strolling with the devil and all." Peter quipped. Lou bowed. "Despite the sarcasm, I thank you for the consideration." Lou retorted. Peter gestured to the door. "After you. Lou nodded at the invitation. Proceeding out the door, Nayla stopped beside Peter and held his hands as if they were lovers. "You ready for the night of your life, lover?" She inquired seductively. Peter found the gesture very intimate and didn't release her hand. "As long as I have my life at the end of it." He quipped. Lou called over his shoulder. "Safety guaranteed, my man. You'll never be safer." Lou promised. "I asked, but do you know where we'll go?" Peter asked again. Lou spun, staring at Peter intensely, making Peter nervous. "We are going to a place where the party never ends, my man." Lou rasped. Nayla giggled. "Yay." She cheered quietly. Lou smiled a perfect smile and turned around, exclaiming. "Let's go, lets go." Exiting the building, they walked to Broome street. Crowded with the night revelers, Nayla, dressed in a long black gown with a double strand of pearls, clutching Peter's hand possessively. "Tonight, you're my guy." She whispered seductively. Seeing the Williamsburg bridge Nayla squeaked. "Do we get to cross that?" She asked excitedly. "Yes." Lou agreed. That's our bridge Over Troubled Water." Lou responded by quoting the famous song. Nayla clapped her hands and ran ahead. As they crossed the street to the bridge's footpath, a suspicious Peter asked. "Why did you call this bridge a Bridge Over Troubled Water?" Lou smacked his forehead. "Thanks for reminding me." He stated without further explanation. Stopping suddenly, Lou spat in his hands and roughly rubbed Peter's forehead. "What?!!" Peter exclaimed. "Shh," Lou stated emphatically. "You'll know the why in a moment." He stated with an air of mystery. Under a Pale moon that reflected off of the choppy waters below, Peter noticed a man walking toward them on the path. There was something odd about the man; a dark shadow surrounded him. "What the hell?" Peter exclaimed, amazed as he noticed. The dark shadow that enveloped the man seemed to pulsate as if alive. Peter shook his head as if that would help. The stranger stopped in front of Lou and pulled out a knife. "Give me all yo money bitch." The man demanded coldly. "Fool, you do not know who you impede. Nayla declared," Declared. Lou shook his head for her to cease. Turning to the criminal, he spoke. "I Would love to, but I can't." Lou protested. The man looked at Lou like he was crazy. "Can't or won't." The stranger complained. "Six of one," Lou retaliated. "I, you know what? I'm gettin sick of you rich folk thinking you run shit up here." The assailant complained. Peter looked nervously between Nayla, Lou, and the thief. "Why don't we give him what we have? what's with the macho crap? Peter argued. Lou smiled. "Pete, are you afraid"? Lou asked. "No, just responding logically." Peter clarified, "You should listen to your friend." The thief warned. Lou's smile grew. "It's about to get real interesting."

Nayla's arrival

Nayla arrived as directed. She materialized in the bathroom of the lobby of the Holland. Exiting the restroom, An employee at the front desk looked up and noticed her. He miraculously prevented his jaw from hitting the floor as the beautiful succubus walked across the lobby. Glided would be more accurate. She wore a pearl green dress that opened three-quarters up her leg; her long black hair hung loose and flowing. "Ma'am?" He called out. She stopped and looked at him with sensuality oozing from her pores. "Are you okay?" He stuttered. "Why wouldn't I be?" She asked in the sexiest voice the man had ever heard. "Well, it's just that you came out of the men's bathroom." He responded, trying not to stutter. Nayla's smile was dazzling. "Oh, my," She exclaimed, sounding surprised. "Excuse me; I had to go so bad I never looked at the sign." She answered innocently. "But, ma'am, I didn't see you walk by the desk." The front desk clerk responded. "Well." Nayla retorted. "You seemed very busy, and I had to go." She explained. "Of course." The desk clerk responded, not wanting to be confrontational. "Do you know what room you're going to?" He asked. Nayla stepped closer to the desk sending the clerk's heart racing. "In fact, I don't." She admitted shyly. "who would you be looking for?" The clerk asked. Another step closer found the clerk having difficulty in both breathing and focusing. "I'm looking for Lou Cyphur." Standing directly before him, she whispered, her bosom perky, inviting, and succulent. The clerk didn't even look at the registry. "Ohh, Mister Cyphur can be found in room 999." The clerk informed Nayla, who giggled at the room number. The clerk looked up, bewildered by the laugh. "Ma'am?" The confused clerk inquired. "Oh, it's nothing at all." She said dismissively. The clerk nodded, still confused. "The elevators are down the hall." He pointed in that direction. "Thank you." Nayla responded in her sexy voice. "I'm sure I'll be seeing you soon." She replied. He saw the accumulated evil on his soul, which acquired a bit more damnation as his imagination ran away to lewd imagery as he misunderstood her departing statement. "I certainly hope so." The lustful clerk responded. Nayla walked seductively to the elevator adding weight to his damnation. A knock at room 999 brought an angry Lou to the door. Opening it, Lou, unfamiliar with the face but not the nature of the visitor, asked. "What are you doing here?" He demanded. "My Lord." Nayla replied. "The high mistress Lillith sent me to keep you company." Lou looked perturbed. "Company?" He responded angrily. "I do not need company." Nayla responded carefully as Lillith warned her. "Never presume with the Master. Never speak for anyone but yourself; if you cannot convince him that you should stay, accept his dismissal immediately with no backtalk. return to me and accept your punishment for failure." Lillith had threatened. Nayla nodded. "Of course, you don't, my Lord; I begged for the opportunity to walk beside you, and if you found me pleasing to your eye, then please you in a manner a mortal would be unable to." Nayla posed. Lou narrowed his eyes at his succubus. "I must say

Lillith has chosen well. Are you prepared to obey without question?" Nayla bowed her head. "I am my Lord." Lou tilted his head. "even if you disagree with me or find the situation untenable?" Lou queried. "My Lord, who am I to cast doubt upon the Lord of evil?" Lou smiled. "Well said. You are fresh from the flames." Lou noticed. Nayla did not respond. "Did you not hear my question?" Lou asked. "My Lord, I thought it more an observation than a question." She quipped. "And why is that." Lou asked, pushing the issue. Nayla finally looked at Lou and was struck by his good looks. "My Lord, you are the Master of evil. Nothing touches your flames that you don't know about." She deftly responded. Lou's smile broadened. "Again, well said, young succubus. You have earned the right to accompany me, only remember the strictures placed upon you." Lou demanded. "As you say, my Lord." She responded. "Very well, enter, and I shall inform you about our mission here." Lou stepped aside, permitting her entry to his room. Inside the suite, Lou began explaining his purpose there. "You see, my young succubus, the initial reason I came was to do an on-sight inspection of the foul spirits I had released in the mortal sphere." Nayla interrupted Lou asking, "Foul spirits, my lord?" Lou's head snapped in her direction. "Normally, I would cast you off for interrupting me, but since you asked an intelligent question, we'll let this one pass. Yes, foul spirits. Demons are on Heaven's radar, but foul or damned spirits did just as well, if not better than demons. One reason is Demons frighten, Spirits; once alive, they know how to coerce a living being better, so they prove to be more effective. As I said before being interrupted," Lou gazed at Nayla, who gestured a closed mouth. "I began to catch a feint whiff of something I had not smelled in a long time." Lou paused as he poured a drink for himself and Nayla. Listening intently, she failed to see the gesture. Lou paused, drink upon his lips, staring at Nayla; his eye contact shifted to the glass He had set in front of her. Seeing the gesture, she looked down and saw the drink. She raised her glass which He gently clinked with his toasting. "To all that is malicious." Nayla smiled. "Malificently." She returned the toast. Lou smiled. Wonderful amalgamation, Magnificently malicious." He cheered. "Lillith has done well sending you." Lou said, giving a rare compliment. "As I was saying." He continued. "I smelled something I had not smelled in a long time." He paused again, and despite Lillith's warning, Nayla pled. "My Lord, please." Lou smiled. "Good to see some compulsion in you, my dear. Well, what I smelled was a genuine good intention." Lou paused, waiting for the question he knew was coming. "My Lord, do you mean to say there is no good intention in the world?" She inquired. Lou nodded. "There is no doubt that there is, but we are not in the world. We are in the heart of capitalism, and all who have power have ulterior motives akin to secrecy and greed." The look of ignorance vanished from Nayla's face, "Ahh." She exclaimed in understanding. "Ahh indeed." Lou repeated. I followed the smell to a clinic that specialized in helping the depressed and found the smell of a sanctuary." Nayla was mildly surprised. "What did you do, My Lord?" She asked. Lou smiled. "What I do best, I found the proprietor, A disgustingly good fellow who charged his clients only what they could afford." Lou said. Nayla tilted her head. "But what if they were poor and couldn't afford it?" Nayla posed. "That's the disgusting part," Lou complained. "He wouldn't charge at all." Nayla's brow furrowed. "But how did he stay in business?" She asked, sounding surprised. Lou smiled. "This is where he fell short of sainthood. He would shame his richer clients and had many as he is renowned for his efficacy." Lou snorted. "Master, if he faltered there, what qualified this place as a sanctuary?" Lou smiled. "Excellent question. He began advertising his free services on television, radio, and the internet. unheard of!" Lou griped. Nayla nodded. "what is to be done with one so well-meaning?" Nayla asked. Lou smiled. "While you go to the cow for milk, it is not the cow you squeeze." Nayla thought a moment. "You found a weakness among his people?" she asked. "Three of them. The one whom we shall visit tonight is amongst the best of them. Still, his mind is open and closed, making him the ideal candidate for corruption." Lou said gleefully. "Ahh, to see the Master at work." Nayla said in what passed for idolization among the demonic. Aroused by the praise, Lou looked to the bedroom. We have time." Nayla raced him to the room, where they engaged in wanton sex.

CHAPTER 12

THE DEVILS' YO YO

n the Williamsburg bridge footpath, Peter saw a black emanation pulse from the thief. Confused at what he saw, Nayla leaned over to explain. The Master has temporarily removed the mote that blinded your eye. Now you may see what no other is permitted to see, the evil that surrounds you." She clarified. Peter was both fascinated and frightened as the logical part of his brain fought with the superstitions inherent in most human beings. Looking at Nayla, Peter could see her demonic form. While still beautiful, there was something about her that was very frightening. It could have been the savage look in her eyes, and It could have been the reddish tinge her normally copper-toned skin emanated. Time seemed to slow down as he watched the thief threaten Lou with his knife. "Ya wanna die bitch? gimme your money." The thief sneered. Nayla remained quiet. Lou turned and looked at Peter. "What do you think, Peter? Should we humor this fool and give him our money, or should he be punished for arrogance?" He inquired." The thief retorted in a hushed whisper. "Are ya stupid? What are ya asking him for? Can't you get that I'm the one with the knife?" He waved the knife in front of Lou's face threateningly. Lou remained to look at Peter, who remained silent. Afraid of the thief and astonished at Lou's lack of concern for the knife being wielded. Losing patience, the thief uttered. "Fuck it." and struck forward to stab Lou. Suddenly

Lou's attention was focused on the thief, who seemed to freeze. "Whispering but loud enough for Peter to hear, Lou uttered, "My name is Lou Cyphur." Lou revealed. "Now, say my name, and you shall learn the truth of your destiny." The still thief, as if compelled, whispered. "Lou, Cyphur." Lou smiled. "Faster." He prompted. The thief seemed to internally struggle against Lou's demand which Peter witnessed as a fluctuation in the black aura Peter saw surrounding the thief. "Ohh, you want to fight?" Lou challenged. Suddenly it seemed as if the Earth opened, and clawed fingers and flames stabbed at the thief. "My name." Lou ordered. The terrified thief whispered. "Lou, Cyphur." Lou called for the flames, which stabbed the thief again. "Faster." Lou ordered. "Lou, Cyphur." The thief whined. "Faster." Lou demanded. "Lou Cyphur, Lou Cyphur, Lucifer!!" The thief screamed. Peter stood, mouth wide open in disbelief. Lou, with sinister glee, did not allow the thief to die but instead dipped his writhing soul in and out of the flames of damnation. Like a demonic yo-yo, he shrieked in agony. Suddenly a gray cloud appeared, and from it came an entity that bore an awesome aura of authority. "Really, Lucifer?" It prodded. "Since when did you begin torturing souls before their damnation?" The powerful being inquired. "His damnation was set upon him when he approached me with evil intent." Lou argued, indicating the dangling thief. The powerful entity looked upon Peter, who felt he would wither and die under such scrutiny. "I did not mean the thief." The entity responded. Lou followed his gaze, which was fixed on Peter. Smiling, Lou retorted. "He is a fruit being prepared for the picking." The entity shook his head. "Such a thing will not stand." He warned. "Azrael, do your job and permit me to do mine." Lou demanded. "Your job is not to torture the living in such a manner." The entity called Azrael responded. "You know then the perimeters of cleansing the field as commanded by the Creator? No. yours is not to say, Angel of Death, be about your business then begone." Lou demanded. Azrael looked upon the suffering thief. "Release him; allow him his judgment. Azrael demanded. "As you wish, Reaper of souls, he shall be mine upon judgment. Lou released the soul, and Azrael gathered the soul as the thief's body fell to the ground, his face reflecting terror as his death mask. "Should make for a lovely funereal, don't you think?" Lou asked as he looked upon the contorted face of the now-dead thief. Azrael turned in disgust. "Fallen star, the Creator shall judge you." He exclaimed in departure. "Blah blah blah." Lou mocked. The air cleared, and Peter stood in shock beside the beautiful Nayla. Lou clapped his hands gleefully. "That was fun." Lou observed blithely. Unsure of whether he was hypnotized or sneakily given a hallucinogen, Peter shook his head, trying desperately to rationalize what he had just witnessed. "Hard to believe, isn't it?" Lou asked flippantly. Peter wanted to scream, but a morbid curiosity took hold of him. "Truth is not objective as humans believe." Nayla whispered in his ear. Turning to look at her, Peter saw her clearly for the first time, a demoness with horns, still beautiful but with a horrifying center molded in the flames of Hell.

"Why? Why did you torture that man?" Peter pled. Lou stared at Peter disbelievingly. "You did see he not only wanted to rob us but was willing to, at the very least, maim, if not kill, us for what he desired?" Lou queried. "Yes, but you have the power to deal with it less dreadfully," Peter complained. "I do, but I didn't." Lou countered, pointing out the obvious. "But you could have. You could have shown.." Peter faltered at the last word. "What, mercy?" Lou prompted. "Yes, exactly." Peter agreed. Lou stared at Peter impatiently. "Peter, seriously, who I'm I?" Lou posed. "What?" Peter responded uncomfortably with the answer. "You heard me," Lou responded angrily. "Who the fuck I'm I?" Peter gulped, trying to moisten a dry mouth. "You are the Devil, Lucifer. The accursed angel cast out of Heaven." Peter quietly admitted. "That's right!" Lou shouted. His countenance seemed to grow until a giant Demon stood before him. "Wrong zip code for mercy!" Lou boasted. "We don't do mercy. We are the punishers of evil humans without mercy. Without consideration of the pain they are suffering, such has been my duty since my expulsion. Accept or deny it. I am the ultimate, unyielding in my ferocity to accomplish my duty. Pay heed, mortal; your acts of kindness are an act. I am the reality for those gone astray." With terrified eyes, Peter looked at Lucifer, revealed in his proper form. "Why me?" Peter whispered, and although Lou heard him, he asked Peter. "What did you just ask me?" Peter found his voice and asked again. "Why me? Of all the people you could have chosen, why choose me?" He demanded, regaining a measure of confidence. Lou smiled. "Because of the fire that burns so brightly inside you, the fire you try so desperately to contain. To control. Lou whispered. Nayla approached her Master, whispering in his ear. "My Lord, is it your intention to damage his mind?" She inquired. Lou looked at her sharply. Softening slightly, Lou shook his head. "No, that is not my intent. Well-spoken demon." Lou gave another rare compliment. Looking at Peter, he whispered, Good night Peter, until we meet again."

Peter bolted upright in his bed, mattress covered in sweat. His sheets were on the floor as if kicked off. *That could not have been just a nightmare!* He thought to himself.

Evil by nature

Lou paced his suite. Nayla sat in meditation to report her status to Lilith. *"My Lady."* She greeted formally upon making psychic contact. *"Loyal servant, what have you to report?"* Lillith inquired softly. *"My Lady, the Lord Lucifer is about his business but seems distracted by a mortal."* Nayla shared. *"What concern is that to us? He's always had his hooks in humanity's affairs."* Lillith responded dismissively. *"As you command, my Lady, I am only reporting my observations as you ordered me,"* Nayla replied. Lilith responded defensively. "I did not command you to spy on our Lord." Nayla did not flinch. "My Lady, you ordered me to watch over our Master concerning physical desires. So he would not find himself unsatiated and anything that might compromise his status, am I incorrect?" Nayla respectfully inquired. Lillith seemed momentarily surprised by the young demoness's sense of confidence. *"It appears we understand one another, servant,"* Lillith admitted. *"See to this mortal that you say has been, as you say, disconcerting to our master. If he poses a threat, eliminate him. If not, let Lord Lucifer enjoy his quirks."* Lillith ordered. Nayla bowed her head in acknowledgment. *"Has our Lord inquired after his scouts?"* Lillith asked. *"The Master has made some initial inquiries, and I believe he seeks out more to command them upon their next set of instructions,"* Nayla reported. *"Curious,"* Lillith commented. *"What is curious, my Lady?"* Nayla posed. *"I find it curious how you came by these observations when we know the Master to be very secretive with his comings and goings."* Lillith spat. *"My Lady, you sent me here for my powers of observation, was it not?"* Nayla posed. Lillith glared at her, and even through the distance, Nayla could feel her scorn. *"Child, never forget who raised you above the flames of your damnation."* Lillith hissed. *"I will never forget my lady, which is why I attempt to do your will to the best of my abilities, not to anger but to please you."* Nayla capitulated. Lillith appeared to relax. *"Of course, child. Proceed with your task and report to me if you feel there is something worthy of my attention."* Lillith commanded. The psychic form of Nayla bowed before Lillith. *"As my Lady desires,"* Nayla responded.

Coming out of her meditative fog, she found Dazz, her imp helper staring at her. "Why are you staring at me?" Nayla inquired. "My lady, was that Lady Lillith?" Dazz asked. "And if it was?" Nayla responded. Dazz stared at Nayla, causing her to feel uncomfortable. "Dazz, why are you looking at me as if I've recently been added to a menu?" Nayla posed. Dazz bowed. "My lady, I mean no disrespect. It's just that I've never served under a prospect before." He stated. Nayla looked at him, curiosity growing. "Dazz, what are you talking about?" Dazz rose from his sitting position to his full three feet height. "My lady, belonging to the imp class, we are given low-level servitude positions. We are the unsung, the unheard, and the unnoticed. We are rarely given a chance at glory or to serve one destined for glory. However, with you, I believe that's about to change." Dazz stated. Nayla stared at her imp companion with a look of disbelief. "Why would you say such a thing." She lightly reprimanded. Dazz bowed. "My lady, if I may speak bluntly?" Dazz requested. Nayla nodded. "Please do." Dazz appeared to consider what he was going to say. "My lady, The first time I met you, you appeared to me the exact type The Lady Lillith would recruit. Pretty in the face and body but weak in the mind and emotionally insecure." Daz began. Nayla cocked her head back, disliking the reference. "Dazz." She complained. "I guess that's my fault for saying for agreeing to your blunt speech. Dazz shook his head. "No, my lady, you misunderstand. As I said, it was what I thought upon first meeting you. Dazz began to pace. "You were so grateful to Lady Lillith. She seemed pleased with you; I understood that Lillith wrought herself another empty vessel to pour her petty jealousies. However, as I watched your conversation with her, your posture was never slouched. Your shoulders never sagged. You sat upright with pride and determination." Dazz iterated. Nayla laughed. "I'm not sure what you're trying to point out, my little imp demon. "See, that! That right there." Dazz pointed out excitedly. "What right where?" Nayla asked, somewhat confused. "Even a lowly creature such as myself you speak and treat kindly. No, perhaps that is the wrong word, respectfully, yes respectfully, and that earns you the loyalty of others without you asking of demanding it." Dazz confirmed. "Dazz, are you toying with me?" Nayla grumbled. Dazz shook his head. "No, my lady, never with you. Nayla stood up from her meditative position. "Why are you telling me these things, Dazz? Isn't your loyalty to Lillith?" Nayla queried. "No, my lady. My loyalty is to Lucifer. It is by his command that I serve the lady Lillith." Dazz clarified. "But are you not now going against his wishes by speaking badly about her? Dazz hid a smile. "I see you are still unfamiliar with diplomacy in Hell. Allow me to summarize." Dazz requested. "Please do." Nayla accented. "Diplomacy in Hell consists of desire, opportunity, and resources to acquire the desire. "Sounds like living." Nayla observed. "Oh, it is, except more diabolical and cutthroat. For the living, it's about getting or maintaining status or material gain with a loss being a setback or termination from employment;

in Hell, it's more about suffering and torture of the body and soul." Dazz shared. "And what has any of this to do with me?" Nayla asked incredulously. Dazz held his finger up in warning. "Beware, my lady." Somewhat frustrated, Nayla whispered fiercely. "Beware? Beware of what?" She demanded. "The lady Lillith." Dazz whispered. Nayla looked shocked. But why? She is my benefactor; why would she bring harm to me?" She naively demanded. "My lady is not familiar with Lillith's origin?" Dazz inquired. "Please, every woman that has walked the road of prostitution knows how she rejected the notion of Adam being her superior and got her banned from Paradise." Nayla responded. "In part, yes. But you either left out or don't know the reason." Dazz stressed. "Inform me then as to the reason." Nayla insisted. Dazz looked around to be sure no one or thing had snuck into the room. "What are you doing?" Nayla demanded. "Looking for spies." Dazz answered. "Part of Hell diplomacy we were talking he concluded. Satisfied no other imps or minions were slinking about, Dazz whispered. Lillith is the queen of the jealousies." Dazz stated bluntly. "She is only now beginning to see how clever you are. She also is watching how the other demons respond to you. It disturbed her when all the demons clamored for you in desire, not that she'd ever allowed them to lay with her. She was still upset when the demons howled for you." Dazz informed Nayla. "Be mindful, my lady, be very mindful. Dazz warned. At that moment, Lou called for Nayla to attend to him. "I would have words with you." Lou advised Nayla. "As you desire, My Lord.

CHAPTER 13

THE LIES WE TELL

"Hey, old man." Patty called out to Pedro, who was making sandwiches for a customer. "What do you want, old woman?" He teased in return. "Is that the Doc out there?" Pedro made it to the window just in time to watch Peter dodging cars as he frantically pumped the pedals on his bicycle, presumably to work. "Looks like him." Pedro agreed. "This is the first morning since he moved here that he didn't order a breakfast sand-which from us." Patty observed. "I think you're right." Pedro agreed. "Of course, I'm right, idiot." Patty retorted. Pedro shot her the evil eye. "Watch yourself, old lady." He warned. "Or what? You'll drink a gallon of milk and fart me to death?" She replied. A customer could be heard snickering. "You know what you're going to do tonight?" Patty asked Pedro. Pedro's shoulders sank. "No, but I'm sure you'll tell me." He quipped. "You're going to go to Doctor Petes' place and ask if he needs our help." Pedro shook his head. "I don't think so, Patty; he's a goddamn therapist; for God's sake, how am I gonna look asking him if I can help. Patty stared hard at Pedro. "You're gonna look like a friend," Her voice softened. "And the caring, compassionate man I fell in love with." The customer who had finished his meal and gone to the cash register to pay for it looked at Pedro and uttered, "Check, mate." Pedro nodded. "You're right about that, amigo." Pedro admitted. Dipping and dodging traffic, Peter rode to work. Pumping the pedals on his bicycle furiously anxious to talk to William. Arriving early, Peter punched in the security code giving him access to the building. Ignoring the shower room, he went straight to William's office to wait for him there. Twenty minutes later, he heard the rest of the staff file into the building. Maria walked into William's office to bring in his mail as part of her normal duties. She was shocked to see Peter sitting by the window. "Doctor Dayaggi," She gasped. "Doctor, you surprised me. Doctor Payne isn't in yet; should I inform Nancy when he arrives?" Maria posed. Peter shook his head. "No, thank you, Maria; I'll wait for him here." Peter responded. "But Doctor," Maria began. Peter interjected. "I'll wait for him here. That will be all, Maria." Peter said dismissively. Maria exited the office with a look of concern; she had never seen Doctor Dayaggi in such a state. He looked disheveled and in a state of agitation. Doctor Payne arrived fifteen minutes later and was informed of the situation. "I've never seen Doctor Dayaggi in such a state before." She reported revealing concern. "Don't worry, Maria," William said, consoling her. "The good Doctor has been stressed; I'll talk to him. William went straight to his office, side-stepping Doctor Zhang, who asked why Peter was pacing in William's office. "I'm about to find out, Doctor, if you'd excuse me." William walked passed Doctor Zhang and headed for his office. Opening his door slowly, William found Peter on the floor doing push-ups. "Peter." William said in greeting. Peter jumped to his feet. "William, thank god." Peter stated. "Peter has something happened?" William asked, referring to last night. Peter's eyes seemed to glaze over. "Everything happened." Was the ambiguous response returned? William realized Peter was terrified. "Peter, please sit down." William invited. "Can't do that." Peter said in refusal of the invitation and began pacing the room. "Okay, Peter, I'm going to need you to calm down and explain to me rationally what is going on." William requested. "Rationally?" Peter echoed. "William, you don't understand there is no such thing as rational." Peter stated emphatically. Williams's eyes narrowed as his focus on Peter sharpened, much like his look when he realized a client was about to suffer a nervous breakdown. "Don't look at me like that." Peter protested, catching the look in his boss's eyes. "Excuse me, Peter, but you are acting completely out of character, causing me great concern for your well-being." William countered. Peter paused, closed his eyes, and went through some deep breathing exercises; calming himself, he opened his eyes. "William, forgive me." Peter requested, sounding calmer. "Of course, Peter. Can you talk about what happened?" William asked. Peter paused again. "You're going to find everything I say unbelievable," Peter began. William remained silent, waiting for Peter to begin. "Well, last night, after talking to you, I rode my bike home and waited for the call from the guy we identify as Lou Cyphur." He began. "Wait," William interjected. "What do you mean who we identify as?" Willam responded. Peter looked around as if being spied upon. "He's not Lou Cyphur." He exclaimed. "Yes, if I remember correctly, you said he thinks he is the devil." William repeated the claim Peter had made in his office the previous day. Peter shook his head. "No, William, you don't get it. He is the Devil." William exclaimed in terrified anger. "Peter, listen to what you are saying." William requested. "Yes, I know. It sounds like I've succumbed to his delusions, but hear me out." Peter then retold the story of the unexpected arrival of the beautiful demoness, Nayla. To the slaying of the thief on the Williamsburg Bridge. "But Peter, I haven't heard any reports or news of a crime on the bridge, much less a murder." William protested. Peter clenched his hands into fists. "I'm telling you there was one, and beyond that, the Devil is real and is among us!" Peter insisted. William took a breath and motioned to a chair. "Peter, please sit." He asked. Peter sat, legs fidgeting. "William, I know how this sounds, but you must believe me." He pled. "Peter," William began. "Right now, I believe you believe it, which is my only concern. Peter stared at William. "I would ask you to refrain from condescending if you would." Peter requested. "Peter, I want you to stop and think about what you ask me to believe." William replied. Peter nodded. "Don't you think I know!" Peter exclaimed. William nodded. "Yes, I do, Peter. Listen, why don't you compose yourself for the rest of the day? We'll talk more after I call the police to find out about that body you alleged was murdered by the bridge. Peter bit his tongue, wanting to scream at his boss. The only fallacy was that the Devil didn't exist, but sitting there in the modern air-conditioned office began to make him doubt himself. Peter took a deep breath. "If you don't mind, William, I'd rather finish my paperwork. I apologize for acting like a newbie. I must have been drugged or something." Peter pondered. "Besides, I have a client this afternoon, and I'm finally gaining his trust. William looked at Peter a moment. Peter stood still, accepting the scrutiny. "It is against my judgment, but okay," Peter sighed. "Thanks, boss." He said gratefully. William held up his hand to forego any other words of gratitude. "Under the condition." He continued. you calmly tell the rest of the staff and me the events of last night, not just the highlights but in full detail." William compromised. "Peter reluctantly nodded. "Of course." Peter complied. Exiting the office, Peter went to his office to wait for his appointment. William contacted Maria. "Maria, please find out what police precinct patrols the Williamsburg bridge." He requested. "Of course, Doctor." She replied.

Suicide by design

Errol Tandy sat in his room eating his medication of Zoloft as if it was candy. The anxiety building for the last two weeks grew powerful last night and peaked around midnight. Looking around his room, he kept thinking, "Talking it out doesn't work; meditation doesn't work. Fucking Doctor doesn't know his ass from his elbow. Errol thought he heard the soft pattering of small feet in his apartment. The sun could not penetrate his darkened apartment. Usually, the dark was a place of escape for him. Now it seemed his last refuge was being taken away from him. He wanted desperately to escape the dark room, but his anxiety and underlying agoraphobia left him unable to do anything. Errol sat in the middle of the room. He began rocking back and forth slowly, casting thoughts of desperation out to the ether. *"What I'm I going to do?"* He silently pled. No response other than his fear turning into terror. He tried a tactic Doctor Dayaggi taught him. *"Identify the fear."* He could hear Dayaggi say. Errol took a deep breath. *"Okay, Errol, what are you afraid of?"* He asked himself. The silence was the only response. "Are you so afraid you can't give me an answer?" He demanded of no one, or so he thought. *"Do you want to know"* A voice only he heard responded. Errol quickly looked around the apartment. "Okay, boy, it's official; you've lost your fucking mind." He declared. *"Funny people deny what they know when they approach the truth."* The unidentified voice replied. Errol froze. "This aint happening; it's all in my mind." He insisted loudly. Popping a few more pills, Errol started humming a song his Mother used to sing to help him sleep. Her voice was very comforting, and Errol found solace briefly. That moment was viciously snatched away by an evil snickering. *"Aww, look at little Errol looking to hide behind Mommy's dress again."* The voice teased. Rocking harder, Errol ate some more pills. *"I will drive you out of my head!"* He screamed internally. The snickering faded, and a voice asked. *"Why would you do that, Errol?"* Errol stopped rocking. "Because you're not real." He posed aloud. *"If I'm not real, why are you answering me? Do you think you're crazy?"* Errol paused. He paused because he didn't think of himself as crazy. Sick, yes. Confused? Without a doubt, but not crazy, please god, not crazy." He pled in the darkness. *"Now that's just plain rude."* The voice exclaimed. Curiosity overcame fear, compelling Errol to ask. "What's rude?" An exhalation of impatience followed the silence. *"You call out to the darkness, the darkness, in sympathy of the loneliness you're suffering, answers back, and then you rudely call out to the light."* Came the explanation. Errol reflected on that for a moment. *Ahh, but we won't hold it against you. The dark always has frightened humanity, but that was never our intention or fault."* The voice insisted. Curious beyond reason and far better than the isolation he felt, Errol continued the conversation. "Really?" He asked aloud. "Whose fault was it then?" He inquired. *"Well,"* The voice responded. *"If you believe that God created everything, then that blame would also belong to him; if that is too much for your tastes, then somebody can blame Nature, who endowed you with fear. Fear of the unidentified. Fear of the superb. Fear of death. Fear of me."* the voice claimed. Feeling the fear creep back, Errol stammered. "And wh, who are you, you?" The silence that followed felt alive as if it would snatch the life from him. *"come on, you know who,"* The voice said almost playfully. Errol tried again to calm himself. *"Go ahead, take a few more. You know they help."* The voice insisted. Errol looked at his pills. "Fuck it." He exclaimed. Grabbing the bottle, he grabbed a handful and swallowed them. The fear intensified, and beginning to feel dizzy, Errol looked at his meds and thought about taking a few more. *"That's not going to help you?"* The voice warned. *"Why not?"* Errol slurred. *"Because silly,"* The voice teased. *"You're at the maximum safe dosage. What you need now is courage."* The voice demanded. Errol's laughter sounded self-deprecating. Remember to whom are you speaking? If I had the courage, I wouldn't be locked up in my room. "You know, for a figment of my imagination, you don't know me at all." Errol mocked. A snicker came forth from the darkness. *"Of course I do, Errol. I know you so well I remember where you get your courage from."* The voice insisted. Errol laughed again. "Really? and where would that be? Chanting? Praying? Meditating? It isn't these fucking pills. I can tell you that," He mumbled mockingly. The voice snickered again. *"No, nothing so spiritual."* The voice suggested something to Errol that he was missing. "Listen, a voice in my head, if you're not going to tell me what the hell you're talking about, get the fuck out!" He slurred, words thickening, becoming almost unintelligible. *"Really, moron, you haven't figured it out yet,"* The voice scorned. *"You are an idiot."* Errol was taken aback by the venom in the tone of the voice. "You know, voice in my head, you're not very helpful. You finally spoke up when I cried out, but when I need an answer, you shut down; now, why that is? or can't you answer that?" He mumbled, confused and irritated at himself. *"No,"* The voice retorted. *I can answer because you already know the answer. It is simple;*

you were given free will and the right to exercise that will. I can only guide, not reveal. You must make that discovery yourself. "Errol marveled at the depth of his imagination. "Well, color me stupid because I don't know what the fuck you're talking about." he mumbled quietly. *"Okay, maybe one more clue, then that's it. If you don't want answers, I have to move on."* The voice claimed. Errol chuckled. "Move on? where the Hell would you be moving to? you're only a voice in my head." Errol insisted loudly. "The voice chuckled. *"Well, you're right about one thing and wrong about another."* Confused, Errol mumbled. *"What?"* The voice rose in volume. *"Look, moron, do you want the clue or not?"* The voice demanded. *"Yes, please."* Errol giggled. *"The courage you seek never came from you; the gold liquid entered you."* The voice claimed sounding friendly. Errol's face lit as if striking an epiphany. Staggering, Errol stumbled to the cabinets, yanked open its door, and looked at the whisky bottle inside. Despite the Doctors warning of never mixing the two, Errol took a big swig of the liquid courage. He then laid down on the floor and asked internally, "Are you the Devil?" The voice responded. "No, just his shadow. "Time to come home now." The voice responded. The following morning the unanswered pounding on Errol's door forced the Landlord to call the police. "What was the reason you entered the premises, sir?" The first police officer asked. "As I told your partner, I got a complaint from his downstairs neighbor that water was dripping from his ceiling. When I knocked on his door, Mister Tandy didn't answer, which worried me." The officer took his notes, inquiring further. "Why would that concern you?" The Landlord shrugged his shoulders. "I think he had a mental problem. He rarely ever left his apartment." The cop nodded. "Okay, a detective will want to speak to you. The Landlord nodded, looking again at the terrified stare of his tenant, who clutched a liquor bottle to his chest. surrounded by water and vomit.

CHAPTER 14

RECONCILED

The group of therapists, or the bomb squad as Bruce called them, gathered outside William's office. Maria, William's receptionist, invited them to sit and wait. "Doctor Payne will be with you momentarily." She informed them. Bruce looked at Helen for an explanation. "Do you know what this is about?" He inquired. She responded by shaking her head. "You know as much as I do." William shook his head. "I find that hard to believe." Helen tilted her head smiling. "I don't doubt there are many things you find hard to believe." She repeated mockingly in return. Looking around, Bruce asked the receptionist. "Maria, wasn't Doctor Dayaggi invited to this shindig?" Maria smiled. "Doctor Payne will be with you momentarily." She repeated. Doctor Sable narrowed his eyes at the perceived slight. "Know any other tricks?" Bruce whispered. Leave her alone. She's only doing her job." Helen argued in defense. Maria looked at Helen. "Doctor Zhang, Doctor Payne will see you now." She informed Helen while ignoring Bruce. "What am I?" Bruce asked, feeling slighted. "Sorry, it's not in our bag of tricks to solve mysteries." Bruce looked confused. "What?" He posed while shrugging at Maria's response. Helen laughed as she rose to enter William's office. "That went right over your head, didn't it?" Helen teased Bruce, who also rose to enter the meeting. "What did I miss?" He called Doctor Zhang back. "Doctor Sable, are you causing a ruckus out here?" William asked, opening his door and inviting them in. "No, sir." Bruce quickly responded. "Busted." Helen whispered. William gazed at Helen and winked. Helen lowered her head smiling. The group filed in and waited for William to return to his chair. "Please be seated." He asked politely. Helen and Bruce sat, and without hesitation, Bruce inquired. "Where is Peter? Another late date?" he teased. William smiled. "Once again, your flare for impatience rears its head." William exclaimed. Bruce quickly recanted. "Sorry, boss, it's just that," William cocked his head as if listening intently. "Just what, Doctor Sable?" Bruce took a moment before responding. "Doctor Dayaggi has been under tremendous stress lately, and he seems to be carrying it alone." He responded, sounding concerned. Helen grinned. "Nice save." She replied. William nodded. "I agree; not bad, Bruce. William sat. "That is exactly the reason I've called you here today." Helen leaned forward, a look of concern on her face. "What do you mean, William? Payne took a moment before responding. "Doctor Sable was correct in his assumption. We need to pool our collective expertise in aiding Doctor Dayaggi." Bruce interjected. "What's going on, boss?" He inquired. William paused again as if trying to find a way to say what needed to be said. "I'm having cause for great concern for the mental well-being of Doctor Dayaggi." William admitted. Helen and Bruce looked at one another with surprise and shock. "I don't think it's a secret that Peter and I have a professional rivalry between us, but between us, he's one of the healthiest, mentally and physically, people I know." Bruce admitted. "What's going on, William?" Helen asked. "It would seem that Peter has a client that believes he is the devil." William divulged. "The client thinks Peter is the devil?" Bruce probed. "No." William replied. "The client believes that he is the devil." William clarified. Bruce shrugged. "So, it won't be the first person who," William trailed off as the unspoken implication set in. "Wait, are you telling me Peter has also bought into that fallacy?" Bruce asked. "That's exactly what I'm saying." William confirmed. Helen sat with her mouth open in a state of disbelief. "Doctor Zhang, anything you want to ask?" William posed. "I just find this all very disconcerting; I mean, I would have thought one of us would have suffered, you know, this transference before Peter." She conveyed. William nodded. Bruce leaned forward. "Doctor Dayaggi has always been so meticulous. It seemed unlikely that someone could pull him out of his state of certainty. What do you need from us, boss." William sat back, relieved to see his team pull together. "I've invited Peter to come and share his findings, submit a possible diagnosis and observe his actions. If anything he says or does strike us as suspect, he gives professional suggestions on a course of action to help our colleague." William suggested. "No doubt, boss." Bruce intoned. Helen nodded. "Of course, anything for Peter." She agreed. William looked over at Helen, who seemed caught up in thought. "Doctor Zhang, are you alright?" He inquired. "It's just that, it's only," She stammered. "It's okay, Helen. Take your time." William reassured her. Helen nodded. "I have a patient that insists that the Devil has been through here, and he looks like Peters's patient. She's terrified to come back." Helen admitted. "Is this someone we need to talk to?" Bruce asked. Helen shook her head. "No, I think it would only reinforce the idea in her mind slipping her into a deeper state of anxiety." Helen explained. William nodded. "We'll follow that advice for now, Doctor Zhang. For now, I want us to prepare for Peters's arrival. I asked him to stop by this afternoon." William informed them. William stood signaling the end of the meeting." I look forward to seeing you all this afternoon." He concluded. After the meeting, Bruce Looked for Helen. Stopping at her receptionist's desk, Bruce inquired after her. "Debra, is Helen in her office?" Debra lynx, five feet five inches tall with shoulder-length brown hair and brown eyes, was intellectual and ever-busy helping Helen as a Lead therapist, looking up from her work. "I believe she went to the patio upstairs." Bruce nodded his thanks and went to the roof, where William had their outdoor lunch and relaxation area. Helen sat alone, peering toward Manhattan. Bruce quietly approached her. "Are you okay?" He inquired. Helen looked up, visibly shaken. "Bruce, I'm very concerned." She admitted.

"We all are Helen." He consoled. Helen stared away. "Peter is the most organized, grounded person I've ever met." She expressed sadly. "I know Helen." Bruce agreed. "I don't think you do, Bruce; if Peter, in a single session with the man, was so quickly taken by his delusions, what would happen to us?" She asked, deeply concerned. Bruce cocked his head to the side. "Shoo, girl. What are you talking about? We're the bomb squad! Together we take on all comers." Bruce postured. Helen smiled. "Was that you being ghetto?" She asked. Peter smiled. "You know it." He responded while striking a pose. Despite her concerns, her smile deepened. "Don't do that anymore, and stop standing like that." She exclaimed, ridiculing his pose. "A tad ridiculous?" Bruce asked. "A tad." Agreed Helen. Bruce sat next to her. "What are we going to do, Bruce?" She inquired. "Whatever we can." Bruce responded.

Spy vs. Spy

Nayla entered Lou's suite. You summoned me, Master?" Lou looked at the beautiful Nayla. "To whom were you speaking?" Lou inquired. Nayla cast her eyes down as a show of respect. "My Lord, I spoke with the imp demon Dazz." She responded promptly. "Do not toy with me, Demon." Lou exclaimed in a threatening tone. "Master?" Nayla responded, her voice carrying a questioning note of ignorance. Lou grew angry, which revealed itself physically as his eyes grew red. "What was the first thing you were told upon your directive to serve me? Nayla fought to remain calm. "To serve you with all I am." She responded quietly. Lou stared hard at his consort, seeming to penetrate her soul. Nayla dropped to her knees. "Master, I have displeased you; how may I garner your grace again?" Nayla begged. Lou took a breath calming his rising anger. "Who do you serve?" Lou demanded. "Master, I serve," You know," Lou interjected. "A psychic projection leaves traces of plasma, especially if the participants adapt." Lou shared. Nayla bit back her response, knowing any deception on her part could be dangerous. "Master, I spoke with Lady Lillith." Nayla admitted fearing the repercussion. Lou smirked. "That might have been the smartest thing you'll ever do." He conceded. With her head still bowed, Nayla questioned his response. "My Lord?" Lou's smirk turned into a mischievous grin. "Knowledge." It was the one-word reply Lou shared. Nayla peeked up. "A thousand pardons, my Lord, knowledge about what?" Nayla begged. "Oh, about everything. Your colleagues, What are their ulterior motives and overall goals." Lou added. "Begging your pardon, my Lord, but I'm still confused." Nayla admitted. "From the day we came to be acquainted, Lillith has shown the inclination that she is second to no one. She disobeyed Adam. She dared to argue and disobey God, and from the moment she entered Hell, she acted as if it was her kingdom and that we jointly ruled." Lou revealed. Nayla sat down, stunned, learning about this aspect of her patrons' nature. "She is the queen of the jealousies and master of envy." Nayla was secretly impressed by this powerful woman. As if trading her mind, Lou spoke. "Do not be overly impressed by her. She leaves herself exposed in her single-mindedness. It is not difficult to surmise her desires." Lou criticized. Nayla bowed her head again. "It is true, my lord," Nayla admitted obeying the one rule of Hell everyone existed by. Look out for yourself; a sell-out is often well off. "My Lord, I've contacted Lady Lillith regarding your actions in the mortal realm." Nayla admitted. Lou nodded. the glow of his eyes subsided as he calmed down. "My Lord." Nayla continued. "Lillith wanted to know if you were contacting the foul spirits you deployed, their responses, and if you have been doing anything out of the ordinary." Lou nodded slowly. "I see, and what did you say to that particular query?" Lou probed. "I reported that you have begun to see a therapist." Lou gave a malicious grin. "That must have given Lillith a jolt of optimism." Lou chuckled. Nayla's face reflected confusion. Lou smiled softly. "Ahh, my poor naive little demoness, you just don't get it do you?" Lou posed. Nayla looked down, embarrassed at her naïveté. "Forgive me, lord, for my ignorance." She whispered. Lou waved away the seeming disappointment. "You are a young child; pay attention." Lou commanded, straightening up. "It is time for a formal education in the politics of hell." Lou formally exclaimed. "Rule number one of Hell is to do unto others before they do unto you. Rule number two: You are always number one, even regarding whatever Lord you serve. If you don't put yourself first, the Kings and the subjects of Hell will use all you are and leave a dry husk of your remains. So the only loyalty you'll find in Hell is loyalty to yourself." Nayla's mouth dropped open upon hearing these revelations. A perfect example of that is Lillith." "Lillith, my lord?" Nayla interjected. "Yes, youngling. Lillith is formidable because she has vast experience and very little fear." Nayla opened her mouth to interject with a question. Lou raised his hand to ward off the query. "If you would allow me?" Lou posed. Nayla bowed her head. "Of course, my Lord. "As I was saying, Hell is a place that constantly seeks to usurp my position. Her Kings and demon lords are always seeking advantages to dethrone me." Nayla looked to be in shock. "But my Lord." She began. "You are the Founder of Hell; without you, what would happen to the damned?" She asked, sounding frightened. Lou raised a finger. "Excellent question, and the answer is no one knows. I've had some philosophers and scientists consider that. No one has reached any real conclusions because it has yet to happen." Lou surmised. "My Lord, if that is so, why would Lillith apply herself to such a task unaware of its outcome?" Nayla queried. Lou nodded. "Good question; I surmise that Lillith is self-destructive. Her sense of independence is so strong that she would rather see everything cast aside and destroyed than live with something that doesn't treat her as she feels she deserves." Lou pointed out. "And what might that be?" Nayla inquired. "That she is among the first-born of humanity and deserves nothing less than a throne and title of Mother of humanity." Lou responded. Nayla whistled. "She must have been furious when Eve was formed and regarded as the Mother." Nayla observed. Lou nodded. "She not only was but still is." Lou clarified. Nayla shook her head. "Talk about holding a grudge." She spouted. "Indeed." Lou agreed. "Master, what will you do with me knowing I was spying on you?" Nayla boldly asked. Lou fell silent. Nayla swore she saw his emotions dance across his face as he considered her question. "Aren't you concerned that such a question might hasten my judgment?" Lou inquired. Nayla shrugged her bronze shoulders. "I've never liked waiting for something, especially if it might be bad. I'd rather get it done than wait for something to happen." She admitted. Lou took another moment before responding. "How many times have you broken your word?" Nayla considered the question. "When my parents asked where I got money from, I would lie." She responded. Lou cocked his head to the side. "How is that breaking your word?" Nayla smiled. "My Father would make me promise I would never do anything that would bring shame to our family." Nayla responded sadly. Lou nodded in understanding. "I see. I also see that it still pains you." He observed. "Yes, Master, it does, deeply." She admitted. "In answer to your question, I must ask you one." Lou intoned. Nayla nodded. "Of course, my Lord. "Whom do you serve?" Lou asked. "Master?" Nayla questioned. "It's a simple question." Lou pointed out. Nayla bowed her head. Fear made her voice tremble. "My Lord, I swore allegiance to Lillith for making me as I am, so I suppose it would be her." Nayla closed her eyes, awaiting a fearsome punishment. After nothing happened, she opened her eyes, astonished that she still sat in front of Lucifer unscathed. The look on his face was one of disbelief. "Master?" She queried nervously. "Child, I don't think Lillith would have ever saved you if she had the slightest notion of your capacity. Lou said almost reverently. "My lord?" Nayla asked. Lou stood abruptly. "Stand, demoness!" Lou demanded. Nayla stood, reconciling herself to what she thought was to come. "Nayla, Demon succubus of the order of Lillith, do you from this moment ever more swear your fidelity to me and me alone, with no other coming before me?" Lou intoned. Nayla was in a state of shock. "But my Lord, I have betrayed you and.." Rising his hand, commanding silence, Nayla silenced herself. "Your discipline is beyond measure, as is your courage. Lillith never suspected that I might be attracted to that. She believed once I found out you were spying on me, I would destroy you, and normally I would have. But when confronted, you did not hide behind lies or retreat into excuses. No, you were ready to accept the consequences, whatever they might have been. For that reason, I will raise your station. None in Hell shall have power over you except me." But my Lord, what of Lillith?" Nayla asked. "What about her? She tried doing what you did once, and when she was caught, she had a thousand reasons for her betrayal. Remember the first rule of Hell." Lou warned. Nayla nodded her head vigorously. "I will, my Lord." She responded, wanting to jump for joy.

CHAPTER 15

INSPECTION

Dressed in a black tracksuit, Lou called the front desk to order breakfast. Nayla, who luxuriated in her hot showers, walked into the small dining area to dry her long-flowing black mane. "What are we doing today?" She queried. "at the moment, I'm waiting for them to bring me breakfast. I'm also waiting for you so we can go about my business." Lou informed. Something Lou said she thought of as strange. "Breakfast? Why'd you order breakfast? We do not need to eat." She expounded on the obvious. "It's all about appearances. It would look odd if we stayed here and never ordered food." Lou pointed out. Nayla looked perturbed. "Why should we care.." Lou interjected. "Because we try to leave as little of a footprint as possible. Spirits of malice are expected to act barbarically, even the occasional minion but not one such as yourself, and it's taboo for me to be here by heaven ruling. Even my subjects do not like the notion of my visits." Lou pointed out. Nayla wisely stopped what could be taken as an interrogation. "As you say, My Lord." Lou looked at her crossly. "That's one, Nayla. "She froze in fear, knowing she had just upset the Master of Hell. She revealed her value again as her impulse was to beg his pardon; instead, she replied. "Very well, enjoy your breakfast. I'm going to get ready for the day." She sashayed into the bedroom. *Lillith did well with this one. Lou thought to himself.* Nayla exited the bedroom as Lou was feeding his breakfast to the pigeons that landed on the window sill. She stood there waiting for him. "Almost done." Lou announced. Nayla smiled and sat on the couch, watching the Lord of hell feeding pigeons. "Lou, finishing, turned to see Nayla smiling at him. "Why are you smiling?" He growled. "I think you know why." She responded with a boldness she did not feel. Lucifer smiled. "You are one of very few that got to see my Angelic nature." Lou responded softly. A deep, based voice met Nayla's look of concern. "But never, ever think that you have an effect on me; that is a side of me reserved for Nature and her creatures." Lou exclaimed. Nayla nodded her understanding. "Shall we go?" Lou asked politely as if the last few moments didn't occur. The desk manager was new, and when Lou inquired, he was told that the manager had committed suicide. Lou looked at Nayla, who shrugged off any blame. Walking out of the hotel, Lou sniffed the air. A passerby noticed and commented on the gesture. "Stinks to high heaven, doesn't it?" He posed. Lou smiled. "Ahh, it's not that bad; it smells like New York." He responded cheerfully. "I suppose you're right." The pedestrian agreed. Lou motioned for Nayla to follow him. many eyes turned to stare at the raven-haired beauty dressed in a deep purple tracksuit. "Why do the men act as they've never seen a woman before." Nayla posed. Lou laughed. "Nayla, your powers of seduction are flowing from you. You must learn to dampen it in this domain, or you will signal Heaven of your presence and be useless to me." He advised. Nayla calmed herself down, her first reaction being terrified at the thought of being dispelled. "Master," She whispered. "Lillith never taught me how to do that." Lou nodded his understanding. "It's not a trick; you only have to find these men undesirable, and those emanations will be subsumed." Lou shared. "Thank you, Lou." She said with a smile that Lou returned. "There you go, look, we've entered the influence of Lor, a sprite demon of mischief. Lou explained. "Why, if I may ask Mast, I mean Lou." Nayla apologized, catching herself. "Why exactly are we here?" Lou glanced around. "Tell me, what do you notice?" Lou probed. Nayla looked around, missing at first but then noticing. "It appears as if everyone is extremely focused, but behind the focus is the intention, and beyond that," Nayla paused. Lou watched, impressed with this newly made demoness. "What do you see, Nayla?" Lou pressed. "Greed. Malignant, barely restrained greed." She exclaimed in a near whisper. "Yes, daughter, exactly right." Lou conceded. "For what purpose?" She inquired, sensing something far more sinister than mere damnation. Lou looked at her curiously. Unnerved that she might have offended him, she bowed her head. "Master, have I given offense? Lou shook his head. "No, and it's Lou. No, I was wondering if Lillith fully realized your potential or if she saw you as another harlot, trainable to do only her bidding?" Lou responded. "But Lou, is that not the purpose of my creation?" She inquired. Lou smiled. "First of all, I did not, nor did Lillith, create you; in the flames of perdition, you were relegated, and while that may have been Lillith's purpose, it may not be mine." Lou answered vaguely. Nayla gazed at her surroundings. "I don't mind admitting that I'm confused." Lou smiled again. "A natural response to anyone with only partial information, Nayla." Lou pointed out. "I shall share a part of my plan; if you figure out more, that would be to your credit." Lou said in a complimentary tone. Lor's job is to entice and incite greed, mischief, and envy. The demon sprite called Diz is to entice and incite hypocrites, traitors, and blasphemers. In contrast, The demon Andrax does the same among arsonists, rapists, and murderers." Lou explained. Nayla's brow furrowed in deep thought. "I know it is much you're not revealing." She expressed. "Correct." Lou said. Nayla raised her eyes, looking at the people they walked amongst deeply. "What I'm I missing?" She asked herself quietly. Come, let us visit the lair of Diz." Lou prodded. Lou approached Rockefeller center and guided Nayla to the subway to catch the D train. In the noisy subway, Nayla leaned toward Lou. "Reminds me of home." She shouted. Lou grinned. "Yes, the wail of the second circle." Lou agreed. The train arrived and carried its passengers to their destination, where Lou prompted them to disembark. Nayla looked at the sign. "Wall street?" She said in an interesting voice?" Lou grinned. "We seek Diz, The fabricator. from a realm of hypocrites, traitors, and blasphemers." Lou espoused. "What am I missing?" Nayla voiced in frustration. "Lou laughed aloud, making some passersby on the busy street look at the man with the baritone, boisterous laugh. "I'm sure you'll figure it out Lou claimed, surprised Lillith would allow one as observant as this demoness out of the fires.

The unraveling

Peter stared into his closet. His difficulty in something as simple as choosing what to wear indicated his muddled thinking. *"Get a hold of yourself, man." Peter chastised himself. "Just pick a pair of pants and a shirt and get moving."* Slowly getting dressed, Peter dreaded presenting his diagnosis to his colleagues because he knew the reactions he would receive. He could envision William asking him to stick to the facts and not let his over-active imagination take control of his thought process. Conversely, Bruce humors him just to set him up for a condescending joke, while Helen pukes motherly support. Peter sighed. In slow motion, he showered, shaved, and dressed for work. He called a car service refraining from his usual mode of transport. Exiting his building, the gathering dark clouds perfectly reflected his mood. Sitting in her chair by the window of Her restaurant, Patty watched Peter slowly climb into the cab. "Pedro," She called to her husband, who, as usual, was in the stock room restocking shelves. "Pedro!" Patty called louder after not receiving an answer. "What?" Pedro called back, sounding irritated. "Did you do what I asked?" Patty asked ambiguously. "Pedro gasped. "Patty, what the hell are you talking about now?" The restaurant was empty, so Patty left her seat and stomped into the store room. "You never listen to me." She accused, entering the room. "I avoid it whenever possible," Pedro responded sarcastically. "Doctor Pete, you ass." Patty cussed. Pedro placed a can he had on the shelf before turning to face his wife. "For the love of everything holy, what the hell are you talking about?" Pedro pled. "Remember last night; I asked you to visit Doctor Pete?" Patty asked. Pedro nodded. "Yeah, I remember." He conceded. Patty glared at Pedro. "And?" She demanded. "And what?" Pedro responded while returning to stacking the shelves. It was obvious to Patty that Pedro wished to avoid the issue. "Well? Did you see him?" She demanded. Pedro remained quiet. He knew his wife well enough to know she would be extremely dissatisfied with his answer. Patty was extremely loyal and woe unto those who tried to harm those she cared about. Pedro stopped stacking and turned to his wife. "I didn't go." He admitted. Patty's glare sharpened. "You what?" She asked, anger mounting. "Listen, baby," Pedro began his explanation. "The man has a staff of professionals at his fingertips if he needs help. I'm just a deli owner." Pedro protested. "What do I know about helping people with emotional issues? What if I say the wrong thing and make it worse? I didn't feel," Pedro searched for the word. "Qualified." He exclaimed. He was taking the steam out of Patty's argument. She hugged her husband. "You're right, honey; I shouldn't have asked you to do that. He has been good to us, so the next time he stops in the store, tell him you're here for him." Patty compromised. Pedro nodded. "Of course, baby."

Peter's cab pulled up to the clinic. Stepping out to ever-darkening skies, Peter looked up and wondered if it were an omen. Peter entered the clinic and went directly to William's office. Maria was at her post. "Good morning, Doctor Dayaggi." Maria greeted him warmly. "Good morning Maria, is Doctor Payne available? She nodded in response. "He is. If you, please be seated, I'll let him know you've arrived." She replied. Maria called William on the intercom. "Doctor Dayaggi has arrived, sir." Maria paused a moment. "Yes, sir, I'll tell him." She said before hanging up. She gazed at Peter while punching numbers on the phone. "Doctor Payne will see you momentarily." She conveyed. Peter nodded acknowledgment. "Doctor Zhang, Doctor Payne is ready for you and Doctor Sable now," Maria informed the therapeutic supervisor. Doctors Zhang and Sable entered Doctor Payne's reception area a moment later. Seeing Peter sitting, Helen had difficulty hiding her shock as Peter looked thinner, his face gaunt with dark circles forming under his eyes. "Hey, old man, how the hell are you?" Bruce called Peter. Doctor Dayaggi stared at Bruce, then at Helen. "Still keeping bad company, I see." Peter jibed. Helen smiled as she saw and heard a flash of the Peter she knew and cared about. "Someone has to look out for the strays." Helen returned. The smile on Peters's face grew from the hint of normalcy being offered during this awkward moment. "Peter," William called. "If you'd be kind enough," He gestured into his office—a silent beckoning. Peter grinned. Rose from his chair and strode into William's office. The Doctors filed in behind Peter, and William stopped at the door. "Please hold all calls, Maria." Maria nodded her understanding.

The Doctors sat at the large oak rectangular desk that Doctor Payne had in his conference room. Doctor Payne sat at its head while Doctors Zhang and Bruce sat on his right with Peter on his left. A picture of Doctor Payne in front of Memorial church at the university of Harvard. Encased in a frame that matched the conference table was etched with gold dust bearing the slogan of Williams's alma mater, "veritas." Truth or a fragment thereof was hoped to be found in today's meeting. "Can I offer anyone a refreshment before we get started?" William asked. True to form, Doctor Sable spoke up. "Can we, by any chance, get some cappuccino in here? I thought we would do this later in the day." Peter smiled. Bruce caught the smile and got defensive. "What? He offered, and I'm hungry." He complained. "Really, Bruce, decide. Client or employee, you can't do both." Zhang complained. William buzzed his receptionist. "Maria, would you please send for a light breakfast please." William requested.

"Any store in particular.?" She probed. "Yeah," Bruce interjected. "Yeah." William interrupted, "The quickest one." He said, giving Bruce a look of displeasure. Bruce quietly sat with no further complaints. "Well, that should take about twenty minutes; let us get started." Payne suggested beginning the meeting. Peter stood and began his presentation. About four weeks ago, a walk-in arrived. It was mid-afternoon; I'd have to refer to my papers for certainty. This man introduced himself as Lou Cyphur. The Client initially presented himself as well-educated, highly intelligent, sophisticated, and well-traveled. He lived independently and seemed very confident. Although appearing to be a well-rounded individual, his psychological integrity revealed an outstanding deficit. "And what was that?"

Sable inquired. Peter glanced up from his notes, noticing how his colleagues were looking at him. Shoving his feelings back, he continued. "Well, Doctor Sable, in answer to your question Mister Cyphur has many Father issues beginning with abandonment, oppositional defiance, Anger management, Identification disorder, homicidal and genocidal ideation, and Tourette's syndrome. Peter paused. He felt the tension in the room rising. "I strongly suggest we seek a court order to issue a summons to Mister Cyphur to appear for a psychiatric evaluation to ensure his ability to function safely in the community. Bruce shifted in his seat. William looked over at him. "Doctor Sable, is there something you'd like to say? Bruce's gaze went from William to Peter. "Forgive me, Doctor Dayaggi, but this all seems slightly extreme. What proof do we have other than your evaluation?" Bruce leaned close to Peter. "Why are you so convinced? Peter returned Bruce's stare. "Lou Cyphur believes that he is Lucifer." Peter barked flatly. Bruce shrugged dismissively. "So what." Bruce retorted. "So I believe him," Peter responded.

Lou & Nayla

"Master, are you ready?" Nayla inquired. Lou shook his head. "No, we shall wait a bit longer to have the full cover of night." Lou ordered. Nayla nodded in acceptance. "May I ask what tonight holds?" She inquired. Lou smiled. "Tonight, my dear, we summon the foul spirits I had released from hell. Tonight they get their marching orders." Lou said with a malicious grin. Nayla's grin reflected her master. "Do we release havoc, my lord?" Lou shook his head. "Not yet, my little demon, there will be a time for them to be loosed, but first, others must pave the way to maximize their results. Lou gloated. Nayla felt a perverse joy seeing Lou delight in his plan. "Will it be like the bridge, my lord?" Nayla enjoyed Lou's display of power and disrespectful treatment of the Angel of Death. Lou's grin faded. "No, demon, that was a mistake." Lou admitted. "My Lord?" Nayla queried, surprised at the admittance. "A mistake." Lou repeated. "The purpose of me releasing foul spirits into the world is because their spiritual footprint is insignificant. In the past, I used demons, devils, and monsters to terrorize people and force their idolization on me. Still, when Heaven took notice, they set up a form of demon radar that spied out on any incursion upon the world. Reacting to Heaven's repression, I used a lesser demonic force. "Did it work, Master?" An intrigued Nayla asked. Lou nodded. "Indeed, that was until that night on the bridge. I was so consumed with rage at the audacity of the thug that he could rob me. Me! I was livid, and the opportunity to take a modern man of science and twist him," Lou trailed off. "But it was folly to allow me to get carried away in such a manner. I nearly undid decades of work in a single night by dangling that fool's body over the flames of hell and torturing him, forcing the Angel of Death onto the scene, thereby alerting Heaven that Evil had forged unto the mortal realm. "But Master," Nayla began. Lou stared at her. "Pardon, Lou." She corrected. "What does this mean for us, Lou." She inquired curiously. "That's what we will be finding out tonight, whether my presence has brought the full attention of Heaven or not." Lou pointed out. "If not?" Nayla probed. Lou smiled, revealing a perfect set of teeth. *He looks very handsome in his mortal guise.* Nayla thought. "Well," Lou began. "If we've managed to escape Heaven's scrutiny, I will show you what kind of results patience can garner, my little demoness." Lou chuckled. Nayla's gaze became distant; upon her refocusing, she saw Lou staring at her. "Well?" He asked. Nayla stared back at Lou. Lillith summons me, my Lord. Lou clapped his hands together. "Excellent. Attend to her and then report to me." Lou commanded. Nayla nodded in obedience, unsure how she let herself get caught between two powerful entities of darkness. Exiting Lou's room, she returned to her bedroom and began meditating for psychic communication. "Sister." came the distant calling. "I am here, My lady." Nayla responded. "what have you to report." Lillith inquired. "My Lady, I have serviced the Master, although he seems more preoccupied with his mission here on Earth than any dalliance with me." Nayla dutifully reported. Lillith appeared to lose patience. "I don't care how often he screws you, little girl!" Lillith shouted. "Are you so dense that you don't understand I care about the completion of Lucifer's plans?" Lillith scolded. "My Lady, you told me my assignment was to assure the Master was kept sexually sated so he wouldn't bring harm to a mortal woman." Nayla reminded Lillith. Anger resounded in Lillith's admonishment. "Foolish girl, your job is whatever I tell you your job is. Remember, I raised you out of the flames. I gave you relief from the pain. You owe all that you enjoy to me! never forget that." Lillith warned. Nayla bowed her head. "I shall never forget my lady." Nayla responded, sounding grateful. "Very well, my sister; now I need to know which spirits Lucifer is contacting, their missions, and when he plans to implement them." Lillith ordered. "As you wish, my lady." Nayla complied. Coming out of her trance Nayla tapped on Lou's door. "Come in." Lou responded. "Well?" He asked. Nayla sat cross-legged on the floor. "It is everything you said it might be, Lou." She reported hesitantly. Lou stared at Nayla. "Is there a problem?" Lou inquired, a threat left unspoken. "No, Lou, I feel uncomfortable with the betrayal." Nayla admitted. Lou barked a laugh. "Demon, betrayal is the language of hell. I highly recommend you get acquainted with it very fast, or you'll find yourself at the end of it repeatedly, do you understand?" Lou asked. Nayla nodded her head. "Tell me your impressions?" Lou requested. Nayla thought a moment. "For whatever reason, it seemed she wasn't alone," Nayla began. "And what gave you that impression?" Lou probed. "It seemed that every time she began a new topic or line of questioning, she looked elsewhere for input." Lou nodded. "A conspiracy for sure," Lou exclaimed while rubbing his hands together. "Lou, isn't the notion of a rebellion abhorrent?" Nayla innocently inquired. Lou smiled. "Not at all. Every thousand years or so, some demon lord or King gets a wild hair up his ass and gets it in their tiny mind that they could run hell better." Lou explained. "It's somewhat refreshing." He admitted. Nayla didn't hide her confusion. "How so?" She asked. Lou took a deep breath before explaining. "Imagine five, ten, or even twenty thousand years of peace! The mundane sameness of everything would render hell as boring as shit. However, hell is constantly in flux with the periodical turmoil, making the realm insecure and frightening. Heaven is the place of stability." Lou finished. "Ohhh." Nayla exclaimed. "I think I get it. So who do you think is scheming against you? Lou considered the question. "I have my suspicion, but I need to investigate more before I'm sure." He explained.

CHAPTER 16

TRAITORS

The never-ending Tempest wailed. The moans of the lustful could be heard as pleasure turned into agony. In her private suite, Lillith stared at the reflecting pool allowing contact in the mortal world. Visibly upset, Lillith threw a mirror against a wall. The mirror shattered. Sitting, enjoying a cup of blood wine, the Lord of the second circle barked. "Good thing you're not superstitious, or that would mean seven years of bad luck." He snickered. "Asmodeus. What do you want?" Lillith demanded. The tall, white-eyed demon lord looked up from the mirror at Lillith. "I want what we all want." He responded ambiguously. "Oh, and what might that be?" She responded. Stroking his wispy chin hairs, Asmodeus approached Lillith. "First, of course, is to bed you," He began. "Yeah, Not ever." Lillith snapped. "Second," Asmodeus continued. "Is the mastery of hell, which you are going to help me get." he posed. Lillith shook her head. "As I told you, this must be done with sublime tact. Lucifer will not surrender his throne." She complained. "Yes," Asmodeus agreed. "However, if we can prove to Heaven Lucifers' incompetence and reluctance to follow the divine plan, he might be usurped by a power far mightier than our own." Asmodeus stated calmly. Lillith stood and walked over to a window that overlooked the dry, arid Realm's dry plains. "Well," Began Asmodeus. "I've sought an alliance with one clever enough to devise a plan sublime enough to go undetected and powerful enough to dethrone Lucifer." He bragged. Lillith looked at him sharply. "What is this plan you speak of?" She queried. Asmodeus shook his head. "Why should I trust you with that vital piece of information?" He asked suspiciously. Lillith narrowed her eyes. "Do you want my trust? My help? My silence?" She threatened. Asmodeus bent down and began picking up pieces of the broken mirror. "Much like this mirror, a commonality was reflected upon us: Lucifer's terrible managing of hell. Now the mirror lays in pieces because anger caused it to be hurled at the wall." Lillith sighed. "What's your point." She complained. "I would have thought that obvious," Asmodeus responded evasively. "Yeah, well, so much for that. Look, you either trust me or you don't, and I strongly suggest you do, or the first thing I'll do is tell Lucifer what you're planning." She threatened again. Asmodeus considered for a moment. "Alright, fine." He exclaimed. Asmodeus leaned toward Lillith conspiratorially and began whispering. "I have spoken to and struck a deal with Valak," Asmodeus told Lillith. She responded with a gasp. "Are you insane?" Lillith asked wide-eyed. Asmodeus scowled. "Did you or did you not say we needed a sublime plan? Sublime enough to fool even Lucifer?" He insisted. Lillith nodded in compliance. "Asmodeus, what would posses you to think Valak could get anywhere near Lucifer undetected? Asmodeus grinned wickedly. "The plan is ingenious." Asmodeus bragged. "Plan? What plan? We never decided on anything." Lillith demanded. Asmodeus tapped his temple. "I've been thinking for this to work; the fewer who knew, the better." Off-handedly accepting Lilith's complaint.

"Tell me this plan." Lillith grudgingly accepted the fact that Asmodeus had already set things in motion. "As you pointed out, Lillith, the plan must be sublime. The problem comes from Lucifer knowing every demonic trick in the book, but what if the trick didn't originate in hell?" Asmodeus posed. Lillith grew curious. "Okay, you have a captive audience; what are you talking about?" Lillith demanded. Asmodeus cackled. "You are going to love this," Asmodeus bragged. "Out with it!" Lillith ordered. "Valak also concluded any idea born of hell would carry the stench of hell," Lillith interrupted. "Yes, we know that already." She insisted. The whites of Asmodeus's eyes glowed. "What if Lou himself is the reason for his dethroning?" Asmodeus queried. Lillith's expression registered shock. "Have you lost your fucking mind?" She screeched. Asmodeus looked offended. "I assure you I most certainly have not." He protested. "Listen, as he likes to call himself now, Lou is becoming enamored with mortality. He has, of late broken restrictions about revealing evil to mortals. Lou has introduced a succubus to a mortal, and he's even gone so far as to torture a living soul, forcing Death's specter to appear before a mortal! Now, if we can utilize this mortal, he has become so forthright to get Lou to agree with his humanist view. perhaps that would be enough to incite an insurrection among the Kings of hell." Asmodeus concluded, nearly frothing at the mouth. "And when the battles are concluded?" She inquired. "Valak will lend us his legions to subjugate whoever survives," Asmodeus concluded. Lillith took a deep breath of impatience. "And you think that once all of hell is laid open and all that stands between the throne and Valak is you, you think he's going to cede power to you?" Lillith began laughing. Asmodeus faced Lillith. "Why are you laughing?" He demanded. Lillith struggled, but she started laughing every time she looked at Asmodeus. After a moment of struggle and Asmodeus's growing anger, Lillith gasped. "You can be so foolish!" She gasped. Asmodeus stomped around the room. "I don't hear you coming up with a better idea." He hissed. Still fighting to regain her composure Lillith responded. "No idea is always better than a bad one." She hissed in return. Asmodeus cut his eyes at Lillith. "No matter, the plan has been set into motion. Lillith's eyes widened. "What have you done?" Lillith whispered harshly. Asmodeus looked around as if searching for someone. "To whom are you speaking? Me? Unbelievable, since I'm so stupid, why would you waste your time talking so, as you put it, so incredibly stupid." Asmodeus complained. Lillith looked at Asmodeus in disgust. "What the fuck happened to you?" She queried. Asmodeus looked confused. "What do you mean, what happened to me?" He posed. Lillith stared at him. "What I mean is, your Mother is one of my chief Succubus, and your Father was King David, who your Mother seduced! That Lineage nominated you as the master of the second circle of hell. You were fierce and ambitious enough to threaten Lucifer for his throne in your first cycle as circle ruler. But that was long ago, and it appears that the passage of time has also stolen your courage and cunning." Lillith reprimanded. Asmodeus appeared to shake with rage. "How dare you whore!" Asmodeus shouted. "You dare to judge me? I am your King, and you're nothing more than a subservient slut that bends in whatever direction your master slaps you in!" Asmodeus retaliated. Lillith stopped laughing and grew in indignation. "Worm!" She shouted in return. "Son of a wanton Father and demonic Mother. Remember to whom you speak. I am Lillith. I was Created alongside Adam, his first wife—the one with enough courage to stand In front of the Creator of all. Even before Lucifer became Satan, I defied the Creator. When He told me to submit to Adam, I questioned his divine wisdom by asking, Was I not raised from the Earth alongside Adam? By what right has he now become my Master? For this, I was exiled from the golden city. Never address me in such a manner again, demon son." Lillith demanded. The conspirators stared at one another for a tense moment. Lillith exhaled and calmly asked. "Do you think it will work?" Asmodeus chuckled. "We can only hope." He remarked dryly. "I must reach out to our contact," Lillith exclaimed. "For what purpose?" Asmodeus asked. Lillith smiled. "I'm thinking the best way to hide Valaks huge footprint is using her as a go-between for Valak and the therapist," Lillith explained. Asmodeus nodded. "Yes, genius! I will inform Valak immediately."

Asmodeus declared before vanishing. Lillith sat in a meditative position, preparing to contact her agent Nayla.

CHAPTER 17

LOU'S NUMBERS

The room fell silent. William cleared his throat and asked. "Do you mean to say that you believe him when he says He believes it?" Peter looked at William. "I mean to say that Mister Cyphur may have skills we are unaware of." Peter clarified. "What type of skills might you be referring to, Peter?" Helen inquired. Peter paused a moment. "It can range from hypnosis to con-man to a chemist." Peter responded. "The implication is that he uses these skills in tandem to fool his victims?" Bruce asked. Peter nodded. "That seems most logical to me." Peter paused. "It is impossible, the things I saw. Flames of hell, a demoness. an entity of Death; I'm not sure how he did it, but Lou must have drugged something I consumed and, in my weakened state, hypnotized me to accept everything he said as truth." Peter said softly. After a moment of silence, Helen asked the unspoken question. "Peter, do you believe this man when he tries to convince you?" She inquired in a soft-spoken voice. Peter looked out of the window. He stared at the quickly gathering clouds. "It looks like it's going to rain." Peter remarked off-handedly. "The weatherman said there is a chance of afternoon showers." Bruce replied. "Peter?" Helen called gently. Peter raised his hand in acknowledgment. "I heard you, Helen." He responded. "The fact of the matter is, when I'm amongst you, my colleagues, I know everything Lou says is at least delusional," Peter began. "And when you're not? Among us, I mean." Bruce asked. Peter spun to look at his associates. "When I'm not what? Among you? Well, Doctor Sable, I find myself in a state of confusion and perplexity. I'm unsettled as all my training screams against the evidence of my senses. The one that calls himself Lou has a gift of manipulation far surpasses anyone I've known, heard, or read about. He makes Rasputin look like an amateur. He could teach P. T. Barnum because Lou has the greatest show on earth." Peter confessed. "So you believe him?" William asked. Peter stared at his employer. "Sometimes." Peter admitted. William nodded. "Well, there is only one thing to do." The group grew quiet, waiting for his decision. "We will not abandon a colleague while he suffers an existential crisis. Peter, we fully support you. I recommend that you inform Mister Cyphur that his case is profound. seek his permission to allow what we'll call therapeutic shifting. You, Peter, sit as a lead therapist, and your colleagues sit as wingmen in shifts so that only you will have extended exposure to his influence. That would give us a chance to have fresh perspectives." William announced. The therapists shifted in their seats. Peter, who was still standing, leaned over Doctor Payne. "But William, I don't know if he'll approve of that." Peter argued. "Well, Doctor Dayaggi, perhaps you should ask the devil if he honestly believes one therapist is wise or intelligent enough to help the incarnation of Evil all by himself? If so, he was never serious about getting aid as opposed to trying to frighten the poor mortals again. If that's the case, he is not the fearsome bogeyman he is reported to be." William stated. Peter's facial expression conveyed doubt. "I don't know," He muttered. William looked up at Peter, who still hovered over him. "Peter, you have to try. Don't you see what he's doing to you?" William pled. Peter nodded. "You're right, William. Fuck him if his feelings get hurt." Peter exclaimed. Helen placed her hand on Peter's forearm. "Peter." She whispered. Peter looked down at her, eyes ablaze. "Peter, don't you see how he is affecting you?" She inquired. Peter continued to stare at her with eyes burning with unresolved anger. "Peter, you suggested that a patient be damned. You forget, my friend, we are

Doctors; we don't fuck our clients; our job is to cure them." The anger in Peter's eyes diminished. Peter smiled. "Sweet Helen, your words are soothing; thank you for grounding me." Peter espoused gratefully. "And that's why I think our approach to this matter in the manner I suggested would work." William concluded. Peter nodded in agreement. "It is agreed then." Peter resolved. "Do you have a recommendation on how to proceed?" Peter asked for the first time in the meeting, sitting beside William, to whom he directed his question. After a moment of consideration, William spoke. "I think since this is Peters's client, he has established a relationship with the man. Peter should inform him of our suggestion with me beside him, giving Mister Cyphur the impression that it has the full support of Management; I'll then explain the importance of having shifting therapists." He explained. The group nodded in compliance. "Do you think he's going to accept any of this?" Bruce asked. William nodded. "I do." He responded. "Why, why would he accept such a premise?" Helen inquired. Doctor Payne smiled. "Have any of you read Milton's Paradise lost?" William inquired. Peter smiled. "Pride." He said softly. William smiled in return. "Yes, Peter, pride. If your, Lou, truly is Lucifer, the incarnation of Evil, it would be easy for his pride to accept that he is so convoluted that it would take a group of mortals to come close to understanding the depths of his mind." William concluded. "You're a fucking mad genius, William!" Peter whispered, leaning close to him. William winked at Peter. "Now, all you have to do is set it up." William reminded Peter, who smiled. "This should be fun." He exclaimed. "Are you nervous about doing this, Peter?" Bruce asked. Peter looked at him. "A bit, but I assure you the deed will be done, Doctor Sable. William looked over at Helen. Doctor Zhang, I'd like it if you could go over a strategy with Peter on the best way to convince Mister Cyphur that this approach would be most effective for his treatment." William suggested, to which Helen nodded in agreement. Peter shook his head. "I'm not thinking that is a good idea at all." Peter claimed. "And why is that?" William inquired. Peter reflected a moment. "Lou is a very personal character.

If we keep this, at least the informing part, more personal, he might go for it, but if he smells like I've been coached, he will refuse. I think it has to do with his issues with authority figures." Peter expressed sincerely. William gave thought to Peter's recommendation. "You've been with him the longest, alright, fine. We'll follow Doctors Dayaggi's suggestion and allow him to disclose to Mister Cyphur our recommendation for his continued treatment." William agreed. "You have a phone call to make, Peter." William said in dismissal. Peter nodded in agreement. "Yes, boss, I do." Peter agreed. "We'll await Peter's signal that Mister Cyphur has been informed and agreed to our stipulation. William espoused. "Until then."

Lord & Lady of Lust

Asmodeus sat in his castle, staring out a window overlooking his domain. The unceasing winds blew their hot breath across the arid plains. The pale, bleak sky is symbolic. The colorless, never-ending hot wind of desire that never ends painted the domain in its empty expanse. "My lord," a demon said, announcing himself. Asmodeus turned to find his chamberlain kneeling. "What is it?" The Lord of Lust queried. "My lord Lady Lillith requests an audience with your magnificence." The Demon reported. Asmodeus tilted his head, staring at the Demon. "Crave, how long have you served me?" Asmodeus inquired. The Demon answered immediately. "My Lord, you recruited me just before the usurpation of Peitho, the lady of persuasion." He responded. Asmodeus nodded. "So, since the beginning of my rule," Asmodeus clarified. "Yes, my Lord." Crave agreed. "Tell us, Chamberlin do you feel you know your Lord will?" Asmodeus posed. Crave nodded slowly. "Only as much as my Lord let be known. Crave responded wisely. "Tell us then your thoughts on Lady Lillith." Asmodeus demanded. "My Lord?" Crave asked in a subdued manner. "You heard and understood the question, don't you?" Asmodeus's demand had a ring of anger to it. Knowing his master is not known for his patience, Crave quickly qualifies his seeming confusion. "My Lord, I meant to ask only if you mean her character, loyalty, or desire." Crave quickly expressed. Asmodeus seemed to consider the response. "All of the above." He decided. Looking out the window, Crave saw the sector's vast emptiness and remembered that this King's mercy was as empty as the Plains of this circle. "My Lord, Lady Lillith is among hell's most devious citizens. She has no patience for failure and would send her Mother to the fires for an opportunity. I think this speaks to her loyalty," Asmodeus interrupted. "In what manner?" He asked. Crave took a moment. "She is loyal only to herself and her desires." Crave answered back. Asmodeus nodded. "Could you hazard a guess what that desire might be?" Asmodeus probed. Crave looked around nervously as if afraid they might be overheard. "Why are you apprehensive?" Asmodeus asked his Chamberlin. Crave looked into the white eyes of his Lord. "My Lord, we are in hell." Crave responded. "Yes and?" Asmodeus questioned, becoming upset at the implication. "My Lord. Lillith has spies everywhere, and I don't wish to be on her bad side." Crave responded, frightened. "Tell us, demon, why do you sound more frightened of a demoness than your Lord?" Asmodeus accused. Crave bowed. "Nothing could be further from the truth, my Lord. Asmodeus nodded. "And if Lillith rose against me?" Asmodeus left the question unfinished. Crave looked around again, looking for shifting shadows. Asmodeus roared. "Slave! Do I need to seek out one more courageous than you?" The Lord of Lust demanded. Crave sank lower to the floor. "My Lord. I do not know the extent of her power; She is Lucifer's Mistress, and I don't wish to offend his Majesty. Asmodeus fumed. "You are a coward Crave. You think I can't shield my domain against intrusion?" Asmodeus charged. "A thousand pardons, my Lord. Any conflict you face, I face with you. Any challenges against you have me for an enemy as well. The Demon swore. The face of Asmodeus bore contempt as he addressed his servant. "If such is the case, be forthright in your answers to me and stop equivocating." He demanded. Crave struggled with the impulse to look around again. "My Lord, in answer to your question. Crave paused, reluctant to put himself in such a vulnerable position by speaking openly against a power of hell. Asmodeus stared impatiently. "My Lord, I believe she desires the throne for herself. She wants the title of Grand Empress." Crave said softly. Asmodeus's look of anger changed to curiosity, analysis, realization, and finally, back to anger. Emotional discharges danced across the face of Asmodeus as he considered what his Chamberlin revealed. This is what I believe to be her desire." Crave concluded. The chamber was quiet. To clarify, it was silent. Not even the howl of the infernal winds could be heard. Crave looked up at Asmodeus, who was staring into the vast Plains. "Your foresight is keen, Chamberlin." Asmodeus grumbled. "Perhaps I shall raise you to the rank of Majordomo." The King continued. "Bring forth the Mistress of Hell." Asmodeus ordered. Crave bowed to his Lord and slowly exited the tower chamber. He descended stone steps. His apparel changed from a flowing black robe to the golden red of the Majordomo of the house of Lust. The former officeholder was terminated for lack of productivity and misappropriation of estate assets. Trumped up charges, undoubtedly, but this is hell. The ousted administrator awaited the new officeholder to render and execute judgment. Such are the niceties of hell. Crave arrived in his new quarters and immediately summoned Lillith, who was in her blood ruby tower. (a gift from Lucifer when she joined him in damnation. It also served as a symbol of her status as the first bride of Evil.) Kuru, a demon servant and acolyte of Lillith, approached her Mistress (who lay facing a huge window overlooking a small cavern where Lillith occasionally entertained.) in a bejeweled room of Onyx, Jade, and marble. A couch of silks covered a bed of nails that held the prone form of the Succubus Lillith. The room was warm and musty. The smell of sex was pervasive. In a blood-red gown that swept the floor as she walked, Kuru approached her Miss tress. "What is it?" Lillith cooed as the acolyte approached. "My Lady. Your presence has been requested at the Palace." Kuru reported. Lillith rolled over to look at her servant. She quickly sat. "What did the idiot Peitho want?" Lillith inquired. Kuru shook her head. "It was not Peitho, my Lady. The house of Lust has a new Majordomo, an elevated demon called Crave." Kuru reported. A look of curiosity crossed Lillith's face. "Why was I not notified? She demanded. "I was not given time to ask. The Majordomo himself came with the summons and, as quickly, left. Kuru noted. An inflamed Succubus transported herself to the Palace of Lust. Arriving, she found herself in the presence of the new Majordomo. "My Lady." He bowed in greeting. The simple gesture of respect diffused some of Lilith's anger as Crave knew it would. "My Lady, forgive the manner of my visit and announcement, but here at the Palace, we are more secure from celestial eavesdropping. "And why would the Celestials wish to listen to the conversations of the hell-bound?" She asked. Crave bowed again. "My Lady, that would be for the Lord Asmodeus and yourself to discuss." Crave replied. Lillith gestured at the room. "Except one has to be in a room to converse with another." She pointed out. At that moment, Asmodeus appeared. "That will be all, Crave." He announced. The Demon bowed, first to Lillith and a deeper bow to his Lord, then vanished. "Want to tell me what's going on, Asmo?" Lillith inquired, using a name of familiarity. Asmodeus tilted his head in response. "Seriously? I thought you were going to report something to me." He responded abrasively. "I'm sure I don't know what you are referring to." Lillith retorted. Asmodeus paused. "We've been working at cross purposes." He claimed. "How are we doing that?" Lillith posed. "Lucifer is about to kick off World war three, and the harvest will be rich. However, I do not like this mortal he keeps visiting. Asmodeus complained. "Yes." Lillith agreed. "What do you recommend we do?" She inquired. "We should wait and allow Lucifer to affect his plan if it works out great. If he fails, however, the Celestials will be very displeased and may be open to a change in Management." Asmodeus spoke, whispered with a conspiratorial wink. Lillith smiled. "You know they would not aid.." Asmodeus interjected. "Not directly, no. However, they would not oppose the change if we had the demon power to back us up." Asmodeus charged. Lillith's smile grew. "So all we have to do is quietly assemble an army, sit back and wait. Lillith highlighted. "Exactly right." Asmodeus agreed. "But then?" Lillith asked. "But then what? The Demon king inquired. Lillith furrowed her eyebrows. "Not, but then what, rather, but WHO rules?" Her question demanded. Asmodeus rubbed his chin. "I've given that some thought." Asmodeus revealed. "And?" Lillith exclaimed. "I think we should rule jointly. Me as the King of hell and you as her Empress." Asmodeus submitted. Lillith smiled.

CHAPTER 18

RELEASE OF THE FOUL

Lou sat impatiently. Nayla tried on an outfit. "Are you ready?" He grumbled. Nayla preened in front of a mirror. "This outfit is so cute." She squealed. Lou shook his head. "I'm ready," Nayla announced, leaving her bedroom. "It's about damn time." Lou huffed. Nayla giggled. "What's so funny?" Lou demanded. Nayla hugged Lou. "We're like an old married couple." She quipped. Lou pulled Nayla at arm's distance. "I need you to focus. Today is a busy and important day, my pet." Lou emphasized. Exiting the room, Nayla pouted. "Can't we take one day and enjoy what this realm has to offer?" Lou shook his head. "Have you forgotten our purpose here?" Lou inquired. Nayla shook her head. "No, Lou." She responded softly. "Good. Now we must seek out the three vile spirits and have them engage their marks. The streets were busy as Lou and Nayla walked to the train station. The evening was hot and humid. It was the type that had New Yorkers on edge. An evening where the heat invited the worst in Humanity to expose its raw, violent nature. Horns blared, sirens screamed, and people yelled at one another in a crude and aggressive manner. On the train heading uptown, Lou and Nayla walked up on three teenagers harassing an older man. Seeing Lou and Nayla, the teens ceased maltreatment of the gentleman and moved to another part of the train. Viewing the couple as his savior, he thanked them profusely. The older man got off the train at the next stop, waving and thanking Lou and Nayla. The train stood at the platform, doors open, allowing people to enter and exit. The teenagers sat halfway down the car, watching their would-be prey escaping. Lou turned to the boys. "Hey, hurry up if you want to catch him before he gets to the streets." He coaxed. The teens looked at each other, back at Lou, then bolted after their target. Nayla pinched him. "You're such a tease." She quipped. Lou smiled. "I am the father of temptation." He bragged. Getting off the train on wall street, Lou turned to Nayla. "Do you remember the demon Dizz?" Nayla nodded. "Keep an eye out for him. It is who we seek." Lou informed her. It took no time to find the demon Diz who was plying his trade of deception. He was seen by Nayla, sitting in a coffee shop convincing a banker to readjust the lending rate to an underdeveloped Country. The banker was trying to explain how the Federal oversight committee would launch an investigation against his firm if he were to do such a thing. "We just don't need those headaches." The banker complained. Recognizing Nayla as she entered the establishment and approached him, Diz appealed to the banker with a tempting lie. "Fine. If you're too frightened, I'll move on to my next client, who sees the multi-billion dollar proposition I'm offering as well worth the risk." The demon lied, bringing Nayla into the con. "Miss Angst, good to see you again. Let me introduce you to Mister Paulson of the International foreign exchange." Nayla slipped into her role easily. "Guten abend Mister Paulson. I will be graced with your professional acumen as a business colleague?" She asked, flashing a brilliant smile and exuding her power of sensuality, which the maleness of the promiscuous and lewd banker immediately reacted to. The banker stood and pulled out a chair for Nayla to sit down. "I am sorry, Fraulein, but Mister Paulson feels uncomfortable with our proposal and fears indictable repercussions," Dizz said, sounding disappointed. Nayla looked sadly at the banker. She slowly sat in the proffered chair. "Say this is not true, Mister Paulson." Nayla whined. Grimacing, the banker nodded. "I am truly sorry, Fraulein Angst. My organization cannot risk ruining its reputation or possible legal entanglements which may cause distress to our clientele." Nayla shook her head sadly. "Such a shame. What if I sweetened the deal by offering your Company assured, wealthy German clientele? Citizenship anywhere with a non-extradition clause as an escape vehicle in case it gets legally uncomfortable here in the states?" She proffered. The greed behind the banker's eyes lit up. "You have that kind of clout?" Paulson prodded hopefully. Nayla narrowed her eyes and leaned close to him, close enough that he could feel her heat. Paulson gulped. "Ja mein Liebling. Our organization has ties that extend throughout the developed world. Your efforts on our behalf will be well rewarded. However, if you are afraid of taking a small risk for such a large return...." Nayla left the sentence hanging and watched as the banker's greed steered him to a wrong decision. "Well, if you can guarantee my safety and immediate removal of fraulein Angst, then yes. Send me instructions via courier, and I will see your requirements." The banker assured them. Dizz pumped the banker's hands in a vigorous handshake. "You will not regret this, Mister Paulson, and I assure you, you will be a very wealthy man." The demon in the business suit promised. Paulson gazed at Nayla. "Perhaps fraulein Angst, you will give me the privilege of escorting you to dinner when the deal is finalized?" Paulson advanced. Nayla smiled. A wicked smile that Paulson misread. "I will look forward to that, Herr Paulson." Nayla responded softly with a wink. She stood to leave, and Diz stood alongside her waving back at Paulson. "I'll start the process and contact you in the next day or so." He informed the banker.

Once outside the coffee shop, Nayla looked at Dizz, who immediately tried to recruit her. "Succubus, I don't know what you're doing up here, but if you are looking for work, I could use someone as beautiful and quick thinking as you." He complimented while leering. Nayla snickered. "I know who and what you are, spirit," Nayla said quietly. "Really?" Diz rebutted. "Tell me then, who am I?" The demon asked. "How quickly we forget." A voice from behind the monster rang out. Turning quickly, the demon's mouth dropped open, seeing the conveyor of the criticism. Quickly the devil bowed his head discreetly. "My Lord." He gasped. Lou grinned. "So you do remember?" Lou observed. "Master." Diz began. Nayla nudged Diz. "He is Lou while in this guise. She informed. Diz nodded and began again. "Lou, you'll be glad to know I brokered a deal. One that will remove much-needed food from one Country, shifting it to an arms shipment to another to support their civil war," Dizz reported proudly. Lou nodded. "Well done. Your new assignment has you taking the skills you've refined here and taking it to the Country's capital and filling the politicians with your greed." Dizz looked confused. "There, of course, would be the reward of an ignoble title for your successful completion." Lou enticed. Diz bowed. "As you command, Lou." Diz winked. Lou grinned. "Perhaps I'll speak with Lillith about getting you a personal assistant." Lou hinted. The smile on Dizz's face broadened. "Come, Nayla; we have other agents to find," Lou commanded. "Dizz, do you know the whereabouts of the demons Lor and Andrax?" Nayla inquired. Dizz shrugged. "Last I heard, Lor has been around the United Nations, and Andrax was at the Pentagon. I don't know if they are still there, but that was the last I heard." Nayla nodded, turned, and she and Lou walked into the darkening streets.

Agents of war

To avoid celestial detection, Lou and Nayla took an early morning flight to Washington, D.C., to find and instruct Lor. This foul spirit was exceptionally talented at finding keywords in a conversation and exaggerating the aggravating effect it caused—a dangerous tool in a war room. Exiting the plane, Nayla quietly inquired. "Why the cloak and dagger, Lou?" Nayla naively asked. Lou looked at Nayla intensely. "Do not concern yourself with such matters. Suffice it to say all I do for our home." Lou looked at the crowd around him to signal Nayla that this was the wrong place and time for such discussions.

Leaving the airport, Lou hailed a taxi. Enchanted by Nayla, the driver asked, "Where to, ma'am?" Nayla slid into the cab, followed by Lou. "The Hyatt regency." He ordered. The driver ignored Lou and stared at Nayla, waiting for her answer. Nayla looked to Lou, who nodded. "The Hyatt regency, please." She echoed Lou's order. She looked at Lou, confused, as she had never seen Lou ignored before. They arrived and checked in without incident. In their room, Nayla asked for an explanation of the cab driver's behavior. Lou smiled. "That poor soul is so damned, he is a lustful creature, and I wouldn't be surprised that he winds up as one of Asmodeus's lap dogs," Lou explained. He walked over to the mini bar and grabbed a couple of mini bottles of whiskey. "But I still don't understand how he could ignore you the way he did," Nayla complained. Lou cracked open the seals of the mini bottles and poured the golden fluid into the clear plastic cups the hotel provided. "For the same reason, a man would take the food out of his family's mouth to buy clothing or jewelry for his Mistress. Nothing can displace that which we adore." Lou clarified. Nayla nodded as if finally understanding. "So, in a way, he's more my slave than yours?" She queried. Lou smiled. "In a fashion, yes." Lou conceded. Nayla looked at Lou and grinned. Lou drained the glass of its contents only to look up and see Nayla smiling at him. "What?" Lou asked. "Did I spill on myself?" He probed further, checking himself for spillage. "I was just wondering." She responded evasively. Lou squinted at her. "Stop that." Lou insisted. "Stop what, my lord?" Nayla posed, sounding confused. "See that?" Lou complained. "That right there. Nayla looked blankly at him. "Right there!" Lou demanded. "Where you act like you don't know what I'm talking about or referring to," Lou complained. Nayla smiled. "As always, you are correct, Lou. I was just wondering if it was me that was helping you to smile or perhaps the completion of your quest?" Nayla added, realizing the reason Lou was acting happy. Lou responded by smiling, grabbing the remote control, and turning on the news. He plopped down on the couch and got comfortable. "Good morning Washington. This is Jeff Nicoles." "And I'm Trisha Dusky. Today the Foreign Exchange Committee, in an unexpected policy shift, has denied food relief efforts to Haiti. The Haitian ambassador is demanding an investigation." Lou turned off the T.V. with a grunt of satisfaction. "I see Diz completed the first part of his task. Lou jumped up. "Let's go to the library," Lou suggested. Nayla looked confused. "I'm sorry, but did you say?" "Library," Lou interjected. "Yes, let's go," Lou exclaimed apprehensively. "Now, now, now!" Lou followed her around, clapping his hands to hurry her along."Okay," Nayla capitulated. "Anyone in particular? She nagged. Lou sneered. "There's only one." Lou insisted. Hailing a cab, Lou instructed the driver. "Library of Congress," Lou ordered. Nayla nodded, the mystery solved.

Upon arriving, Lou asked the cab driver to drop them off on a corner. Exiting the cab, Nayla peered at Lou. "You realize they will drop you off at the front door anywhere you ask. Lou watched as the cab pulled away. "Yeah." He agreed. "While that may be true, I did not spend the past quarter of a century planning only to have it blow up in my face because I got lazy. Secrecy is the key for most intricate plans to succeed." Lou pointed out. Nayla absorbed the lesson. "Where are we going?" She asked. Lou led them to a cafe named Le Bon. Entering, they found a corner booth and sat. Lou ordered coffee and a roll. Nayla looked at him blankly. "I would have thought you'd be too excited to eat." She teased. "Gotta keep my strength up." Lou cracked in return. Five minutes after their arrival, two dressed in conservative black suits and neatly groomed gentlemen entered the cafe. The two men, seeing Lou walked up to his table. One of the men commented on the weather. "It feels a bit cold, wouldn't you agree?" Lou stopped eating. "I've felt colder." Was Lou's reply. "Yes, but have you seen it wetter?" The other gentlemen asked. Lou nodded. "Much." Nayla looked at the men as if they had lost their minds with such nonsensical statements. Lor. I see you've brought Andrax; that is excellent. "I have sent Diz here." Lou began causing a look of confusion to pass between Lor and Andrax. "But Sire," Andrax began. Lou held up his hand for silence. "What I need from you, Andrax, is to go where Diz was, Wall street. Spread the desire for Corporate, military action. In the meantime, Dizz will be here spreading greed into the hearts of the Military. In contrast, you Lor spread discontent into the civil population by meddling in their humanitarian cause, frustrating the people and causing them to lose confidence, resulting in civil war. The two demons in disguise looked at Lou, concerned. "I'm not sure how all of this will do anything of consequence," Andrax said off-hand. Lou's eyes blazed with fury as he whispered. "The plan does not require you to understand, only that you fulfill your part in it, understood?" Lou demanded. Andrax slowly nodded. "We understand, but you need to understand as well; nothing good waits for you should you fail." The demon casually threatened. Lou smiled at the threat. Andrax, I know you serve Valak the deceiver, and his might is a force to reckon. However, you are not he, and I would have no qualms about deporting you to the darkest pit of my Realm for your insolence." Lou threatened in return. Andrax complained. "Lucifer, you misunderstand. I was not trying to threaten you. I only reminded you of the consequence of failure behind such a monumental task." Andrax complained. "It's Lou." Nayla corrected the demon. "What?" Andrax queried. "In this guise, we call him Lou." She clarified. Andrax looked back at Lou. "Fine. Lou, it is. The two well-dressed demons rose. "By your leave, we shall prepare for the next phase," Lor exclaimed. "Excellent. I shall return and prepare my human sacrifice." Lou declared, causing a patron at the diner to turn and look in their direction. "Sleep," Lou whispered. A silverware clattering crashed to the floor, a waitperson dropped a full tray of food as she passed out, and the patrons' faces slammed into plates and tables as all obeyed the command of sleep. Nayla glanced around and then back at Lou, who smirked. "Not as elegant as I would have liked, but there we are, shall we?" Lou asked Nayla, gesturing toward the door.

Peter sat in his office. An uneasy feeling tugged at him. Since the last meeting, his colleagues have been walking delicately around him. Even Bruce, with his callous attitude, has been irritating in his attempts to soothe Peter. Wondering if Lou would contact him, Peter desperately needed to prove to his colleagues and, yes, even to himself that he was not crazy and that everything he reported had happened and was not a clever ploy. The phone rang, causing Peter to jump. Peter answered, upset by the intrusion. "Nancy, I told you I didn't want to be disturbed." He reminded his secretary. "Are you avoiding me?" An eerily familiar baritone voice asked playfully. Peter drew a breath before responding. "Mister Cyphur?" He asked, not wanting to seem overly familiar. "Oh my." Lou gasped melodramatically. "You are not going to cast a spell of Taurus caca." Peter was baffled by the response. "A spell?" He echoed. "Not just any spell, but one that is used to give the recipient of the spell the notion that the caster is so unimpressed by his deeds, or even his presence that he begins the dialog with bullshit." Peter chuckled. "Did you just call me a bullshitter?" He inquired. "I did." Was Lou's curt reply. "Fair enough." Peter conceded. "You can be a bit overwhelming." He admitted. "True." Lou agreed. "The reason for the call, Doctor, was simply to ask if you would like to join me for lunch." Lou invited. Peter paused. "Will Nayla be there?" He inquired. "She could be if you'd like." Lou responded teasingly. "Lou." Peter paused, hoping to entice Lou's curiosity. Lou remained silent. "Hello? Peter said, thinking Lou had hung up on him. "It could be said that Lou is my name, and temptation is my game." Lou quipped. Relieved that Lou had not hung up, Peter replied. "No doubt about that." A tap at the door made Peter lift his head to see William in front of the rest of the staff. Peter put his finger to his lips, indicating for them to be quiet. "Lou." Peter began, only to be interrupted. "Peter, I advise you to be straightforward with me from here on in; I am the Tempter, not the tempted. "I see that I've offended you, and I apologize; it was not my intention." Peter offered as a gesture of reconciliation. "What do I smell, Peter?" Bruce, thinking Peter was losing control of the conversation, looked at Peter with concern. "What do you mean, Lou?" Peter asked. Suspicious that Lou was somehow catching on that he was being set up. "I mean, Peter, I get the feeling that you have a backdrop going on I don't see at the moment." Lou admitted. "Can't you use your powers and see what you want?" Peter challenged. Lou snorted. If you knew anything about Celestial influence, you would know that because Mars is retrograde with Saturn, the force I would have to use to penetrate the veil of the ecto-verse would reveal only the terrifying image of myself. I'm not trying to give your colleagues a heart attack and scare them to Death." Lou complained. Peter thought Lou's counterargument was more than sufficient to prove him competent. "Forgive me, Lou, but," Lou interjected. "Excuse me, I'm not sure how often I must remind people, but we are not in the forgiving business." Lou exclaimed. "Yes, you have said that. I stand corrected. If I may propose a counteroffer to your lunch invitation?" Peter inquired. "What do you have in mind?" Lou countered. Peter looked at his colleagues, who sat staring at him nervously. "I want you to come to the clinic so I can show you off to my staff." Bruce fell out of his chair, causing Helen to spill her beverage on Williams's lap, who sat there bravely trying not to yelp in pain or thrash as the hot coffee spilled onto his crotch. Lou heard the clamor on the other side of the phone. "Peter?" Lou spoke in a tone that suggested he was losing his patience. "Again, I apologize, Lou. My colleagues heard me speaking to you and rushed into the office." Peter explained. "To what end?" Lou posed. "They wanted to know if you'd come in because they say my reports on you are too fantastical." Peter admitted. "Is that a way of saying crazy?" Lou teased. William slowly got up as his face portrayed one of sufferance. "So your staff wishes to meet the devil?" Lou challenged. "If you wouldn't mind." Peter implored. "Very well, but it must be tonight." Lou insisted. "I'm sure they'll agree." Peter capitulated. "Until then, Peter." Lou said in a voice that had a backdrop of crying children. Peter shook his head, realizing Lou was trying to shake him up. "I've played basketball in New York Parks, asshole; you'll have to do better than that." Peter complained to a dead phone. "I think he hung up." Bruce presumed. Back in Lou's room, Nayla looked incredulously at her Master, "What the hell was that?" Nayla insisted heatedly. Lou put his hand up in a gesture of warding. Nayla crossed her arms. "Lou. You are on the brink of wreaking havoc on Humanity, damning millions of souls to Hell; why are you bothering with this human?" Nayla asked, exasperated. Lou looked at Nayla squarely; she shuddered in response, afraid she had gone too far. "Nayla, what did I tell you about loyalty? Nayla gave a short head bow. "It is and always will be as my Lord orders; I'm just concerned that my liege does not lose all to the rebels who only await a mistake on your part before striking." Nayla admitted in submission. Lou grinned. "Lillith got more than she bargained for when she took you from the flames." Lou responded in observation. "Thank you, Lou." Responded a grateful demon. "The conversation about spells was my way of saying stop the bullshit. Lou clarified. "Then why not just say that?" Nayla dared. "Ahh, not as clever as you thought, little demon. A straightforward answer would not have confused him, and a confused human is an emotional, illogical creature that is easy to defeat." He explained.

Visitation

Lillith made her way through the pleasure Palace of the Realm of Lust. Looking for Asmodeus, she felt the power was already beginning its corrupting effect on the King of the second circle. She found Crave in his gilded office; Asmodeus's Majordomo spoke to Peitho, the former Master of the second circle until Asmodeus ran a successful campaign and usurped the throne, making him the Lord of Lust. Seeing Lillith approach, Crave stopped speaking and watched the self-proclaimed Empress of hell approach. "Demon, I seek your master," Lillith exclaimed. Crave blinked slowly to hide his contempt for her, who he called "The harlot of hell." Never aloud, of course, and never to her face. "My lady, Lord Asmodeus, is giving final instructions to the insurrectionist demons." Crave asserted. "Without me?!" Lillith whispered harshly. "Where is he?" She demanded. "As I told you," Crave began. "You told me what he's doing, not where." Lillith insisted. "He is in his throne room," Crave reported. Lillith narrowed her eyes. "The Palace of Lust has never had a throne room." Lillith pointed out. "Indeed," Crave responded, then looked down at Peitho, the former master of the Realm. "The King has demanded your immediate demotion to minion status or self-exile to the realm of the abyss." The Majordomo stated coldly. Peitho looked up at Crave in desperation. "I have the right to face my judge and would be executioner!" He demanded. Crave looked down in contempt. "Those old laws will no longer be valid by the orders of the new regime," Crave exclaimed dismissively. "Go now to your doom lest we send ravagers to hunt you down." Crave threatened. He then turned to Lillith. "Follow me." Turning, I walked toward a newly constructed flight of stairs built toward the rear of the majordomos office. The stairs were spiral in design with gold leaf reliefs of lovers embraced in passion. Lillith became more disturbed by these signs of decadence. Entering the throne room, Lillith was appalled to see Asmodeus sitting on a massive golden throne. At his feet in three golden chairs facing the throne sat Andrax, King of deception, Aeshma, the spirit of violence, and Tiaminicus, the spirit of confusion. "By what authority do you issue commands of movement?" Lillith demanded as she ascended the steps of the throne, of which there was much further evidence of corruption as Asmodeus attempted to separate himself from the familiar demon. "Why, by the authority of my crown lady empress," Asmodeus responded while bowing to Lillith. Lillith halted her ascension of the stairs, halting beside the three foul spirits. Realizing Asmodeus was not yet thoroughly corrupted, she issued a warning. "Be mindful, your Majesty, corruption awaits all who don the mantle of power. Gesturing around him at the new furnishings, made mostly of gold. Asmodeus asked. "Do you mean this? Seriously Lillith, I thought you would be pleased with the upgrade; after all, you love beauty."

Asmodeus explained. "And we are to rule jointly as agreed?" Lillith pursued. "Of course, that was the deal." He responded smoothly. "Then why is there only one throne?" She snapped. Asmodeus stammered a moment. "Well, after our spies did their work and we finally confronted the traitor, we could do as we pleased knowing we had each other, so if you wished to visit the mortal world, you could know I am here watching over things," Asmodeus explained. "And I would do the same for you?" She inquired. "Of course." He replied immediately.

"You forget," Andrax grunted. "We are loyal to Hell. If it is, as you say, that Lucifer is relinquishing his power to a mortal, then he must be expelled as the Lord of evil. However, if his plan of inciting world war three goes unimpeded, we stand beside him as our Lord. We serve Hell." Andrax pointed out. Asmodeus nodded. "Of course, mighty Andrax. The lady Lillith and I are setting up an interim government so that Hell continues running smoothly. At the same time, Lucifer is evicted, and your many legions will be invaluable if Lucifer resists." He explained. Andrax leered at Asmodeus. "You cannot deceive the King of deception, Asmodeus. I am aware of your true intention. However, as I said, we serve Hell, and if Lucifer is compromised, then his removal would be necessary." Andrax pointed out. "It is as you say, Lord Andrax." Piped Lillith. "We serve Hell not one entity but our Realm. Our reports indicate that the master seems to have succumbed to the ravings of a mortal doctor. This is unacceptable. We believe that Lucifer began an expedition, but the forces of Good discovered Lucifer's attempt to start a third world war and interfered by putting the Doctor in his way. It was a subtle and effective intervention as Lucifer was tempted to break Celestial law by introducing a mortal to the immortal Realm." Lillith charged. "Yes." Tiamanicus agreed. "We saw that and were concerned Lucifer would call down wrath upon us from on high." The demon of confusion admitted. "You see why Lady Lillith and I took the steps we did? Asmodeus interjected. Not to threaten the Realm but to preserve it." Lillith exclaimed. "In either case, Lucifer now has Lor and Diz in positions that would allow them to leverage their influence and instigate his grand design." Andrax pointed out. "Mark my words, Andrax, Lucifer, or his corrupted mortal guise of Lou, will cease all hostilities, and the war will never come to fruition." Lillith countered. "I, for one, would like to be ready for that day so Hell does not suffer because of Lucifer's lapse. Andrax nodded in understanding. "I go to my assigned post in case Lucifer goes through with his design." Andrax stood, and Tiamanicus and Aeshema followed their Lord's example. Turning to leave Andrax, he called over his shoulder. "But my general, Tiamanicus." Andrax gestured at the spirit of confusion and Aeshema, a spirit of violence. I will have legions with stand-by orders to reinforce you on my command. He said gravely before departing. The two conspirators watched the spirits of Confusion and Deception as they descended the new golden stairway, exiting into the Majordomo's chamber. Asmodeus swiveled on his throne to look at Lillith, who sat in one of the golden chairs around the throne. "That was exhilarating!" Asmodeus raved. Lillith looked sadly at him. "Asmodeus, please." Lillith pled with anger in her voice. Asmodeus looked at her petulantly. "I don't understand you, Lillith. First, you complain about not being properly appreciated then you go on about little demons with petty ambitions. Well, here I am with the grandest of ambitions with a feasible ploy to attain those goals, and all you do is find a reason to complain. I am making you the grand Empress!" Asmodeus spat. Lillith tilted her head at him. "What you have not realized is that you are under the delusion that the spirits of Violence, Confusion, and deception are at your beck and call, but what you have done is soak yourself in oil and wish to use fire as a weapon. I will go to my tower and watch from there, send for me if you need me." Lillith posed and, descending the golden stairs, began what every astute denizen of Hell does when about to engage in a dubious plot, start planning an exit strategy.

CHAPTER 19

LOU IN HOUSE

Nayla heard Lou muttering to himself in his room. The adjoining rooms gave a semblance of privacy, but that's all it was. After a hot shower, Nayla dressed in blood-red shorts, a pink top, and black running shoes. Tying her hair into a ponytail, Nayla checked and smiled at her reflection. Knocking on the door that separated their rooms, Nayla entered as Lou gave permission. Nayla sashayed into the room, preening as if on display. "Well, what do you think?" She asked while posing. Her voluptuous breasts tested their restraints, her curvaceous body designed to illicit the provocative beast. Eyes that burned lustfully. Nayla was a sight to behold, with full lips and long, flowing black hair.

Without looking up, Lou replied to her query. "What do I think? About what?" He asked, non-committal. Nayla took offense. She shifted from her pose to another, noticing Lou staring at papers. "Wow, that honeymoon was short.' She huffed. Lou looked up from his work. "What are you bitching about?" He demanded. Nayla put her hands on her hips and grunted. "Lou?" She inquired sarcastically. "There, but for the sake of form," Lou complained. "What?" Nayla asked, confused. Lou shook his head. "Nothing; you look great, by the way." He complimented. Nayla felt her anger dissipate. "Do you think me shallow?" She probed. Lou shook his head. "I would have, but according to the human, we all need some form of recognition to verify our existence," Lou recalled. Nayla's brows furrowed in befuddlement. "That sounds right." She admitted. They looked at one another, concerned. "We have a job to do." Lou barked. "One that you've planned for so long," Nayla confirmed. "Come, the sorcerers of this modern age have extended an invitation to listen to their spells." Lou teased. Nayla laughed. "Sorcerers. Ha. As if." She mocked. Lou pulled on a pair of basketball shoes. White high tops, black sports tops, and a Knicks cap. He spread his arms as if on display. Nayla clapped her hands. "You're crushing that look." Nayla gushed. Lou frowned, unfamiliar with the vocabulary. "You look good." She said by way of explanation. "Let's do this to the sorcerer's lair." Lou called out. They exited Hotel and walked up the street at 42nd and 5th ave. to catch the train. Walking up the busy avenue, Nayla was intrigued by the seemingly never-ending crush of Humanity and their self-imposed sense of purpose. Aboard the train, the passenger crush was less than a rush hour but still ample. One rather disgusting individual looking to perpetrate his creepy behavior rubbed his hardened pelvis against Nayla's well-formed, sexy ass. She spun and stared furiously at the man, almost unleashing the furies on him. She felt a tug on her arm, and Lou pulled her closer to him. "Don't do that." He whispered. Nayla looked up, her eyes revealing ignorance. "I'll explain later." Lou promised her. He then set his eyes on the pervert who assaulted Nayla, whispering. "Off you go." The man turned and quickly left their side, moving down the train. "What the fuck Lou." Nayla complained. Lou stared at Nayla. As I said, I'll explain later." Lou insisted. The train speaker crackled. "Next stop, grand street." The barely understandable speaker declared. Lou shuffled to the door with Nayla in tow. They exited the train at their stop. Walking out of the station Nayla was assailed by a strange odor that stopped her in her tracks. "What the fuck?" She complained while holding her nose. Lou smiled. "That is the odor I was smacked with upon my arrival here. I was shocked that this place could carry such a smell. "Lou, what the hell is that?" Nayla asked about the unfamiliar odor. "I keep forgetting this is your first assignment, so you wouldn't know this smell." Lou observed. Nayla nodded. "You got that right, so tell me, what is that awful smell? The succubus demanded. Lou smirked. "What you smell, my dear is the funk of sanctuary." Nayla shook her head in disgust. "You want to go to the source of this smell?" She challenged. Lou nodded. "That's where we'll find Peter." Lou quipped, sounding anxious. Nayla did not look well. "This smell is making me nauseous." She complained as they walked toward the clinic. Lou stopped walking and turned to Nayla. "Listen." Lou began. "I'm going to need you to focus on the terrible smells that are the underbelly of this city. You have the power to ignore, so ignore this shit. We have work to do." Lou demanded. Nayla nodded obediently. They walked down the block until they stood at the source of the emanations. The sign read, "Less stress Clinic." Nayla shuddered. Lou shot her a glance. Entering the building, the first thing Nayla noticed was the attractive receptionist at her desk. Curious, Nayla approached her. Molly looked up from her paperwork to see a stunningly beautiful woman approach her. Unable to look away, she inquired. "May I help you?" Nayla looked at the pretty woman but was captivated by her blue eyes. Being new to the mortal world, Nayla had not yet discovered her full powers. One of those powers was mimicry, the ability to look however she wanted, which at this particular moment was terrifying to Molly as she watched Nayla's eyes change from a smokey brown to a brilliant blue. That trick caused Molly to stammer her questions. "Wh, wh, who are you here to see?" She gasped. Seeing her discomfort, Lou glided up to the desk. "You haven't forgotten me already, have you?" Lou teased. Molly's apparent discomfort vanished as Lou's magnetism tempted her. "Well, hello, Mister Cyphur." Molly gushed. "So very good to see you again. You have the staff waiting for you in the conference room." Lou smiled. "The entire staff, huh?" Lou entreated. "Yes, sir." Molly responded. "If you're ready, I'll inform The Doctors that you're coming." She offered. Lou looked at Nayla, who nodded. "Can we get this shit over with?" She pled. Lou returned his gaze to Molly. "Ready when you are." He agreed. Molly got on the office intercom, alerting the conference room staff that they were on their way. Molly led Lou and Nayla to the conference room, where the Doctors sat around a circular table. Doctor Payne stood as he saw the couple approach. "Okay, team, remember our purpose today. Do not allow yourselves to be drawn into arguments or clashing ideologies." Payne warned. "We are not amateurs, William. Doctor Sable complained. Doctor Dayaggi looked over at him. "He'll get to you by your ego, be mindful, Bruce." Peter warned. "Like he did to you?" Bruce countered. "Goddamn it! He isn't even in the room yet and has us fighting already." William complained. The room got hushed as Lou and Nayla entered. "Well, I see the gangs all here." Lou exclaimed as they entered the room.

The Session:

First, I'd like to welcome you and your companion, although we are only now acquainted?" William paused, not realizing that Nayla was unfamiliar with human nuance. "Her name is Nayla." Lou said for her. She turned to look at Lou, who winked at her. "Doctors, I suggest that you direct your questions at me." Lou recommended. Bruce looked at Nayla. "So you're telling me if we want to know anything about this lovely woman accompanying you, we may not ask?" Doctor Sable inquired. Lou smiled at him. "Your motives have nothing to do with professional curiosity Doctor." Lou pointed out. Taken aback, Bruce argued. "I'm sure I don't know what you mean." He complained. "This one has balls." Nayla observed. "He would teach his grandmother to suck eggs." She laughed. Bruce looked offended. "I'm not sure why I'm being treated in such a rude manner." He complained. Lou looked at Bruce. "Do you know who I am?" Lou asked Bruce. Sable looked directly into Lou's eyes, earning him a pinch from Doctor Dayaggi. Bruce ignored the warning. "I do know who you are. You are Lou Cyphur. A gentleman who suffers the delusion that he is the devil." Bruce said bluntly, causing William to wince and Peter to frown. Lou smiled. "Correct, and knowing that I am the Father of lies, you would still try to lie to me?" Lou queried. Doctor Sable shook his head. "But you're not the devil, so that's not something I have to concern myself with." Bruce pointed out. Lou smiled. "How arrogant." Lou looked over to Nayla. "Do you understand now why I chose Peter to reveal myself?" He asked. "I don't understand." Helen chimed in. "Doctor Zhang. It was nothing personal against you, but you all have reasons why I didn't choose any of you. Doctor Sables' arrogance would have made him ridiculously easy to corrupt. Doctor Zhang, you lead a good life, and I saw you with your daughter, and despite what might be said, I am not a heartless ogre; that's my P.R. dept. that spreads all those rumors about me. Doctor Payne, The fact that you took your Ivy league education and found a way to help the poor made you disgustingly untouchable as you gain status in Heaven as a good soul. I have no use for good souls. You Peter. You have a unique blend of goodness and an I don't give a fuck attitude that made you a prime target to corrupt. Lou explained. "You honestly believe you're the devil? Like Satan in the garden and all that? Bruce inquired. "I see you've studied a bit." Lou observed. "A bit." Bruce said in agreement. So you're supposed to be a mental health therapist?" Lou posed. "I am, and a good one at that." Bruce boasted. "Not very modest, though." Nayla pointed out. "So tell me, my good Doctor, what diagnosis would you give someone such as myself?" Lou inquired. Bruce paused as if thinking over the question. "Come now, Doctor, no posturing; tell us your thoughts." Lou stated softly. "I don't posture." Bruce denied it emphatically. "He said while posturing." Nayla replied. "Fine." Bruce said flatly. "You want to know my diagnosis of you? Here it is. The entity known as Satan suffers from abandonment issues, a God complex, Oppositional defiance, anger management, identification disorder, and homicidal, genocidal, and xenocidal ideations. As Lou Cyphur, I assume you had an abusive childhood and suffered from low self-esteem." Sable concluded. "It sounds as if he knows you well."

Nayla injected. Lou laughed. "Not far off the mark, am I?" Bruce insisted. "Light years off, but that is of no matter." Lou stated boldly. "Why doesn't it matter, Lou?" William asked. Lou smiled. "Because mortal, I've set my legions in position. They will activate my signal and begin to take actions that will instigate World War three. All that you know will soon perish. My demons shall rise and lay waste to the world you despise." Lou growled. "Mister Cyphur." Helen called out. "Yes, Doctor Zhang?" Lou acknowledged. "Are you telling us that you're going to kill everyone?" The fear in her voice came through in her question. "No, dear. I'm not killing anyone. It's your people. Your species invited almost insisted upon this wholesale devastation." Lou demanded. "You befoul the air you breathe, the water you drink, the very ground that supports you is treated with malice." Lou whispered, making the proclamation much more terrifying. "Seriously? Please don't tell me you're buying into his bullshit." Bruce complained. Lou smiled. "Not very professional of you, Doctor." He claimed. "First, you didn't come here for treatment. You came to scare the hell out of us," Nayla looked at him. "Pun intended? She inquired. "Pun?" Bruce asked. "No. No puns, this aint a game, and why is it that you can't speak except to make nasty asides you think are clever? Nayla turned her demonic attention on Bruce. "Do you want to talk to me?" She asked, locking eyes with him. Bruce fell silent as he was caught in the stare of a hell-spawned succubus. "Lou, please." Peter begged. "Nayla, enough. Nayla released her hypnotic gaze on Bruce, who began to shake. "Doctor Sable, are you alright." William asked. Bruce nodded weakly. "All that you threaten," Helen began. "Promise." Lou interjected. "Fine, promise. Can you tell us why?" She begged. Lou smiled. "Of course, my dear. Your race was given a grand gift, and what did you do with it?" Lou posed. "Yes, we have been poor custodians, but you must see our vast improvements in understanding the world around us. We've been gun-taking steps, too," Lou interrupted. "Too little too late." He insisted. "So, let me see if I understand this; God has decided it was time for us to be annihilated and the earth destroyed?"

Lou stood up and reached down for Nayla to take his hand. "I have said all I will say. Prepare yourselves; the time is upon us. Lou looked toward Peter and winked. Lou and Nayla strolled out of the office and clinic leaving a stunned staff behind. "Lou?" Nayla softly spoke his name as they walked to the train station. The sun began its gentle transition into evening. "I'm not sure the point of all this." Lou cupped Nayla's face in his hand. "I promise all will be made clear." Nayla nodded. "I trust you, Lou." She relented. Lou smiled. "And well, you should." He boasted. Back at the clinic, the Less stress staff was dumbfounded. "What was that?!" Bruce exclaimed. "I tried to warn you." expressed Peter. "Doctor Sable, are you alright? Bruce nodded. "Yeah, but now I know why Peter was taken by their parlor tricks. The woman." Peter interjected. "Nayla." Bruce agreed. "Yes, was she present when you had those visions?" Without hesitation, Peter concurred.

"That's what I thought. She is a world-class hypnotist." Doctor Sable concluded. "Possible." Peter agreed. "Whether that's the case or not, we have a potentially dangerous, delusional man on the streets; his access to hazardous materials is unknown, and we may have to alert the authorities." William conceded. "Let me seek him out." Peter requested. William shook his head. "I don't think that's a good idea, Peter." Peter shrugged. "I never said it was a good idea; it's just what I'm going to do," Peter explained as he grabbed his jacket and exited. Helen, who felt Lou was speaking truthfully, abruptly stood. "I'm going to get my daughter from school. I can be reached at home." Helen picked up her purse and left. William and Bruce looked at one another. "I'll be at my desk. Bruce commented as he slowly rose. Like so many leaves before a strong wind, William watched as his staff scattered.

CHAPTER 20

A SEASON OF REASONS

A full moon filled a clear sky. Washington D.C. pedestrians strolled alongside the banks of the Potomac River, and tourists filled the streets of the nation's Capital peacefully, unaware of the burdens that their elected officials were contending with. While the citizens walked, talked, and laughed in their oblivious state, the committee chairman for foreign affairs sat disturbed by new policy shifts reassigning important foodstuff with a Caribbean destination manifest to an Eastern European Country. Military arms that were earmarked for a middle eastern Country had also been reassigned to the same Eastern European Country that was receiving the food supply meant for the Caribbean destination. Upset by the new directive, the Chairman launched a query that nearly ruined his career as a memo answered his complaint from his supervisor, stating that the issue was not open for debate. He was ordered to allow the process to continue unhindered because any other action was unacceptable. That refusal to comply would hasten a termination under the "Patriot act."

The Chairman was experienced enough to know that invoking the Patriot act meant that whatever action was planned under the policy would come to fruition. The Chairman sat with his head in his hands, agonizing over his duty. From the quiet came forth a voice. The voice seemed to come from everywhere and nowhere. He was alone, or at least thought himself to be. *"Why are you giving yourself a headache? The voice asked, sounding concerned. Don't you understand if the Europeans don't end their fighting, it will spill into other countries, setting the stage for a war no one is ready for?"* The disembodied voice pointed out. Shrugging his shoulders, the Chairman decided at that moment that discretion was the better part of valor (as well as being a surefire way to keep your job.) He signed the authorization that permitted the process to continue, feeding and arming some while starving another. *"fuck it."* He thought. *"I gotta take care of myself and make sure I keep what's mine."* He thought selfishly. In the shadows, Lor grinned wickedly. "Nothing like self-interest to get a good person to do something they know to be wrong." He mumbled softly. Now we strike at the nerve center." The foul spirit of greed mumbled before vanishing.

In the Pentagon war room, General Frank Peel, Commander of the G.T.O. (Global Tactical Operations), Stared at the situation map, highlighting the European conflict. Currently active, the map showed their borders were being threatened as lines of tanks massed in attack formations. He stood to stretch his six-foot, two-inch body, which was begging to cramp up. He turned his head, looking at another section of the map showing hostile activities escalating in the Middle east. A Captain approached the General, who was wrapped up in thought. "Begging the Generals pardon." The Captain requested. "Yes, Captain?" The General acknowledged the Captain's presence.

Locking his dead brown eyes on him, causing him some discomfort. "Sir, my apologies, but General Schmidt wishes to know your orders, sir." The Captain reported. General Peel locked eyes with the young officer. "Inform the general that we are a go as soon as the President approves." The young officer saw the moment's intensity reflected in his Commander's eyes. "Yes, sir." He quickly responded. Peel was approached by brigadier general Oscar Donovan, second in command. "Sir, we might have a problem." Peel looked at the General with a stare that loudly said, "Take no prisoners." His second in command shook his head. "Now, General, I aint come here to upset you, but the situation requires your tact." General Donovan solicited smoothly. Peel narrowed his brows in a scowl. "Donny," Peel uttered. "Sir." Donovan snapped.

"I got Schmidt in the middle east with artillery division ready to rain destruction and Delta waiting for a go-to acquire leverage over a Saudi oil deal. And as if that wasn't enough, I have to direct strike force Alpha who," Donovan interjected. "Strike force was who I was going to report on, sir." Peel stood quiet a moment. "Let's have it." He ordered. "Well, sir, it appears as if Colonels Jones and Salazar of the fifth and seventh special forces wish to proceed with their missions, citing an unrelated and fortuitous power outage giving them excellent concealment," Donovan reported. Peel grimaced, spun on his heel, and marched to the communication bank. An officer indicated the phone the General was looking for. Picking it up, he barked his name. "Eagle's nest here." He barked. "Eagle nest, this is Rain man," The colonel responded. "My comrades and I would like your permission to engage." Peel waited a moment, awaiting valid reasons for accelerating the timetable. Hearing none Peel responded. "That's a negative rain, man, and big poppa does not want the playground approached until the order is given; copy rain, man?" Peel inquired, confirming the complete comprehension and obedience of the order given. "Copy Eagle nest. Negative on the early breech. Awaiting further orders, Rain man out." Colonel Knowles terminated the conversation. "You think he'll obey, sir?"

Donovan asked. Peel turned back to his three-D, high-definition map and muttered. "Knowles is a good soldier. He looks at this as a skirmish, not what it is." Peel iterated. Donovan considered the cryptic implication behind the Commander's words. "Sir, what the hell is going on?" Donovan pled. Peel remained staring at the glowing map. "Sometimes Oscar, the greatest unknown, becomes known most horrifically," Peel said quietly enough that only they heard it. "Not sure what you mean, sir, but if you were going for assuring.." Donovan let the unfinished sentence hang there. "Son, I'm a Lieutenant General in the United States Army, and the only thing I can assure you of is if an enemy would do us harm, it is our job to make them regret it," Peel said with ice in his voice. "Sir, yes, sir." Donovan acknowledged.

Secrets unfold

Lou sat Nayla down on a park bench. They had ridden the train to Murray street, where they exited and walked to Rockefeller Park. Nayla stared at the statue of liberty. She had begun to remember her love of Nature which showed in the softness of her look. "Demon." Lou said with a rasp. "It is time that I inform you of what will occur." Lou grumbled. Nayla's attention snapped back to Lou. "I have shared with you only some of the reasoning behind our actions; I will clarify." Lou intoned. "The demons, Lor, Diz, Aeshma, Valak, and Andrax, are the emissaries of violence, greed, and deception. While I call them demons, it is a promised status, not an actual one. They are foul spirits that have perpetrated much evil. I use them because of their low Ecto disturbance when they manifest themselves to humans. While they have the same effect a demon does in their manifestations, they do not disturb Heaven's guardians enough to cause a reaction." Nayla held up her hand. Lou looked at her, puzzled by the gesture. "What are you doing?" Lou inquired. "I wish to ask a question?" Nayla quietly responded. "So ask." Lou snapped, irritated by the interruption. "Why are the spirits harder to track?" She inquired. Lou grinned. "Good question Nayla." Lou complimented. "The spirits are not made of the substance of hell. A hell-born demon is a fallen Angle who Sired his offspring in hell. "Then why call me demon?" Nayla inquired. "A demon of dread is a class of demons formed in the flames of hell. After committing much evil in life, they need to show that they are non-repentant, prove their corrupt nature by committing acts of maliciousness." Lou explained. Again Nayla raised her hand. Lou stared at Nayla intently. "Why do you keep making that ridiculous gesture?" Lou probed, irritation mutating to frustration. Nayla lowered her head, grinning. "I have seen children do it to capture the attention of their adults. She explained. "Well, I find it very annoying, so please desist." Lou huffed. "But Lou, how can the spirits possibly prove themselves if they are dead?" Nayla posed in confusion. "I grant them a special dispensation to haunt the living. If their intent is sincere and their haunting effective, then and only then may they be considered candidates for promotion to demon novices. As I was saying." Lou asserted. The spirits have tremendous influence over people that already follow the course of corruption." Lou continued. "Through their baser instincts, we prompt their feelings. This is our back door to human behavior." Lou explained proudly. Nayla, many eons passed before The Creator sent his breath in the aspect of Nature to the world. When the Earth was in its infancy, Nature relegated the task of preparing the world for life. So she went about capturing the purest waters the cosmos had to offer, began her biological construction of the world, and gathered all the necessary materials. As the world was molded and ready to cradle the infant of life, Nature realized the complexity of the assignment. Her first attempt was disastrous as life grew wildly and uncontrollably. Nature was forced to allow the death of her first child as the planet killed herself by poisoning. The grossly overpopulated seas consumed the oxygen, and the Earth choked to death with a few well-timed volcanos. The next time had her nursing monsters that could never fulfill the plans of the Creator." Lou saw Nayla was on the edge of the bench as she hung on to every word. Lou paused a moment, taking in the city's noise. Nayla sat impatiently. Lou took a breath before continuing. In what was to be her last attempt to bring about the creatures the Creator had envisioned, Nature sought advice from the Eternals. Entities of Creation. I sought her out, knowing she might one day be the key to allow me to dethrone my Father and take my rightful place." Lou gloated. "Nayla was awestruck. "You plan to overthrow the Creator?" she gasped, not knowing, until this very moment, the depths of Lucifer's audacity. "I don't want to, but what choice has been left to me? Lou exclaimed. "I visited the young

Mother Nature and told her that her attempts kept failing because of the lack of guidance." Nayla looked at Lou with her mouth wide open. "You knew Nature?" Lou's grin became lascivious. "Know her? I married her. She was my first wife, although Lillith believes it was her. Anyway, I shared with my wife that the best way to guide might not be through direct commands, so we created the laws of Nature, humans call instincts or the laws of survival. They were as follows. Fight or flight. Kill or be killed. eat or be eaten, shelter, and, my favorite, propagate. These were Universal laws modified to a biological medium. With these laws, Nature brought forth Humans, the pinnacle of the Creator's intentions. Fortunately for me, the Creator left Nature to her own devices in the building of humans. The Creator gave his designs for their form but knew for his intentions to be forthcoming, he should not meddle in their sentience or their cognitive abilities beyond his original design, or they would not become puppets, something he wished to avoid. That absence allowed me unfettered access to Nature. My input allowed for the imbalance of Humanity's thought and emotional process as they always fluttered between one feeling and the next." Lou conveyed. Lou's revelations enthralled Naya. "The morning star," Nayla whispered. Lou tilted his head, hearing the whisper. "Why Nayla?" Lou probed. Nayla, to Lou's shock, had a tear in her eye. "Stop it." Lou demanded. "I'm sorry she whispered. "I understand." Came her soft reply. "What is it that you think you understand?" Lou demanded, unable to describe what was moving him emotionally. "Why the Creator called you the Morningstar." Lou snickered. "Do you? Come now, little demon, enlighten us! Lou demeaned. Nayla shifted her gaze from Lou to the people roaming the beautiful park. Children frolicking with their parents, enjoying the warm summer night. Her look returned to Lou, who was staring at her. "My Lord, Lou. I mean no disrespect. Your luminosity and treachery gave the Creator prophecy, and you became his morning/mourning star. She iterated sadly. For the first time since the divine child was born, Lou was thunder-struck by how subtle the Creator is. To give this demoness, this succubus, the insight to reveal to his wayward son a truth he may have never discovered for himself. It caused Lou more discomfort than he could ever admit. Lou slowly smiled, relieving the Terrified demon from her fear of overstepping Lou's boundaries. "You are a rare gift, Nayla, and I will do well by you. Your insight might be naive, but it is refreshing. I never thought I would mourn any loss of the Creators, but you have dispelled me of that notion with a simple observation. All that is moot as we are prepared to give the signal to our field agents, and the age of man shall soon come to a close, and our Realm shall expand as we consume this failed creation." Lou exclaimed. Nayla looked at Lady liberty again. Lou chuckled. "One last look?" He joked.

CHAPTER 21

HELLISH CONCLAVE

An army of hells legions stood for battle. The commanders of all manner of demons and monsters awaited the signal to charge and burst forth from the gates of hell and seek the vengeance that had inflamed in them. In the Realm of Asmodeus, the Lord of Lust sat upon his newly erected throne and impatiently waited. He knew that if Lucifer stood by his original plans, the days of Humanity ended, raising a serious problem for Asmodeus. The problem was that hell was not known for keeping secrets. If Lucifer's plans came to fruition, not only would hell become exponentially larger, but so would Lucifer's popularity. The danger of Asmodeus's plot to unseat him would eventually become discovered. *"This must not fail."* Asmodeus mused. Asmodeus looked down the steps leading up to the throne as he heard Lillith enter the throne room. "You looked concerned." Lillith observed. "You aren't?" Asmodeus said in return. She shook her head. "Not at all. I'm Lucifer's wife. He would not do anything of a permanent nature. He would punish me; it would be painful, but eternity is a long time to spend alone." She said confidently. Asmodeus glared at Lillith. "So, that's why you joined my cause." He hissed. Lillith smiled enticingly. "You didn't think it was because of your good looks." She laughed. "Coward." Asmodeus spat. "Pray we win, harlot, because Lucifer is insane beyond understanding. If you think he can't replace you, I tell you he won't have to because you've already replaced yourself." He barked. Lillith looked confused for a moment. "Do you mean my servant Nayla? She has sworn to me, fool, Lucifer will find nothing there but betrayal." Lillith mused. Asmodeus squinted at her. "Pray that is the case; if not, pray we win. Asmodeus spat. The generals of the rebellion filed into the throne room Valak and Aeshema, spirits of deception and violence, led their wraith and ravager captains. Lillith spoke out. "Report." She snapped. "All goes accordingly." Valak reported. "Lucifer has my cohorts in strategic positions in various governments. If we receive an attack command from Lucifer, we will dutifully obey his directive." Aeshma added quickly. Lillith bristled. "However, if Lucifer recants for whatever reason, we shall defect to your side, giving you our support." Valak concluded. "And that is all we ask." Piped Asmodeus. "All for the glory of hell." He claimed in praise, which the others repeated. "For the glory of hell." Asmodeus looked toward Valak. "Tell us, spirit of deceit, how can we leverage the odds in our favor? Valak paused a moment in thought. "I have been giving this much thought." He responded. "Lucifer seems somewhat enamored with a human; is this true? Valak inquired. "Sadly, yes." Lillith responded. "My agent tells me Lucifer has taken to a human doctor." Valak did not hide his confusion. "Lucifer knows everything there is to know about the body. Why would a doctor stir his curiosity?" Valak inquired further. "He's not that kind of Doctor. Lillith answered. Aeshma, becoming impatient, hissed. "Tell us what we need to know." Lillith threw him a look of dislike. "He is a psychologist." Seeing the confused look on Aeshma's face, she clarified. "A doctor of the mind. We see him having an apparent and thoroughly unwanted influence on Lucifer. Lillith indicated. Aeshma appeared thunderstruck. "How can such simplicity seduce the Lord of Evil?" He queried. Valak looked at his allies. "As I've been telling you, the mind and the trappings therein are a minefield waiting for exploitation. Lucifer has been doing it for eons." He boasted. We have to plan a scheme that will sway Lucifer to the goal of demonic domination." Aeshma pronounced. "Yes, brother!"

Valak declared. "How do we do that?" Lillith asked, nervous that these two zealots might get Lucifer to follow through with his plans for world domination, foiling them and accelerating their undoing when Lucifer discovered who was behind the plot to dethrone him. Snapping back to the present. "We will not succeed without a plan. Valak grinned wickedly. "I have one." He whispered in glee." Asmodeus sat upright on his throne. "If we can convince Lucifer that his human has betrayed him," Asmodeus and Lillith grinned. "For as much as he promotes betrayal, Lucifer gets very upset when someone betrays him." Lillith pointed out. Valak considered for a moment. "I will assign a highly effective agent to handle this." He pronounced. "As important as this is, shouldn't you handle this?" Asmodeus asked. Valak looked at him with a cold stare. "Lord of lust, I don't come into your domain and tell you how to arrange your pillows." Valak responded contemptuously. Asmodeus grinned widely in an attempt to hide his fury at the insult. "And we are thankful for that spirit of deceit, for if you were in charge, our guests would be exhausted from unraveling lies from simple requests." The King of Lust responded lightly. "I shall dispatch an agent this evening to confound our mortal and end this human meddling. Valak promised. "Send a spirit foul; we believe the human to be very clever; otherwise, he never would have turned Lucifer's head." Lillith pointed out. Valak bowed. "We shall be mindful of doing so." He agreed. "Let us be about our business then." Asmodeus exclaimed. Valak and Aeshma bowed and exited the throne room. Once they left, Asmodeus looked at Lillith. "I don't like where this is going." He expressed, sounding concerned. Lillith looked at Asmodeus. "Who's plan was it to use him again?" Lillith asked snidely. "Yes, point taken." Asmodeus grumbled. "We need a plan, just in case," She pondered, looking at the exit the spirits had just exited. In the hall, exiting the pleasure palace of Asmodeus, Aeshma Looked at Valak. "You're going to give dominion of hell to that beast and his traitor harlot?" He hissed. Valak looked back at his Allies. "We shall do no such thing. We will go along. If Lucifer has truly lost his way, someone should usurp his throne. You and I shall find a new ruler as we will have the strongest forces remaining, as we call our assistance, reserves. Aeshma grinned (which was ghastly on the face of violence.)

Den of iniquity

The Den was a local establishment Asmodeus had built for demons on hiatus visiting the Realm of Lust for a little sensual venture. For the sinners condemned for their desire, it was devastating torture; however, for demons in search of raucous action, The Lord of the Realm had set up multiple brothels for the demons to relax or ravage willing (counting as demonic favoritism and less torment, which of course extended your damnation. Or the unwilling paradoxically cleansing their soul through contemptible violations at their discretion. The Den was partially empty as the last celebration for the second circle's elevation status as the Capital of hell. (A promise/ excuse Asmodeus used to gather support for his cause of usurpation of the Luciferian throne.) The party lasted for an Earth week. The poorly lit bar had a drunken demon snoring his inebriation away. In a corner huddled the administrators of hell's current ruling body. Diz, the spirit of hypocrisy of the house of Lillith, along with his colleague Daz, personal escort of the succubus Nayla. Lor, a spirit of greed of the house of Mammon.

Alongside them sat Lewd and Crave, personal attendants to Lady Lillith. Mistress of hell. "I think that we are being manipulated as pawns." Lor espoused. Lewd blurted. "Are you new to the game?" He asked with seeming sincerity. "Is that sarcasm?" Lor dared. Lewd chuckled. Lor returned the chuckle. "Oh, I see. Someone thinks they are so indispensable they can't get their ass whipped." Lor threatened. "What are you two arguing about?" Lewd complained. "Don't you see what's going on?" Dizz laughed, pointing at Lewd. "Bought and paid for." Dizz accused.

Lewd slammed his hands on the table in protest. "How dare you?" He hissed. "By opening my mouth and speaking." Dizz countered. Lewd appeared confused by the rebuttal. Dizz rolled his eyes. "As the spirit of hypocrisy, one of my prerogatives is recognizing hypocrisy. I see yours." Dizz accused. "In what way am I a hypocrite?" Lewd demanded. Dizz tilted his head in a gesture of bewilderment. "Is it possible you don't recognize the compromises of your demonic nature you have subsumed at her bidding?" Dizz inquired in disbelief. "What the fuck are you talking about?" Lewd demanded.

"There is no desire for the hell we seek. The powers that be wish for totalitarian despotism rendering us as nothing more than enslaved demons." Lor complained. "You don't know what the fuck you're talking about." Lewd objected. With a roaring belch, the demon previously engaged in his drunken stupor staggered to his feet, grumbling. "Hey, fancy pants, your lying friend is right." The drunk spewed. Lewd swung his gaze to the drunken demon. "What the hell do you know about anything? You look and smell like a washout." He said condescendingly. The drunk demon staggered. "Yeah, I'm all that shit you called me, but unlike ugly over here, I don't sacrifice my pride for reward, making me a slut," The demon babbled. Lewd swelled in anger. "Who are you calling," He began only to be interrupted. "I was talking to your friend, but if you're getting defensive.." The demon let the insinuation hang.

"Listen," Dizz began. "I don't know or care who the fuck you are, but you're about to get stomped," Lor gasped aloud, making his company stop trying to understand the outburst. Diz was pointing at the unclean demon. "Oh shit," Dizz uttered while still pointing. "You know it's not polite to point and stare." The drunk complained. Dizz began snapping his fingers while twirling in a circle muttering, "Oh shit, oh shit, oh shit." Lor slowly saw what excited Dizz and gasped. "No way," Lewd shouted in frustration. "Would someone tell me what the hell is going on? "I'm not surprised you don't recognize me." The drunk observed. Lewd looked at the mystery demon. "Should I know you?" He inquired. "Not likely since your new lord dislikes nor encourages curiosity, especially about history." The demon complained. "Someone wants to tell me what you are talking about in everything unholy. "Lewd, you ignorant ass wipe, this is the demon Asmodeus and Lillith plotted against to usurp his position," Dizz explained. Lewd stared at the drunken demon. "I do not recognize you." He admitted. "Because, unlike other rulers, yours is selfish, gluttonous, and lustful, which is why Lucifer did nothing when they sought my throne." The demon pointed out. Lewd was curious. "Tell us your name." He demanded. Lor sneered. "Lewd, you idiot! He is none other than Peitho, former King of Lust. He is from the old order. Why are you still here, Peitho?" Lor queried.

Peitho looked at what he would have once referred to as underlings with distaste—infuriated about how Lucifer, in his quest for dominion, allowed for the degradation of hell—beginning with the substitution of demons for the less powerful, therefore a less formidable spirit. The argument is that the spirits created less of a disturbance upon the Ecto-sphere. The invisible barrier that separates dead souls, spirits, and entities from the living, there-by going about relatively undetected by Heavenly watchers. Peitho knew Lucifer to be crazy when the last of his plan was revealed. It called for unprecedented cooperation and collaboration among mixed demonic classes. Of course, the final straw is the introduction of a mortal on an intimate level.

"So tell us, ancient one, with all this knowledge, why haven't you attempted the throne?" Lewd asked sardonically. Lewd smiled, showing broken teeth with jagged edges as if they'd been ground down from a rigid diet. Noticing the look, Peitho explained. "I thank your boss for the smile. You see, he wasn't just interested in overthrowing me, no. He wanted to humiliate and degrade me. It's one of the reasons I still exist." Peitho explained. The bar remained quiet; only a waitress occasionally came to see if the demons needed refreshing drinks. Crave sputtered. "I can't believe Lady Lillith did any of what you are saying." He argued. Peitho signaled for a drink. "My truth does not require your acceptance as verification."

The disposed ruler slurred. "Be that as it may and may that as it be, The whole fuckin lot of them deserve to eat shit and die!" Peitho cackled insanely. "Somebody could disintegrate you for saying shit like that," Lewd warned. Peitho's laugh became self-pitying. "Have you not listened, young demon? We are less than we once were, and hell will be lost unless our King reclaims what was awarded him." Peitho whined. He waved his hand.

"This way or that, it won't matter to me because I know in his final gesture, the Greedy one shall seek me out and cast me into oblivion before he is cast into the same fate." Peitho moaned while gulping from his cup. Lewd and Crave rose from their seats. "Kinsmen, may our fortunes permit us to sit in revelry again despite the feud that embroils around us." Crave toasted. "From your lips to whoever the hell is ruling hell." Lor laughed, raising his mug in a toast. "To utter destruction." Toasted the drunk Peitho, unaware of the peculiar fate that awaited him.

CHAPTER 22

THE SPIRIT OF FRAUD

Upon returning from the Realm of Lust, Valak summoned the spirit of fraud. "You know that the Lord of lust and his harlot queen have their agenda, Aeshma?" The spirit of violence gazed at his compatriot. "That is your specialty Valak. I prefer meeting enemies in an open field of combat, as opposed to this back room, backstab approach of the diplomats." Aeshma spat. Valak glared at him and laughed. "Color it with all the pageantry you want, Aeshma, but I know that violence loves violence regardless of the decor. Clean, bloody, the more of a massacre, the better." Valak laughed at his wit. "do you amuse yourself?" Aeshma grunted. "You must laugh where you can." Valak philosophized. "Well, what are we to do about the insurrection?" Aeshma challenged. "we shall bide our time. One shall defeat the other, and we shall support the victor." Valak clarified. "And if Lucifer betrays hell?" Aeshma probed. "Then the reign of Lucifer morning star shall see its demise," Valak growled.

"This is very disturbing." Aeshma complained. "undoubtedly, but remember, someone delivered a direct threat to the security of hell, and that gives us authority from up high." He boasted. Aeshma shook his head. "I don't think Lucifer will see it that way." He said doubtfully. "Brother, we can only do what we can do. Attempting any preemptive strategy weakens our already delicate position. I strongly suggest we let the parties involved make the decisions, leaving us blameless." Aeshma shook his head. "Sounds like cowardice to me." He complained. "The humans call it plausible deniability. Valak exclaimed. "So now we're learning from the monkeys?" Aeshma said in disgust. "Do not underestimate the evil these tree dwellers are capable of, comrade," Valak warned. The spirit of violence grunted in response.

Well, what do you think? Asmodeus asked for the third time. "I think the spirits look upon us contemptuously," Lillith responded. "No question about that." Asmodeus agreed. "The question is whether we can trust them to commit to their roles?" Asmodeus wondered. "On this, we agree. It has to be swift and decisive when we strike, as we won't get a second chance." She explained. Valak or his ugly compatriot are not allied to our cause, but they are staunch advocates of hell; all we have to do is keep the impression that Lucifer is betraying the Realm." She espoused. The two conspirators sat, musing, "What if we got your agent to plead with the human?" Asmodeus postulated. Lillith looked at Asmodeus. "Yes." Lillith agreed. "It is time for her to prove her loyalty to our clan." She said with glee. "I will return." She exited the throne room and went to her ruby tower. She chased her acolytes out and retreated to her meditation chamber, where she sat overlooking arid fields. She began the soft probe of gently sending her thoughts through the Ectoverse to minimize her presence. "Sister," She called. No response. "Sister." She called again, mindful that Guardian Angels would detect any stronger and her presence. Finally, Nayla responded. *"Yes, my lady."* Nayla dutifully responded. *"What took you so long to answer me?"* Lillith asked suspiciously. *"I was with Lou and,"* Lillith interjected. *"Lou? Does he now have you fooled as well, sister?"* Lillith asked, sounding concerned. *"No, my lady, I'm just trying to stay in character, so I don't slip up and call him by his true name."* Nayla pled. *"Very well. Sister."* Lillith responded, sounding mollified by Nayla's explanation. *"I have difficult information to share with you.* Lillith paused, allowing for apprehension to play its part. *"Lucifer must not start this war,"* Nayla's face revealed confusion. *"If Lucifer initiates this event, according to a reliable source, the upper regions will get involved, and Micheal shall personally dethrone our master, assuring his complete ruin,"* Lillith revealed. Nayla was stunned by the news that Heaven itself was going to intercede. She slowly realized she loved Lou. Not Lucifer, whose true face she gazed upon when he tortured that poor stupid thief that tried to rob them, but Lou, the teacher. He is an admirer of the arts and delighted with enlightened conversation. She would do whatever she could to save him. She began to ask herself when this unexpected feeling came over her. as a Succubus, she could emulate love in the form of Lust. Still, the emotional aspect, the unfettered concern for another's well-being, was not the make-up of her kind. Nayla knew this was her secret and hers alone; even Lou must never know of her feelings. A tear glided down a perfectly formed cheek of a beautiful and bewildered demon. *"What can I do?"* She thought, afraid to speak out loud. She tapped on Lou's door. "May I come in?" She inquired. Entering, she saw Lou hunched over a table with maps. "What you doing?" She asked, trying to sound relaxed. "These maps mark the locations of my agents. Lou looked at her. His eyes were ablaze with purpose. Nayla saw Lou receding into the shadows. Lucifer's persona was the dominant personality, and that personality was all about domination. "I have what the monkeys," Nayla interjected. "Humans, my lord." Lucifer looked up from the maps sharply. "What? what did you say?" Nayla sighed. "Nothing, my lord." Nayla lied to the Father of lies. "What did you want, Nayla?" Lucifer demanded impatiently. "Lillith is right. He is acting as if he is mad." Nayla thought. "I just wanted to ask if you need me. I want to go for a walk." Lucifer looked up angrily. "I don't have time to take you for a walk," Lucifer growled. Nayla bristled. "I am not a dog, and I don't require assistance. I was informing you in case you needed me for anything." Nayla responded politely. "When have I ever needed you? Go!" Lucifer snapped. Nayla spun on her heel and left silently. Lucifer glowered over the maps basking in a triumph soon to be his.

Intervention

Peter sat in his apartment watching the news. Frustrated by all the talk of war, Peter shut off the T.V. and decided to work off some of his tension. Peter dressed in his workout gear and began a strenuous workout regime. An hour later, bathed in sweat, Peter stripped down and jumped in the shower to rinse off. Peter dressed in casual black slacks and a white silk shirt, feeling slightly better and hungry. Walking out of his building, Peter stopped short, realizing he had not gone to his favorite deli. The warm summer air held a bit of dampness to it. Peter crossed the street and entered his once-often-patronized delicatessen. The familiar tiny bell hanging over the door announced Peter's entry. Patty, co-owner and friend, looked up from reading. She stood up in delighted surprise. "Oh, are you fuckin kidding me? Hey, Chico, look who's here!" She shouted at her husband, who was cooking at the back of the restaurant. "Mija." Pedro complained. "We've been married long enough for you to remember Pedro, not Chico, Pedro." Her husband joked from the back. "Okay, whatever, man, just get your ass out here." Patty insisted. "If you keep interrupting me, I won't get that soup done." Pedro complained while he grabbed a towel to wipe his hands, exiting the kitchen to see the big deal. Entering the dining area, he looked up and was surprised to see Peter standing beside Patty. "Hey, Puto! Where the hell have you been?" Pedro asked sincerely. Peter smiled. I've been to hell and back." He responded seriously. Unable to grasp how serious Peter's answer was, Pedro, walked up to Peter and embraced him. "It is terrific to see you, my friend." Pedro posed. Peter smiled. "It is good to see you both." Peter returned. "Where have you been?" Patty asked. "Patty, give the man his privacy." Pedro interjected. Patty looked at her husband. "Shut up. If I want your opinion, I'll give it to you." She quipped. Pedro shook his head good-naturedly. "No respect." He moaned. Peter laughed. "It's as if I never left." Patty nodded in agreement. "I'll be kicking that beaner in the ass till the day he dies!" Patty pronounced. Pedro hugged his friend again. Give

Patty your order; take a load off." Pedro insisted. Peter shook his friend's hand. "You bet." Peter agreed. Putting in his order, Peter sat in a booth which surprised Patty as his food was always to go. The news was playing on their television. Scenes of war and Countries in a state of chaos. Peter watched the mind-numbing imagery with both foreboding and a sense of responsibility. Patty brought his order. "I'm glad you have your meal here." She expressed warmly. Peter looked up, smiling. "Thank you, Patty." Peter raised the volume of his voice. "And tell Hector it smells delicious." Peter giggled. "Hijo de puta, pendeho!" Pedro grunted from the kitchen. Patty looked at Peter, smiling. "We've missed you, Doc." Peter's smile grew. "I've missed you guys as well. Patty rubbed his shoulder. "You enjoy your meal, honey." She insisted. Peter began the mechanics of eating as his mind was far away. As Peter sat, eating what turned out to be delicious soup, the bell on the door rang. In a partial daze, Peter watched awful images flashing on the t.v. "May I join you?" A silken voice asked. Peter looked up and was surprised to see Nayla slide into the booth. "Nayla, are you alright?" Peter inquired. Nayla shook her head. "I'm afraid not." She responded. Peter glanced around to make sure they had a semblance of privacy. "What going on, Nayla? Why have you come looking for me?" Peter inquired. "It's Lou." She began. Peter nodded. "I figured as much." He expressed unsurprised. "Everyone is in peril." She stated. "Peril?" Peter probed. "Yes. The purpose Of Lucifer's visit was to make sure the spirits he had entrenched in the governments of the major world powers were in a position to strike and cause worldwide conflict allowing the hatred of the world to act as a battering ram shattering the gates of hell and losing her demons upon the green Earth. The demons hate the world and would utterly destroy it, leaving a charred ruin prepared for its new citizens of demons." She exclaimed. Peter was shocked beyond comprehension. "But you are a demon; don't you want this for your master?" Nayla looked as if she was fighting her own demon. "Nayla, what aren't you telling me? Peter implored. Patty walked over to their table. "Can I get your guest something, Doc?" Patty politely asked. "Nayla, would you like something to eat or drink?" Peter graciously asked. Nayla shook her head and stared at Peter. "You have to save Lou Peter!" She demanded. Peter blinked, amazed she would say such a thing. Peter lowered his voice. "Nayla, I'm just a man. Do you want me to interfere in his designs? How far do you think I would get before he tells me what he did to that thief on the bridge?" Nayla was in tears. "But I love him!" She insisted. Peter looked at her with compassion. "I'm sorry, Nayla, but you're talking about someone that argued with God. I'm at a loss. What do you think I can do?" Peter inquired, stunned by it all. "Peter, he listens to you. In his way, he respects what you do. Won't you at least try? Save Lou from Lucifer, save the one I love, I beg you." Nayla pled. Peter sat there in a daze. How could he, a man, talk to the harbinger of evil? worse yet, talk him out of a plan he set into motion half a century ago. Peter looked up at Nayla, who was drying her eyes. "I apologize, Peter, for burdening you, but I didn't know what else to do. "Doc, you just gotta help this pretty lady." Peter spun to find Patty behind him. "Patty!" Peter complained. "I'm sorry, Doc, but when I saw this pretty woman crying like she lost a child, I thought she was the reason you've been away so long but hearing you've been helping her and her man just makes us love you more." Patty expressed. Peter nodded. "Thank you, Patty, but this is not as simple as you think." Peter objected. Patty tilted her head in disbelief. "On one hand, you have a guy named Lou; on the other, you have Lucifer, not so hard." She oversimplified. Peter looked at Nayla, who seemed to have read Peter's mind. "Go ahead, tell her. Peters's eyes widened. "Are you sure?" He asked in alarm. "Can't do any harm, and I truly believe you're the only one who can stop him. "Nayla, you're his confidant. Don't you think he would listen to you before listening to me?" Peter begged. Nayla silently looked at Patty, who still stood behind Peter. "Doc, you gotta help this poor girl. Peter looked at Patty, his frustration growing. "No disrespect Patty but you don't know what you're talking about." Peter complained. At that moment, Pedro came up from the kitchen; he looked around and saw the store empty except for Patty, the Doc, and one of the most beautiful women Pedro had ever had the pleasure of seeing. "What's all the noise in here?" He asked. Patty looked over at her husband. "This girl has a problem, and the Doc refuses to help her." Patty complained. Pedro looked at his friend, who sat with his face buried in his hands. "Doc?" Pedro asked. Peter threw his hands up in surrender. "Fuck it, fine; I'll go. Where can you find him?" Nayla looked up, wiping tears from her eyes. "Thank you, Peter. He might be at the Hotel Holland. If you don't find him there, perhaps you focusing on him will summon him." Nayla imparted. Peter stood, shook Pedro's hand, and hugged Patty. "Goodbye, my friends." He said quietly. "Doc, what are you talking about? You're just," Peter had turned and walked to the door; the tiny bell rang, and Peter was gone. Patty and Pedro spun to look at Nayla. "What the hell is going on? why did Peter leave as we would never see him again?" They demanded. "Because you might not." Nayla responded. "What?!!" The Gomez's demanded. "Please sit, and I'll explain. Nayla offered.

CHAPTER 23

CONFRONTATION

Peter exited the deli thinking about what Nayla had told him. Hailing a taxi, Peter had the cab drop him off at the Williamsburg bridge. *"She said that I could summon him by focusing on him. I wonder if coming here helps?"* He pondered to himself. Peter looked around the area. A partly cloudy sky revealed a full moon. The air had gotten slightly damper than earlier. "Lou." Peter called out. Peter sat cross-legged on the damp pathway. "Lou." He called again. After a few more repetitions of calling his name, Peter sat, trying to focus on what no man wanted to focus on, the incarnation of evil. Peter felt the warm wind brush his face. "You know you'll catch a cold on that damp floor." Lou quipped. Peter looked up. "How are you, Lou?" Peter greeted him with a smile. "We can drop the charade now." Lou spat. Peter tilted his head. "I'm sorry, charade, you say?" Peter inquired. Lou grinned maliciously. "Yes, mortal. The charade of Lou is over." Lou stated with purpose. "So, you are no longer Lou?" Peter queried. The one who called himself Lou stared at Peter with malice. 'Lou served his purpose." He laughed. Peter nodded, disturbed at the deranged coughing laugh. "And whom might I be addressing now?" Peter inquired. "You know me. Everyone knows me. They know and fear me more than the one they call God. I am Lucifer, Lord of Evil." He announced. A demonic fanfare of moans and screams accompanied the proclamation. Untuned trumpets blared a cacophony of notes. Peter fought to maintain his composure. "That was all very impressive." Peter stated dryly. Lucifer looked upon Peter with fury in his eyes. "You dare mock me?" He roared. Peter smiled. "Not at all; I was wondering what your plan was, that's all." Peter stated candidly. Lucifer waved his hand, and Peter saw Demons revealed. Poised to move. Awaiting a command to attack. Hoards of demons paced or stood behind giant gates, the fires of hell roaring behind them. Another scene showed men beside phone banks and others besides what looked like missile command posts. The vision cleared, and Peter found himself beside Lucifer again. "So, you plan to destroy the world?" He asked calmly, hiding the ever-increasing sense of dread. Lucifer cackled. "I will make it uninhabitable for all except the lowest of demons. The Earth shall be stripped to her core." Lucifer shouted in triumph." Peter cleared his throat. "You realize all this is contingent on your flock obeying your commands." Peter pointed out. "Who would have the audacity to betray me?" Lucifer demanded. It seemed the moment froze. As if time stood still. At that moment, Peter saw the paranoid look come into Lucifer's eyes. "It is you." He accused suddenly. "You dare betray me after all I've shown you?" Lucifer roared. He waved his hands, and Peter was manacled to an X-shaped wood block. "Who are you spying for?" Lucifer asked. "Have you lost your mind?" Peter shouted. "If I'm spying on you, why would I call out to you?" Peter queried. Lucifer grinned wickedly. "Good question. Would you mind answering it?" Lucifer probed, increasing Peter's suffering. Through the fog of pain, he groaned. "I called because I had a friend named Lou. You may know him devilishly handsome, very intelligent, and forward-thinking." Peter described. "Sounds like someone I'd like to corrupt." Lucifer boasted. "Lou." Peter called softly. Lucifer spun in a rage. "There is no Lou here! I am Lucifer. Firstborn, the morning star exiled from my home, I shall now burn the Infinite city and all creation." Lucifer roared maniacally, more to himself than Peter, who was still in mounting pain. "What then, morning star?" Peter pushed. "If you destroy heaven and Earth, what will be left for you to rule but ruins." Peter entreated. Lucifer stomped in anger. "I warned him. I told him upon my exile that I would return, and both Heaven and Earth would burn upon my return." Lucifer gloated. Peter moaned as the pain increased. "Now tell me, who sent you? Who are you spying for, little man?" Lucifer pressed. Pain turned into extreme pain as Lucifer focused his malice on Peter. "I'm not spying for anyone." Peter gasped between clenched teeth." Lucifer roared, echoing his maniacal laughter. "You think to lie to the Father of lies?" Peter groaned as the pain increased, doubled, and multiplied. "Fuck you, Lou. I knew you were lying to yourself the day you came into my office acting concerned for the well-being of Humanity." Peter ranted. "What the hell are you talking about? I never said anything remotely akin to the shit you're espousing, numb nuts." Lucifer countered. "You lied to me, yourself, and poor Nayla." Peter wailed as the pain continued to increase. "Not bad, monkey boy; you seem to have a tad of fortitude." Lucifer remarked as the pain increased again. "I don't imagine you'll be able to continue much longer. To be honest, I thought you'd be dead by now." Lucifer off-handedly remarked. "I promised," Peter gasped softly as his vision grew dim. "What did you promise? To whom did you promise?" Lucifer demanded. Peter, who was now hanging on to life by a thread. "Promised a friend I'd save Lou, even if it cost her her soul. Peter whispered. Peter's words shook Lucifer, who ceased torturing and poured energy into Peter, who awakened and vomited. "Who is foolish enough to think that I can be saved? Lucifer mocked. Peter, with renewed energy, sat up and looked Lucifer in the eyes. "Are you not supposed to be amongst the wisest morning star?" Peter mocked. "Be mindful, mortal, now answer my question. Lucifer commanded. "Why? do you care? Don't you want to lie and waste everything good?" Peter pushed. "Do not force me to kill you." Lucifer warned. "Poor Lucifer, he lied so well he began to believe his lie." Peter prompted while feeling the need to throw up again. "What did you do to me?" Peter asked while wincing from the pain. Lucifer grinned with malice. "I cannot create, but I can fortify. I infused you with negative energy to boost your failing vital signs." Lucifer explained. "Then why I'm I throwing up?" Lucifer shrugged. "You're a creation of light, and I used darkness, but only enough to jumpstart the positive energy that was leaving you." Suddenly sounding like a spokesperson on a bad infomercial, Lucifer jibed. "Side effects may include physical discomfort, nausea, flatulence, and violent diarrhea." Lucifer mocked. The look of disgust and trepidation on Peter's face sent Lucifer into a fit of laughter. "Oh man, Peter, you gotta see the look on your face; it's priceless." He choked out. Peter tilted his head to the side, recognizing the behavior pattern. "Lou?" Peter asked tentatively.

CHAPTER 24

"Yes, Peter." Lou agreed with the assessment. Peter unabashedly hugged Lou, who stood there surprised at the gesture. "It's good to see you, my friend." Peter uttered. Lou pushed Peter to arm's length. "Peter, you are admitting to being friends with the devil." He said in amazement. "I don't know the devil. I know my good friend Lou." Peter nearly gushed. "Please remember Lou, You and only you can save the world now. The demons you've gathered are poised to invade the world. At that moment, Nayla appeared and bowed before Lou. "My love." She whispered. Lou's mouth hung open. "You are a succubus. You do not know love." Lou protested. "Don't you think I loved as a mortal, my love?" Nayla inquired. Lou nodded. "Of course, but those feelings are burned away in the flames of hell." Lou pointed out. "Yes, my love, while that may be true, you've kept me among the living long enough to begin to remember. Add to that the interactions I've had with the mortals and the time you've spent with me have restored my sense of love and compassion. I'd rather die the ultimate death than see the throne of power in the hands of Lillith and the lap dog Asmodeus, who now calls himself King and Lillith has dubbed herself Empress of hell." Nayla reported. Lou's brow furrowed together tightly as Nayla made him aware of the plot against him. Nayla, what are you saying?" Lou, taken aback by the duplicity, listened as Nayla unveiled the plot to overthrow him. How the spirits of Deception and Violence were in the wings waiting to see whether they would attack the world or Lucifer. "What would their sign be?" Lou inquired. "If you sent the signal to attack, all would join you." Nayla informed. Lou thought a moment. "And if I didn't send the signal?" He asked, his anger increasing. Then they would overthrow you." Nayla whispered. "Lou, do you want to destroy the Earth? Her beauty? Where would you vacation? Where would you find peace or entertainment? Wouldn't eternity become boring if all you had was the constant arguing and malice of demons? What would happen to the essence of Nayla? What would happen to you, my friend?" Peter asked, choking up toward the end. Lou was astonished. "You care for me, Peter?" Lou was beyond belief." But how is this possible? "Nayla rested her head on Lou's shoulder. Peter wore a huge smile. "We have a song in our world, and its chorus answers your question about how such a thing is possible. It's the power of love." Peter smiled while quoting the old Huey Lewis song. Lou placed his hand on Peters's shoulder and nodded. He warmly smiled at Nayla affectionately, then vanished in a plume of smoke and fire. Nayla stared at Peter. Her eyes were brimming with tears. She seemed to glow with a light that was uncommon to demons. "Are you alright?" Peter asked. Nayla nodded. "I'm worried about Lou." She admitted. Peter took a moment to reflect on the current situation. *I'm caught between defeat and calamity. I never thought I'd say with any conviction that I'm in danger of losing my soul, which upon deeper examination, is selfish as the entire world is in peril. One misstep and Lou's modernized thinking would be rejected. A regression to the old ways would supersede the recent redirecting of the function of evil."* Peter mused. He Looked up at Nayla, who stood silhouetted by the moon; she made a striking image. "What's on your mind?" She inquired. "I realize all that's at stake." Peter responded. Nayla nodded. "Lucifer is in Lou's shadow, waiting for a moment that Lou relinquishes the dominant position." Nayla exclaimed. Peters's brows furrowed in confusion. "How does that work?" Peter posed. Nayla returned a look of befuddlement to his question. "I mean, who is Lou? Where did he come from, and why is he here?" Peter asked. Nayla took a moment to compose her thoughts. "As far as I know, The Lord of evil analyzes a situation knowing that different approaches can gain different levels of success." Peter stared at Nayla blankly for a moment. "I'm sorry, but do you believe you explained something?" Peter jibed. Nayla exhaled impatiently. "You don't send a nurse to fight a fire, or a cop performs open heart surgery." Nayla blurted. Peter nodded. "So, you're saying that Lucifer designs personalities as one would fit a suit?" Peter postured. "Under the situation. Lucifer designed Lou to be able to communicate without terrorizing." Nayla concluded. Peter slowly nodded in understanding. Sensing there was more, Peter probed. "The danger?" Nayla sighed. "The danger being that one or both personalities may deem themselves essential, threatening to overwhelm and become the dominate personality." Peter's curiosity grew. "And that would be bad because?" Nayla slowly arched her back, trying to release some tension. The movement was sensual, with the background of the moon and her long flowing hair. *"Stop it."* Peter reprimanded himself. Suppose Lucifer allows Lou to accomplish his task. In that case, he will come, except for Lou, to relinquish control and go to the shadows of Lucifer's subconscious, where it may survive, waiting to be summoned again. However, suppose the Lou entity refuses to withdraw. In that case, a conflict will ensue. Since Lucifer is the impetus, Lou will more likely than not be cast out as a possessive spirit and go from being a mere thought to an actual entity where he could face recriminations for actions compelling sedition against the state." Nayla explained. "Where does that leave us?" Peter said asked. Nayla shook her head. "In a very precarious position." She muttered softly. Peter raised his arms and dropped them in a gesture of futility, "That's just fucking great. You're saying that the world's fate is in the hands of a being with reality-altering powers with anger management issues. We're screwed." He cursed. Nayla looked off into the lit skyway of Manhattan. "We must trust that Lou can convince himself that for hell to thrive, it must evolve."

Nayla nearly whispered. Peter walked to where Nayla stood, and he gently took her hand. Peter guided her to a spot a few feet further on the path. "Do you know what happened here?" He asked. Nayla nodded. "Yes. This is where that ridiculous man tried to accost you." She responded. "Yes." Peter confirmed. "From your perspective, that's exactly what happened. From my perspective, reality as I knew it ended abruptly as You and Lou confirmed what was once thought of as myth and superstition. You confirmed the existence of a devil and demons. Of an Angel of Death. and though now I'm assuming, A God." Peter concluded. Nayla looked at him. Her beauty was blinding. *She had not grown more beautiful.* Peter mused. *It's her eyes; there is compassion.* Peter realized.

CHAPTER 25

REDACTION

In a flash of lightning, Lou appeared. The demons shifted restlessly as they growled in their blood lust. Appearing at the gates of Hell, Lou stood facing legions prepared for battle. "Loyal warriors. I now revoke the order to attack. Go back now to your realms and stations of duty. An uneasiness spread through the assembled ranks. "You promised us to battle. War. Victory over the cursed mortals. Aeshma countered. Lou peered at the spirit of violence. "I did." Lou conceded. "You promised we could rape the Earth." A demon from the Realm of Lust argued." Again Lou nodded. "I will stipulate that I've made many promises; however, that is not now or ever the point." Lou clarified. "We have obeyed all your commands." The demon Lor of the Realm of greed shouted. "We deserve a ruler who serves our interests!" He shouted above, raising grunts of discontent. "We have one who would rule as is best for hell, not this hypocrisy you utter." The demon Diz, of the order of hypocrites, shouted. Lou began to laugh slowly. The laughter built until it filled the caverns of Hell. "Why are you laughing? Don't you see how serious this is?" Andrax, the spirit of deception, begged. Lou gazed at the spirit. "You, spirit. Return to my pocket where you belong, or suffer the fate of all traitors." Lou warned of the spirit of deception. Lou began to grow. "You wish to destroy a world that gave you notions such as accountability? You think you deserve something, do you? The only thing you deserve is punishment. I am not your leader. I am your warden. You have been imprisoned here, not by me but by your terrible choices in life. You do not get to decide anything of consequence. Who filled your heads with such foolishness?" Lou queried. "Asmodeus shall lead us." A voice called out. Another joined in. "Lucifer is a traitor! dethrone, dethrone!" The demons began shouting. As one, they rushed to the dais Lou was standing on.

Lou grew, towering over all. "You dare?!!" He shouted. Lou whistled, and the dread beast, Behemoth, rose from HellHell. Lucifer appeared on the beast's back. "You wish to battle Lucifer, the morning star? Come and meet your fate." Lucifer roared. Unsheathing Azrael's blade, the demons hesitated to know that blade killed the living but canceled the very existence of any demon it touched. Aeshma, in his element, whipped the demons into a fury. Snarling and biting, they attacked. Lucifer was mildly surprised to see loyalists that battled for him. Lucifer was on a rampage. Extinguishing demons, legions had fallen to his blade. Blood lust grew in Lucifer, who again began suffering the corrupting effects of power. Lucifer raved as he mowed down battalions of demons. In the rear of the battle, Lillith and Asmodeus watched as their allies were either hacked to pieces by the loyalists or disintegrated by Lucifer's blade. Lillith saw the unbridled fury in Lucifer's eyes and realized the depths of her foolishness to think someone could overthrow Lucifer. she watched as the Lord of evil had destroyed half of Hell'sHell's population within moments. In a state of panic, Lillith disappeared from the battle. Asmodeus, seeing Lillith vanish, screamed at his troops. Lucifer seeks to destroy your Empress! He must be stopped."

Lucifer and his supporters continued marching toward the King of Lust. Hacking, chopping, slicing. He was getting closer to the Capital of Lust, where the insurrectionist made his base. In a panic, Asmodeus visited the depths of HellHell. The frozen Lakes of Cocytus where the fell shadow of Beliel was bound. The legend was that the Creator expelled Lucifer during the great rebellion; the loss was such a blow to Lucifer's pride that he went insane and developed an identity disorder. He developed multiple personalities, each with a separate function. Lucifer is lucid and wise with a distinct purpose. Satan, another of his characters, is much darker. He is content with being evil and a plague to Humanity. Beliel, This was a personality of a different order. This shadow wanted nothing but the destruction of everything. The most extreme of evil is what Beliel represented. When this aspect of Lucifer came into being, It was exorcised by Saint Bruno the Carthusian. In desperation, Asmodeus sought out the insane shadow. The wailing was hideous in this Realm of traitors of God, men, and country. The region was dark, with tall drooping trees.

The ground was marsh-like, The air fetid. The only smell was that of decay and rot. A shadow suddenly loomed in front of Asmodeus, who yelped in surprise. "Here, why, pretty King? Is it my strength you seek?" The shadow implored. Asmodeus took a moment before responding. "I seek the forsaken shadow." Asmodeus shared. "Yes, we see. What do you want of us?" The shadow requested. "Your aid in a battle against your nemesis, Lucifer. He wishes to destroy HellHell, hoping God will let him back into Heaven."

Asmodeus lied. Beliel looked confounded. "Foolish, God would not allow. War, yes?" Beliel asked. Asmodeus grinned. "War, yes." He agreed. Beliel looked at the entry that served as an entryway. "Lord only." The shadow hinted. Asmodeus looked confused for a moment. "Ahh, you mean only the Lord of hell can issue a release from this circle?" Asmodeus probed. Beliel acknowledged. "Lord only." He agreed. "Very well then, come along; I am the new master of hell." He proclaimed. As they got closer to the entry, Beliel began to wince in pain. Asmodeus noticed Belial's reluctance to go farther and tried herding him like livestock. In excruciating pain, the shadow of evil turned on Asmodeus. "You not, Lord." The deranged shadow growled. A tearing, shredding, and soul-wrenching scream could be heard from the Realm of traitors, where a traitor (Asmodeus) tried to recruit an insane traitor (Beliel) and was trapped by his treacherous nature. As much as Asmodeus wished to become legendary, he became a tale of caution instead.

Desperation

Lillith appeared on the mortal plane after near capture. Her desperate attempt to flee left her no time for preparations. She was fortunate to have a link to this plane of reality; otherwise, she paused, thinking of her defeated colleagues. Lillith looked around, unfamiliar with her surroundings. She saw a sign that said, 'Welcome to Coney Island.' She heard the gentle lap of water as it splashed against the shore. Noticing she was on a beach, she sat on the sand and focused, reaching out telepathically. *"Nayla, Nayla."* She chanted quietly. After a few moments, she got a response. *"Lillith, where are you?"* Was the response Lillith received. She noticed that Nayla no longer called her My Lady or Mistress. *"I must see you." Lillith demanded.* *"Well, I could meet you in about,"* Lillith interrupted Nayla. *"No. It must be now. Go to the roof wherever you are and focus on me; I'll find you." Nayla thought she knew what Lillith wanted. Nayla quietly exited the room and looked for the stairs leading to the roof. Once on the roof, Nayla focused on her former Misstress. "Lillith, I am here. Follow my essence to me."* Nayla chanted. On the other side of Brooklyn, like a dog catching a scent, Lillith caught Nayla's telepathic message and teleported herself to the rooftop. "Nayla." Lillith said in greeting. Nayla bowed. (out of habit more than respect.) Lillith smiled for the first time in a long time. "It is good to see you remember those who served you." Lillith espoused. Nayla was very suspicious. "What do you want, Lillith." Nayla asked bluntly. Lillith tilted her head in distaste. "Well, so much for courtesy." She sniped. Nayla grinned. "You expect courtesy? Why do you believe you deserve such a luxury? Because you were the first female? Or maybe it is because you were the first to snuff a male's advances? Perhaps it is because you defied The holy One and survived. I'm not sure which of these give you the sense of privilege you carry around, but you." Nayla accused. Lillith bristled. "How dare you." She interjected. "Who saw your potential? Who entreated the flame master to watch for you? Who told him you have gifts that could be utilized, so be extra careful how he handles you? That would be me. Not Lucifer or Lou or whatever the fuck you're calling him nowadays." Lillith complained. Nayla seemed to grow a couple of inches as she walked up to Lillith until they were nose to nose. "You stuck-up bitch." Nayla exclaimed. "The only reason you took me from the flames was so you could fashion me into your spy. You wanted me to weaken him so that you could take the forces he has been deploying and usurp his power by starting rumors of the dereliction of his duties to HellHell and foment a rebellion against Lucifer, so why should I listen to you?" Nayla challenged. Lillith fought an inner battle with her pride versus her common sense. Lillith visibly relaxed. "Why are you here, Lillith?" Nayla repeated her question. Lillith looked at the Manhattan Skyline. "I must speak with the human." She responded softly. Nayla hid her shock. "I'm sorry." She responded. "The Doctor. The human your 'Lou' has been talking to." Lillith clarified. "It might be that you wish to speak to him, but why would he want to speak to you?" Nayla probed, wondering why Lillith thought Peter would meet with her. "For the sake of your Lou, my dear." Lillith responded confidently. "Oh, and how is that?" Nayla asked. Do you know where your beloved Lou is right now?" Lillith pressed. Nayla considered a moment. "Probably setting hell straight." Nayla answered curtly. "If you mean destroying the entire population of HellHell, then yes, he's straightening it, oh by the way, it's not Lou doing the destroying; it's Lucifer, and he's so enraged he summoned the Behemoth from the pit, and it is wreaking havoc, so if you plan to destroy HellHell and have Lou to yourself, good luck. With the destructive frenzy he's in now, Lucifer will never allow the persona of Lou ever to surface again. Lillith said smugly. "And there is a rumor that Asmodeus, in desperation, might seek the aid of the bound, cursed shadow." Lillith hinted with fear in her voice. Nayla stood very still; a gentle breeze tugged at her. "You'll lose him if the human doesn't intervene!" Lillith shouted, revealing her desperation. "I know you only serve yourself, Lillith, and you sought the throne, but I hear your desperation; I shall speak to him." Nayla capitulated. "It has to be now. Hell is in ruins; we must stop him before the destruction is complete." She warned. "Go now to the spot in HellHell where you will need him. I shall call out to you." Nayla offered. Lillith nodded and vanished. Nayla closed her eyes and focused on Peter. *"Peter."* She called out. *"Peter, we need you. Meet me on your rooftop."* Peter jumped off his couch where he stared at a tv while not taking in what he was watching. dressing in a blue tracksuit, Peter rushed up the stairs to meet the stunning Nayla. "Peter." She gasped. "What's wrong?" He inquired nervously; these conversations never ended well. This year has been filled with that question more than any other in his life, "What's the problem?"

He rephrased."It's Lou." Nayla blurted. "What's wrong with him?" Peter inquired. "I mean, beside him being the devil?" Peter added sarcastically. "This is not a joking matter; Lou has learned of traitorous behavior amongst the demons and has succumbed to Lucifer's desire to punish them," Nayla reported. "I don't understand why you need my help?" Peter admitted. "Peter Lucifer has summoned the Behemoth from the pit of HellHell. If he continues, all of Hell will be destroyed; you must speak to him." Nayla insisted. Peter was dumbfounded. "Why the fuck should I speak to him?" Peter asked, shaken by the request. "I'm sorry, but you want me to, once again, face off against Lucifer when he's feeling destructive? So sorry, but that would be a hard pass. Do you know what he did to me last time?" Peter winced at the memory. "Peter, you don't understand; if Lucifer continues, we'll lose Lou forever." Nayla nearly cried. "Excuse me, but how is that my problem?" Peter challenged. Nayla stared at Peter long enough to make him uncomfortable. "You're not going to make me feel guilty, Nayla Peter swore. Nayla vanished only to reappear with a disheveled Doctor Payne in tow. The poor man seems as if Nayla gave him enough time to grab a robe. Nayla cast a spell that allowed William to see her embattled domain."Peter, what the Hell?" William asked while realizing the irony of the statement. Looking around at the disastrous scenario of a war-torn hell, William fell silent, fighting his fears. "William, I'm very sorry," Peter begged. "Could you tell me why I am here? William requested. Before Peter could answer, Nayla told him everything. From Lou's identity to his plan for world conquest to the current dilemma of the persona of Lou being subsumed by the Prideful Lucifer. "Now, why should I involve myself in these affairs?" Peter challenged William. "Well, Peter, Nayla's concerns sound rationale to me," William observed. "Yes, but that is not in contention now, is it?" Peter mocked. "Ohh, and what is? William challenged. Peter pointed to Lucifer on the back of the beast, who was downfield, laying waste to demons and laughing maniacally. "He's the fucking Devil, man!" Peter exclaimed. William nodded. "Yes, but he's also your patient." William admonished. That simple statement reminded and revitalized Peter's sense of professional responsibility. He looked at William and Nayla, shrugging. "Fine. Take me to Lou." He capitulated. "Lucifer, you're going to talk to Lucifer." Nayla clarified. "Fine, I stand corrected. Are we ready?" Nayla looked out over the river calling out to Lillith. "I am here, child. Has he come with you?" She inquired. "He has," Nayla responded. "Fix his image in your mind, and I shall bring you both," Lilith assured. Time seemed to speed up, and the world around them until it dissolved away to be replaced by a war-torn hell. A roar behind them signaled the position of Lucifer and the beast.

CHAPTER 26

HOME VISITATION

Peter and Nayla materialized beside a stunningly beautiful woman; despite the fact she had just been fleeing furious demons and bore scars revealing evidence of an attack, she still radiated a timeless beauty. Peter stood in awe. Peter glanced between Nayla and Lillith and was awed by the beauty contained in this damned domain. Lillith looked at Peter and noticed his envy of her beauty. She immediately reverted to her nature and attempted to manipulate him. "You've come to rescue us." She gushed. Peter was caught by the magic of her beauty (spells of charm magnified that). Nayla immediately countered Lillith's attack with one of her own. "Of his own accord!" She shouted at Lillith, who scowled, seeing her last chance at maintaining her position as queen succubus teetering on failure. She knew all was lost as Andrax witnessing the fury of Lucifer, defected right back to his master.

Nayla gestured to Peter. "Please." She requested while gesturing to the distant spectacle of the beast-riding, demon-stomping Lord of evil. Peter nodded and stepped onto the plains. "Hey, Lucifer," Peter called out. Peter went unheard between the whooping and stomping, with the occasional lancing of a demon by Lucifer. Moving to be more in the line of sight, Peter called out again. "Yo, Lucifer." Silence fell like a shroud. As Lucifer stopped whooping and the Behemoth ceased stomping, the silence was paradoxically deafening. Lucifer stared down from the beast. Seeing Peter, The Lord of Evil held his sword up high. "Hey, what's up, doc?" Lucifer laughed. Peter smiled. "Good one. Hey, you want to come down from there?" Peter inquired. Lucifer looked befuddled. "Why would I do that?" The devil asked. "So we can talk," Peter responded. "I can talk fine from where I am." Lucifer retaliated. Peter changed his expression to one of sadness. "I apologize, lord Lucifer; I just wanted to spend some time in your presence while we spoke." Peter returned. Lillith looked at Nayla and smiled. "Clever mortal." She said, sounding surprised.

"Lucifer, why do you wish to destroy the world?" Peter inquired. Lucifer stared down at Peter's eyes ablaze. "Why shouldn't I? Your kind, treat it like a garbage can. There is so little that you appreciate that has been given to you. Why should you have any of it?" Lucifer roared. Peter thought for a moment. "I never would have thought you a coward." Lucifer flew down with such speed the impact of his landing shook Hell and bounced Peter on his ass. The two Succubi clung to one another, supporting each other. "What did you call me?" Lucifer hissed at Peter in a threatening manner. Peter sat up, wiping dust and dirt off of himself. "A coward." Peter softly repeated himself. Lucifer put the blade of Azrael against Peters's throat. "Prepare to die." Lucifer hissed between clenched teeth. Peter frowned. "Before I die, may I ask something?" Peter implored. "A last wish, very well." Lucifer capitulated. "Tell me the story of when you educated Mother Nature." Peter begged. Lucifer frowned, caught by a memory. "Have I not told you of the time the beautiful Maiden came to an open world with an impossible mission to prepare the world for a life form that would one day walk with the Almighty? Her task was a monumental one. Her first few attempts did not work. Her work with Humanity would have gone down the same path had I not shared the notion of a body of natural, governing laws we called 'instincts.' With these impulses and compulsions, Humanity was able to survive for millenniums. Still, now the time has come for their end." Lucifer pronounced. "Of course, of course, you are a just ruler." Peter lavished. "Can you describe her?" He requested. Lucifer was mildly surprised.

"Of course, I can. I have an impeccable memory. She stood five feet tall, with Eyes as green as grass, Lips as lush as rose petals. Skin as golden as honey. As Lucifer described her, his features began to soften. "You know She was my first wife." He said almost gently. "I've heard something to that effect." Peter said equally as gently. Peter looked at Lou. "Hello, my friend." Peter welcomed with a huge grin. Lou, who appeared calmer and more at peace with himself, looked upon Peter with a mixture of gratitude and what could have been respect. "You have a difficult job ahead of you, Lou." Peter assessed. "That I do." Lou agreed. "I might as well get started. Lou stood on a huge boulder. The silence that fell when the Behemoth stopped its stomping had remained. All of Hell witnessed the exchange between Lucifer and Peter. "Denizens of hell." Lou spoke in a mighty voice. This is the dawning of a new hell. Evil will continue to be punished to cleanse the soul and return to the Creator. We shall return to the original intention of this domain. My future cadre will NOT garner Fiefdoms where loyalists may set up independent stations. Hell will again become a place of punishment, with redemption being the end goal. Some will be angered over my decisions. If that is the case, you will be removed from your station and placed in lower demon status. Unlike my shadow, I will not reward evil of excessive punishment. Any abuse of office will find the abuser cast out of the office and suffer the same abuse they inflicted upon others." Lucifer declared. He looked down at Peter. "What do you think? "Not a bad start at all. You are going to take this to a new level." Peter expressed admiration, which, for whatever reason, made Lucifer smile. "Well, I guess my job here is done." Peter acknowledged. Nayla embraced Peter. "Who could have, would have, ever in a million years guess that the savior of hell would be a mortal." Lou chuckled. Peter blushed. "You're far too kind, and I should be going, as standing in the middle of hell is starting to freak me out just a bit." Peter admitted. The scene melted into Peter's rooftop. Peter watched as the sun broke the lip of the horizon. Peter began to laugh. After a moment, Peter caught his breath. Peter ran down the steps of his apartment building and across the street to the

Gomez deli; a car horn blew. "Hey, asshole, watch where the fuck you're going!" The man shouted. "Yes, sir." Peter shouted happily. "Your right; my bad." He responded before running up behind Pedro, who was opening the store. Grabbing Pedro from behind, he lifted his friend in the air. "It's so good to see you, my friend." Peter cried joyfully. "Put me down, cabron. What's gotten into you?" Pedro asked, never seeing his friend be so emotionally expressive. "It's all good, baby." Peter expressed. "Mijo, you gone loco?" Pedro asked. Peter smiled, grabbed him by his cheeks, and kissed his forehead. "I love you, man." Peter stated unabashedly. Pedro struggled to get free from Peter. "I love you too, man, pause, but not like that." Pedro protested. Peter laughed and hailed a cab. "Say hello to your beautiful wife and my lovely kids." Peter snapped as he entered the hailed cab. "Hey, fuck you, pendeho!" Pedro shouted as the cab pulled away.

Less stress clinic.

Peter stood on the roof of the clinic. Awed by the recent events, the non-religious therapist found a new meaning to existence. "So, what now?" The familiar voice asked. "Kind of early in your administration for a vacation, isn't it?" Peter inquired. Lou shook his head. "Not at all. Every thousand years or so, Hell needs a good shake; otherwise, it would get stagnate." Lou shared. "How's Nayla?" Peter asked. "Nayla is in her element. She has rearranged the regional order so that the closer one gets to redemption, they may now hold a co-advisory position for transparency and ascertain that the punishments do what they are supposed to do, not just meaningless torture. Peter nodded. "You are an amazing entity, Lou," Peter observed. "Alright, that's enough of that." Lou protested. "You are a special person Peter. Don't be overly surprised if I look you up for a session." Lou expressed. Peter grinned, whipping out a card and winking. "You have my number." He replied. Lou took the card, smiling. "You have Hell, her demons, and her master's gratitude mortal. Next time I see you, maybe we'll discuss those abandonment and Father issues. You think I have." Lou confided. Peter grinned. "It would be my honor." Peter bowed. "Of course, it would be your honor." Lou laughed while vanishing in a cloud of smoke. Peter stood still for a moment. Peter massaged his chest; feeling tight, he wondered what was done to him when he was doused with negative energy. "Are you in pain? A silken voice inquired. Peter looked up to see a being bathed in a glowing aura. "You know, if not for the week I just had, I'd be convinced I'm losing my mind." Peter pointed out. "you know, if not for the week you just had, I would not be here." The entity pointed out." Peter grinned. "Point taken." He conceded. "Where does it hurt? The entity asked. Peter showed him where on his chest he ached. The entity touched the spot. "That's not so bad." He said, removing his hand and, with it, the pain. Peter smiled. "You have heaven's gratitude." The entity said softly before vanishing. "What are you doing?" William asked. Turning, Peter saw William standing by the stairwell. "Hey, boss, how long were you there?" Peter asked. "I saw you standing there. You seemed to be in deep thought, so I didn't want to disturb you. William responded. "Hey boss, I know when you opened this joint up, you were not trying to get in the middle of it," William held up his hand, gesturing for Peter to stop. "Peter, what happened here could not have gone any better if we had planned it. Don't you realize the enormity of what just occurred?" Willam posed. "I suppose I do," Peter said modestly. William looked Peter square in the eyes. "Stay modest, my friend. You are more valuable than you know. William observed. Peter waved away the compliment. "What are you talking about? I'm just like any other man." Peter objected. "No, Peter, not only are you more than that, but the world owes you a depth of gratitude as you are distinguished. At your fingertips, you have a force second only to God. Remember the ultimate authority." William posed. Peter frowned before responding. "Violence," Peter answered curtly. Doctor Payne nodded in agreement. "And you, my friend, have access to the most violent entity in creation because no one else can claim to be the devil's therapist.

A letter from Lou

Greetings.

Peter, I Hope this letter finds you coping well with the insanity prolific in your world—enough of the pleasantry. I write to inform you of the latest in Hellish news. It will please you that Nayla is flourishing in her new role as Miss-tress of Hell. Infuriating what remains of the old cadre, she began a demoness support group focusing on strict punishment guidelines. Put simply; it states that no woman shall be taken from her properly assigned punishments for the purpose of pleasuring demons unless specific to their sins, as for Lillith. She has been punished by having her office, power, and proximity to the throne removed. She is now among the minions who are having fun poking at her. She was a terrible overlord, and her cruelty has now returned to haunt her.

Speaking of haunting, I received a report that stated the traitor Asmodeus, in his desperation, in the final days of the war, went down to the ninth circle in a vain attempt to recruit the insane Beliel to his cause. The last anyone heard of Asmodeus was a terrible wail of pain as Beliel attacked him, still tearing him to shreds. Well, that's what's going on in Hell. Keep the world spinning, my friend.

p.s. I was thinking about having a feast and inviting Dad.
Do you think that is a good idea?
I will see you in a month or so; Nayla sends her best, meow.

Your eternal
Lou
Aka, Lucifer, the devil, Satan.

Fin
J.E. Serrano